The Coarse Witchcraft Trilogy

Craft Working
Carry On Crafting
Cold Comfort Coven

The Coarse Witchcraft Trilogy

Craft Working
Carry On Crafting
Cold Comfort Coven

Compiled and introduced by

Mélusine Draco

Winchester, UK
Washington, USA

First published by Moon Books, 2013
Moon Books is an imprint of John Hunt Publishing Ltd., Laurel House, Station Approach,
Alresford, Hants, SO24 9JH, UK
office1@jhpbooks.net
www.johnhuntpublishing.com
www.moon-books.net

For distributor details and how to order please visit the 'Ordering' section on our website.

Text copyright: Mélusine Draco 2013

ISBN: 978 1 78279 285 7

A CIP catalogue record for this book is available from the British Library.

Design: Stuart Davies

Printed and bound by CPI Group (UK) Ltd, Croydon, CR0 4YY

We operate a distinctive and ethical publishing philosophy in all
areas of our business, from our global network of authors to
production and worldwide distribution.

CONTENTS

Dedicated to all those Old Crafters who have contributed their gaffes, indiscretions and bloomers.

Introduction

Readers of the *Coarse Witchcraft* series are aware of the story behind the trilogy. How the authors were unhappy with the proposed ideas for publishing the first book as humour instead of the polemic typescript they had originally proposed. They finally agreed for the text to be given to me (as a fellow Old Crafter) to ghost-write and *Coarse Witchcraft: Craft Working* was duly published – provoking more good natured laughter about British witchcraft than we could have expected in our wildest dreams.

Even esoteric author and long-time chum, Alan Richardson, said of the book: '*Coarse Witchcraft made me laugh out loud in more than a few places. In fact, I think it is the first book of its kind; although it pokes fun at modern excesses and can laugh at itself, it still manages to teach the real stuff at a very high level.*'

There was almost enough material left from the first book to launch a second: *Coarse Witchcraft 2: Carry On Crafting*, with plans for a third. It was dedicated to all those Crafters who believe that reverence should be tempered with mirth and merriment – and was as equally well received as the first.

For reasons that will become apparent, the third (and last) title, *Coarse Witchcraft 3: Cold Comfort Coven* has been a long time in the writing. Despite the popularity of the books, the original authors decided to hand all copyright back to the ghost-writer who had created the series (with the proviso that the real names of the characters should never be revealed), and retire from the scene.

Cold Comfort Coven is written in the same vein as the previous titles, and in its own way continues the unexpected, but true, story of the Coven from the numerous notes supplied by, and lengthy conversations with, the original members. In its own way, I think the *Coarse Witchcraft Trilogy* represents a small but important capsule of Craft history that we have been lucky enough to preserve for the next generation of witches.

As I once wrote about another book, there's always a worry when you've been entrusted with someone else's material that the end product may not meet with their approval. So, you may ask, why presume to undertake the creation of someone else's work? In answer, I would draw on Dion Fortune's sentiments: *'The task is not of my seeking, but as it has come into my hands, I will do my best to discharge it honourably …'*

I hope I have.

Mélusine Draco

Glen of Aherlow – 2012

PART ONE: CRAFT WORKING

RUPERT PERCY AND GABRIELLE SIDONIE

Prologue

St Thomas on the Poke is a small market town, as yet still unspoilt by the march of progress despite its close proximity to the south coast. And, despite an even closer proximity to the New Forest, the Coven lays no claim to any hereditary association with the legendary Dorothy Clutterbuck or the 'New Forest Witches'. The Coven has been in existence for many years prior to the birth of its current members and will no doubt continue long after their deaths. Our family has farmed the land for centuries and, although *that* future can no longer be guaranteed, our branch of Old Craft will survive simply because we prefer to remain in the shadows and keep our teaching pure.

In spite of our 'privacy', our own small group is often beset with problems and difficulties of both a personal and magical nature, just the same as any other close grouping of people. Although head of the Coven, mine is not a blood-right. Three years after my mother's death, father re-married; a year to the day his new wife was delivered of a son and promptly died. Some say the child was so ugly that the poor woman died of embarrassment. Be that as it may, as a result of this brief interlude, my father acquired a second son and a mother-in-law who was to be the bane of both his life and, subsequently, mine.

Local people never understood why 'Squire (as my father was known) married Elizabeth Jay but I can now answer that question in all honesty, since it is no longer of importance. Like Jacquetta, the old Duchess of Bedford who snared Edward IV for *her* daughter, Granny Jay is a witch and, although she's never actually admitted it, she used those powers to get Elizabeth into my father's bed. In fact, Granny introduced most of the local children to the Old Ways (including my wife and myself), weeding out those who had a natural aptitude for careful nurturing when they came of reasonable age.

On my return from agricultural college following the

unexpected death of my father, the old lady (whose personal habits and hygiene had always been questionable but now resembled those of an incontinent ferret) announced that I had been chosen to succeed the dead 'Man'. Since Roger, my step-brother, was of her blood, I felt the honour should go to him but Granny muttered that the boy was a moron who couldn't find his own arse with a road map and a flash-light. She wasn't, she added, having *that sort of person* messing up a hundred years of tradition. Despite her unprepossessing appearance, Granny was (and is still) not a force to be trifled with, as many of her neighbours have discovered to their cost. Mine was not to refuse.

Our Coven at present numbers the traditional thirteen although we have, in the past, had many more and often many less. Apart from my wife, Gabrielle, who serves as Dame and myself, there are our children, Richard and Philly, who are currently trekking around India during their gap year from university. (The Old Witch saw to it that they were introduced to the Old Ways at a very early age, even though I threatened to personally strangle her when I found out.) Guy and Gerry run the esoteric shop cum art gallery in the town centre and serve as our specialists in herb-lore. Priscilla and Adam at Bramble Cottage who, apart from keeping everyone supplied with honey and helping out with the livery stables, act as the Coven's instructors. Then there's Helena, our seer and diviner, whose jams and preserves are legendary within WI circles – but unlike Granny, hers is a tranquil madness.

Newcomers to the town, Madeleine and Robert were discovered like rare blossoms at a pub moot when Pris and Adam were forced to attend, due to Roger's emergency hospitalisation for haemorrhoids. (Granny unsympathetically observed that the doctors had obviously found a way to shut his mouth and give his arse a chance!) There's Gordon, our stable 'lad' – an absolute marvel at animal healing and, finally, of course, there's Granny herself.

Our real difficulties arise from Roger who, despite his grandmother's unflattering pronouncement, formed his own coven in a neighbouring village. This means that Granny migrates between the two and although she disapproves of Roger's modern approach (i.e. to let anyone and everyone 'have a crack at the priesthood') she spends most of her time with his group keeping an eye on things. 'In case the daft bugger goes and kills somebody!' The Old Witch also enjoys the atmosphere of seething hostility because Roger's High Priestess is *not* his wife, and his wife disapproves of the one he's chosen – for obvious reasons. Granny, of course, encourages Roger's extra marital activities, and since Roger will roger anything with a pulse … well … the added spice (for Granny at least) is the fact that Roger's brother-in-law is also the local vicar!

Although preferring to remain 'private', we do not work in isolation and are regularly in contact with other Old Crafters all over Britain. Because of my step-brother's more liberal approach to craft-working on our doorstep, the members of the Coven felt that we should become more aware of what was going on in what is generally referred to as the 'pagan scene' at a more local level. Admittedly in doing so, we have added two new and valuable members to our group – so the effort was worthwhile. Nevertheless, while we prefer not joining anything on a regular basis, we do make an effort to interact with the various goings-on in the area. This book is the result of the many conversations we've have, scenes we've witnessed, gossip we've exchanged and the experiences we've undergone, all in the name of Old Craft.

The names of the Coven members are those by which they have chosen to be known for the purpose of the book, for our true identities are no concern of anybody but our own. Neither will you find us in the telephone directory for we prefer not have our lives disrupted by the idly curious. Those who wish to have an understanding of our ways will seek us out when their time is right.

Rupert Percy

Chapter One

Joining a Coven

Pris hoisted her skirt up over her hips, toasting her buttocks in front of the log fire while Rupert poured a generous helping of *Famous Grouse*. 'The bloody Craft gets more like amateur dramatics with each passing year,' she complained.

Although I'm Dame of the Coven, I prefer to leave Craft spin-doctoring to Pris and Adam. She's a striking looking woman with a slight Gothic bent (which she's gradually growing out of), and there's no one can swirl a cape quite like Adam when he's going for maximum demonic effect. Rupert's trouble is that he's a bit on the conservative side. He's more than likely to mutter, 'Have you got *any* idea what you look like?' when an eager neophyte turns up to the pub moot in full fancy dress and sporting a pentagram suitable for picking up radio waves from the Voyager space probe.

Until Pris and Adam volunteered to act as proculators for the Coven, the envoy was selected by the drawing of straws. This meant, of course, that the senior members, who actively loathe public affairs, used their magical powers to push the short straw onto the less experienced. (*Of course* it was unfair, but there's little point in having witch-power and not using it!) Needless to say, it was quickly realised that the least likely people were acting as the public face of Craft. An hour of Gordon pontificating on the various methods of cause and cure of colic in horses can produce a glazed expression on the politest of people. Pris reckons he did it on purpose, so that he wouldn't be asked again because he's perfectly articulate when working in the stable yard. Granny was *not* an option. So here we sat, waiting for the latest report on the changing face of eclectic, generic, multi-faceted, seasonally shifting paganism.

Having made the wrong response to a telephone invitation, Pris and Adam had found themselves included in an introductory evening for wanna-be witches. Observing the usual custom of never going anywhere empty handed, they arrived to find the party in full swing with five people sitting in animated silence! They handed over their bottle of wine and a generously portioned pizza – simple but plenty being the order of the day on these occasions. The pizza hastily disappeared into the freezer but before the wine could be spirited away, Adam reached for the corkscrew and poured himself and Pris a large glass each. Being seasoned campaigners they can read the signs a mile off.

After the introductions and the invitation to help themselves to food – a plate of Hobnobs, a bowl of crisps, cheese and a bunch of grapes – Pris found herself next to a woman whom she'd not met before but who was obviously not a 'beginner'. Pris was promptly inspected from head to foot before being informed that her fellow guest didn't believe in 'dressing up' to meet new people. She peered closely at Pris's flawless make-up and remarked that she was glad she didn't need to plaster *her* face with the stuff. In the next breath Pris learned that her companion was the Southern Counties star of TV and radio on the subject of Craft – in short, a dreaded Media-Witch.

As Pris said, it quickly became obvious that the five guests were there in the supporting role of awe-struck spectators. The *real* stars of the evening were the Media-Witch and the Host (so named because he elevated himself above all others), who were cast as Duelling Egos for the delectation of the visitors. Desperately vying with each other for mouth-space, they dredged up every interview they'd ever given, bandying producers' names around like a *Who's Who* of popular entertainment.

Pris and Adam tried valiantly to engage the three would-be witches in conversation but they'd all developed a vacant, slack-jawed expression brought on by acute boredom and were incapable of forming a sensible question. Time dragged painfully by and at twenty-past nine, Adam had kicked her ankle for the third time. All the talk about himself had injected the Host with all the compelling fascination of a road accident. It was almost impossible *not* to watch him, explained Pris. His physical jerks and twists with his head had a sort of hypnotic effect, like a ferret performing its macabre hunting dance.

'His hair stood away from his writhing head in huge tufts, not exactly 'retro-punk', more a sort of 'recently escaped' look. His mouth had a horrible bewitchment – two rows of tombstones complete with lichen; tiny blobs of spittle that sprayed out with every 's' huddled together for safety at the corners of his mouth. Oh, the fascination. It wasn't anything to do with the drivel he talked, more the dribble that accompanied it,' she added.

Having put away three-quarters of the bottle of wine, Pris went off in search of the bathroom to while away some more time before making their excuses to leave. The Media-Witch seized the opportunity and followed, continuing to bombard her with a monologue of self-promotion. Nervously Pris eyed the space between the lavatory and the wall, fearing at any minute that she was going to be 'hag-tracked' as she sat.

She escaped and returned to find Adam incoherent with desperation, making excuses about having left the cats out and that it was drizzling! The other three took this lifeline and were last seen scrabbling for coats and car keys as they disappeared into the night.

'I bet that pizza lasted him a month,' said Pris as we went through into the kitchen for supper.

'And I bet none of the new ones will ever be seen again,' I added, pulling a large pot-roast out of the Aga and nearly tripping over the dog.

Rupert assumed his place at the head of the table. 'It's time some of these people were shown up for what they are,' he said firmly. 'Isn't this chap the one who believes that if you've read a book and understand what it means, then you don't actually need to practice magic to qualify as a witch!'

'Ummm,' confirmed Pris, her mouth full of hot, fresh bread.

The Host had been around for a while but there are dozens like him lurking about on the periphery of Craft; people who adopt the outward trappings but who possess little or no *practical* magical ability. The real problem is that these are the contacts seekers were coming across when they tried to find out more about genuine post-medieval traditional British Old Craft.

There wasn't any harm in the Host. He wasn't predatory or anything, except that he did tend to lean over Pris in order to stare into her cleavage whenever he got the chance. By the end of one evening they resembled twin Towers of Pisa until Adam had pushed a barstool under his wife's rear end before she fell over backwards.

'People *prefer* the play-acting,' said Adam quietly. 'They want someone who looks the part and they're not interested in whether it's a complete and utter prat, just so long as they talk the talk. Criticism is only seen as sour grapes.' He doesn't say a lot but when he does, it's usually pretty profound.

'But they haven't got a yard-stick to measure anything by,' I protested. 'Publishers are now accepting an author purely on face value and the book lists have hundreds of different titles giving out this airy-fairy drivel. As a result, the play-actors don't *need* to know any more than what's in the books, providing they can keep one step ahead of those who know nothing. As long as they can cast a Circle and recite an invocation, it's considered to be witchcraft and the newcomer knows no different.'

'I don't think they really believe in the magic, either,' said Pris sadly. 'It's like coarse fishing; it's seasonal; anyone can have a go; there aren't any rules; they can make up their own little rituals; it gets them out of the house for a few hours on a regular basis, and it doesn't actually have any practical purpose other than personal gratification.'

'*Coarse Witchcraft,*' said Rupert, spooning an unhealthy amount of mustard onto the side of his plate. 'A damned good title for a book. It could contain a worm's eye view of what passes for Craft among the uninitiated and warn the wannabes to be on their guard against the poseurs.'

We spent the next couple of hours making suggestions about who and what should go into this fictitious book. We got merrier and sillier. And then forgot all about it …

'Gerry thinks the book is a great idea, providing we stick to fact and only include real-life situations,' said Pris over the telephone next morning.

'What book?' I responded, forgetting my grammar in my confusion.

'*Coarse Witchcraft.*'

'Pris,' I said patiently. 'It was a *joke*. A bit of fun. That's all.'

By the time Rupert came in for lunch she'd nobbled him on the mobile. 'Pris and Gerry think we should go ahead with the book,' he said tucking in to a large slice of cheese.

Rupert is appreciative of fine food and his outdoor lifestyle means that he can enjoy a good scoff, without losing that 'small and beautifully made' look, despite the fact that he's now over fifty. That 'we' was the most ominous sound I'd heard for a long time, particularly as *I'm* the one who earns my living with the pen.

'It's libel, darling,' I said firmly, trying to head him off at the pass.

'Do you honestly think anyone's going to hold up their hands and confess that the idiot on the page is them? Besides, we're not going to use names, and the instances won't necessarily be people of *our* acquaintance. We can go further afield … Josh is always good for some gossip.'

Cynically referred to as the 'Witch of the North', we're never sure whether she attracts the comedians, or whether there's something in the water in that part of the country. Whenever we speak to her, there's always been some hilarity or histrionics to report. Like the instance of the neophyte who managed to almost sever an artery when he was taken out into the woods to cut his staff. He was so afraid of the Magister shouting at him that he didn't mention it until he'd almost passed out. This same lad later set light to his robe setting up the Circle – everyone noticed but declined to say anything.

Of course, there's always a depressing up-surge of interest in Craft whenever a programme appears on television. Which is surprising, considering that the media-junkies (or 'munkies' as we prefer to call 'em) parading around in the contents of the local theatrical costumier don't exactly flatter our beliefs. Or demonstrate a lot of integrity either.

Over the years some rather impressive names have been persuaded to appear on film, making complete idiots of themselves for the benefit of the camera. Some can even be relied upon to skip around the bonfire invoking all manner of peculiar deities, having cobbled together strange rituals for the programme-makers who know no different – but, in their defence, at least they're not giving away Craft secrets.

'Munkies', on the other hand, have no shame in flaunting their ignorance – which is faithfully recorded in print and on film for posterity. Like the silly old fool who appeared on television performing a love spell for two people already in love. This was worked at the wrong hour, on the wrong day, on the wrong phase of the moon, *using someone else's hair* (because it was only symbolic!) to bind the dolls – which were consecrated by appealing to Mars instead of Venus. It was a total magical travesty from an absolute beginner but the 'munkie' soon became a celebrity and appeared regularly on radio and television as a result of this performance.

Everyone has their own favourite performance by the PaGan Tips brigade, but as Pris commented the last time: 'No wonder the media has such a low opinion of us – so had *I* after watching the latest offering of pagan theatre. Why do even the well-known names continue to leap willingly into the humiliation trap? Or is it true – we *are* all barking? Couldn't someone go on television looking sharp, smart and intelligent for a change?'

The answer, of course, is 'no' because it doesn't make for 'good television'. As a result, this sort of media exposure always backfires and the contingent of new hopefuls at the next pub moot usually arrive in full regalia, only just stopping short of having '**WITCH!**' tattooed across their foreheads – just in case the barman misses the point.

On the plus side, the moots ensure that we get to hear from newcomers about what's going on further afield, usually relating the story about a 'friend' who has fallen for the spiel of the charlatan. Like the variation on initiation – of a contemporary nature it can best be described as *à la* Bill Clinton. To attain initiation into the Craft one lass was informed that she would have to perform oral sex on her tutor as 'this is the way magical power is passed on'.

'I hope the poor, misguided girl remembered not to inhale,' Adam had commented dryly to the person telling the tale. The crimson blush confirming that the 'friend' was indeed fictitious.

'I've read a lot of books and performed a few spells but have never got any results. Can you introduce me to an experienced practitioner so I can get initiated?' asked one young man, wondering why Gerry's response was far from encouraging.

In our branch of Craft, no one can be formally accepted until they are at least 28 years of age – and that's the way it's been for as long as anyone can remember. Although our own offspring, Philly and Richard, are accepted as being part of the Coven, neither will be allowed to take their initiatory oaths until they have turned 28 despite their experience.

The cavalier attitude to magical practice is frequently demonstrated by Gerry's customers, who are always calling into the shop and asking to be bailed out. 'I've done a bottling spell to get back at a neighbour and now I've changed my mind. I've emptied the bottle into the river, so that it's no longer in my house. Will that stop the spell or do I need to do something else?' asked one.

'*You can't stop it,*' snapped Gerry in italics. 'Once a spell is cast, it's cast, it's working. It would be like trying to stop a bullet once you've fired the gun. You can't just throw it away and pretend it doesn't exist. And having thrown it in the river, you've no means of retrieving it. Inexperienced people shouldn't be messing around with spell casting.'

The customer didn't like this less-than-subtle criticism of her magical prowess and answered sniffily. 'Well, if I'm *so* inexperienced that means the spell won't work and I don't need to worry, then?' There was a long pause. '*Is* there any chance of the spell rebounding?'

Gerry went into full witch-mode. 'Murphy's Law works in magic, too, so I'll bet you a pound to a pinch of witch-powder that if you carry out a working and then wished you hadn't, that one will work *exceptionally* well. And, there *is always* the danger of a spell rebounding,' continued Gerry warming to his subject. 'That's one of the chances you take if you go off half-cocked.'

'But there must be some way to stop a spell.' A slight hint of panic was detected in the voice.

'Only if you can remember *every* detail and perform the *exact* mirror opposite. But even then there's no guarantee that you'll be successful. Next time, think about the consequences before you start slinging stuff around,' Gerry had replied in best imitation of High Priestess mode, hoping that the spell-caster might have learned a lesson.

I hear the horse box in the yard and the rattle of steel on cobbles that means Pris has bought her horse. It's hardly a prepossessing animal, but Rupert's not looking displeased so despite appearances it must have a half-decent pedigree. I hesitate in joining them because Granny's just pulled up in her battered Volvo and

Rupert, Pris and Gordon are jockeying for position in order that none of them have to stand down-wind. That battered old wax coat and hat will probably have to be removed with a blowtorch when she dies.

I hastily make the coffee and take the mugs out to the tack-room since Rupert refuses to allow Granny in the house after the incident with the Aga. It had been a bitterly cold morning and so Granny pulled up her skirts and coat to toast her behind (I've often wondered where Pris gets the habit from). The kitchen was suddenly enveloped in the *'rankest compound of villainous smell that ever offended nostril'*, as Shakespeare aptly put it. Whatever malodorousness lurked beneath those garments was exposed to the warm air and the rest of us turned green. Pris swears she caught sight of a large and knicker-less, wrinkled bottom; not to mention an ancient snakeskin garter held up by varicose veins!

Rupert's a fastidious soul and a Virgo to boot. This being the final straw, Granny found herself barred from the house without the chance of a reprieve. The strange thing is that she seems to accept Rupert's treatment of her without rancour and actually respects him – probably because he's not frightened of her. Unfortunately, his sense of humour is sadly lacking in Granny's direction, whereas her antics can reduce the rest of us to hysterics.

She slurped noisily at her heavily sweetened coffee. 'There's some young Turk doing the rounds who we'll need to keep an eye on,' she announced having settled herself on a bale of straw. 'He's got an impressive pedigree which I suspect he's written himself but Roger's fallen for it, like the bloody fool he is. You ...' she said, prodding Pris with her stick, '... will enjoy this. Get over there next full moon and see what you can find out.'

'What have *you* found out so far?' I asked, knowing the old girl wouldn't be quite so much in the dark as she would have us believe.

Her insipid blue eyes twinkled. 'Cheeky blighter asked if he could touch my garter in homage but his hand rested a bit too long on my leg for my liking.'

Rupert shuddered noticeably; no doubt the vision of gnarled varicose veins at the forefront of his mind.

'What did you do?' asked Pris.

'Gave the bugger a good clout with m' stick,' she grinned showing an amazing set of white teeth. 'Now, be serious. Calls himself Alan Wicca, would you believe? Probably because he creeps around his betters with an unctuous manner, hoping some of their aura will rub off on him. Didn't get the impression there was *anything* there ...'

She trailed off but we all knew what she meant. What people don't realise is that a *genuine* witch can spot another a mile off. We've tried to analyse it on a rational and scientific level but we've never been able to explain it even to our own satisfaction. Perhaps because a true witch *is* judged by his or her works and keeping silence. They don't find the need to go around proclaiming their antecedents to all and sundry but they will defend their corner when they see fit. Which is exactly what Granny was doing by mobilising her troops. She might have stood down as Dame of the Coven, but she's still sound in her judgement and we respect her opinions.

Granny had met the chap at Roger's last open moot and he'd walked straight over to her, taking both of her hands in his and saluted her as the Lady. No doubt that had gone down like a Jesuit at a Beltaine bash with Vanessa, the High Priestess. Apparently Granny reminded him of his own grandmother, a Hereditary Witch from Norfolk who had some mysterious link to none other than the legendary George Pickingill. And of course, out came that tired old cliché that it was his dear old, white-haired grandmother who'd initiated him into the Craft.

'The bugger's lying but let's let him run for a bit.'

'How do we recognise him?'

'Tall, not a bad looking chap, fifties. Smartly turned out for a change. Told me he'd been in the SAS but I suspect his credential there won't stand much scrutiny either. Best let Gerry know 'cos he'll be in the shop sniffing around before long. D'you want a lift back?' she asked Pris.

'Er, no thanks, I haven't finished here,' answered Pris, gagging slightly at the thought of the half-mile journey in the close confines of the Volvo.

To put no finer point on it, Granny's car stinks … there's a sinister and permanent damp stain on both front seats and we're not too sure whether Granny herself is responsible, or whether it's her decrepit old sheepdog. Either way, no local will ever accept a lift in her car, especially as the windows refuse to open to let in any fresh air. Her kitchen is just as noxious with its ancient Rayburn belching out fumes and heat in equal quantities. Not to mention the bone-idle 'entire' tom cat that occupies an armchair central to that sulphurous stench and contributes his own brand of vileness when the weather is too bad for him to go out.

The *real* source of Granny's own individualistic odour is Baggins, a rather handsome billy with a thick black and white coat. He's the only thing in that fetid dwelling that is immaculate – her pride and joy. Baggins is a Bagot goat, a breed that was brought to Britain by the Crusaders in the 14th century. The animals lived semi-wild at Bagot's Park until the Rare Breeds Survival Trust took over the management of them and no one knows how Granny managed to get hold of this thing. The animals have long shaggy coats, shot through with a variable amount of black, stand about 30 inches at the shoulder and sport an impressive set of curved horns. Baggins is mostly black which, together with his slit amber eyes, gives him a highly sinister appearance.

Rupert loathes goats, maintaining that they're dirty, smelly, destructive creatures and in all fairness, there's nothing quite like the smell of an un-neutered billy goat to foster ill-feeling between neighbours. Baggins lives in the old washhouse adjoining the kitchen but we suspect that he's allowed inside the kitchen after dark in case someone steals him.

'Or shoots the bloody thing,' commented Rupert, having learned of the animal's latest escapade of demolishing an entire greenhouse of potential prize-winning chrysanthemums that were being lovingly tended for the County Show.

Despite his appearance he's a friendly old thing (Baggins, I mean – not Rupert) and has caused more than his fair share of amusement when Granny was asked to prepare a blend of incense by one young lass who was desperately trying to impress.

'I want to invoke Pan,' she breathed. 'I want to experience the true Presence.'

Granny made the incense from goat droppings and it took weeks before the family could get rid of the smell. 'Can't get truer than that,' commented the Old Witch with a grin.

True witches, of course, use witch-power for everything connected with daily living (including finding parking spaces and queue-less tills in supermarkets) and no doubt Rupert and Pris engaged in a little bit of unscrupulous working when bidding for the new horse. There's a preparation they conceal in the hollowed-out end of a walking stick that will cause a horse to act like a 'bad 'un' in order to discourage other buyers and keep the bidding down.

Is it immoral? I don't think so. After all, the animal has come to a good home and will live here in comfort for the rest of its days. Could the same guarantees be made with someone else buying it? Personally, I believe the end justifies the means when a creature's well-being is at stake, although those from the town will often disagree with a countryman's definition of 'well-being'.

Old Craft isn't about pretty little Nature ceremonies at seasonal times of the year – it's having a completely different perspective on life. It's an alternative morality, if you like, which endorses the 'eye for an eye' philosophy of Biblical proportions. Those who are only interested on a superficial level will be uneasy with many of the tenets of Old Craft. We *don't* turn the other cheek; we *don't* advocate universal kinship and we *don't* extend 'perfect love and perfect trust' to a mere acquaintance just because they lay claims to the eco-pagan ideal.

What we *do* teach is respect for the natural order of things in their own time and place. We believe in shielding our own, young and old, from outside interference and prejudices; and in using witch-power to protect ourselves when threatened. We value knowledge and treasure the gift of shared 'secrets'. Above all, we honour the 'gods' as the fount of all knowledge, wisdom and understanding, but whether Old Craft can be looked upon as a religious practice is questionable. Certainly we believe in the powers we call down to do our bidding and we have faith in our abilities to channel that power but religion – personally, I would say not.

Chapter Two

What Witches Do

A large proportion of the work witches are called upon to perform outside their own immediate circle comprises healing. Several weeks after their encounter with the Media-Witch, Pris fielded another boundary when the phone rang with a request for some help with a healing spell.

Apparently the Media-Witch had found herself with a problem she couldn't sort. Her 'personal journalist' and 'novice' [sic] was worried about his wife's health since the doctors couldn't find anything wrong. Pris made vague consenting noises out of politeness, mentally outlining a plan to arrange absent healing, then make sure she and Adam were watching television at the appointed time.

Media-Witch, however, took this vague consent by the throat and announced that she'll be over in forty minutes. Mind reeling … forty minutes! Help – Mother, please have a heart attack – now! Better still, *I'll* have a heart attack – now – thought Pris, who hates being caught out with no make-up and her hair a mess.

'Then I thought sod it. At the 'do' the other week she told me she wasn't into make-up and girly things. She won't notice.'

Adam dashed off to shave and change his shirt, the two cats were ordered not to moult and before the whirr of the vacuum died away, Media-Witch and a man impersonating a grizzly bear were on the doorstep.

Now if there's one thing the Coven is extremely hot over, it's coven etiquette. You don't invite yourself to a stranger's house, unexpected, requesting their magical help and turn up bearing nothing but a large drum and an even larger accomplice. In they swept, Media-Witch's gold emblazoned cowboy boots setting off her skin-tight jeans. Smiling sweetly at Adam, she coyly accepted a seat, batting her immaculately made-up eyes at him and tossing a tendril of glossy curl over one shoulder. Handing over her jacket, she daintily smoothed the black plunge-line top over her curves.

Bitch, thought Pris seething inwardly. However, the combination of having lank hair, no make-up and an expression of boiling hatred were guaranteed to give her the appearance of an extra from *Buffy the Vampire Slayer*, so she beetled off to the bathroom to repair the damage. Through the door she could hear the journalist enthusing about Bramble Cottage, the fire, the beams, the atmosphere, the olde worlde charm. How soon could he come back; could he feature them? Real working witches in their charming country cottage – yeah, great, just what they needed!

By the time Pris came back, Media-Witch had brought all this enthusiasm down to earth with a sniff, conceding that it's okay *if* you liked that sort of thing. Personally she preferred her wind-swept maisonette on the edge of the salt-marsh, because it was so atmospheric and handy for her clients (Oh, I bet it is darlin' – muttered Pris under her breath). The journalist hardly glanced up since he was hanging on to his mentor's every word as she expounded her vast knowledge of just how healing spells work.

'I was having a bit of difficulty getting into the right frame of mind but I thought sod it,' Pris continued. 'I don't even know the stupid bag who's daft enough to let her husband trail all over the country drooling over this silly slapper, but she deserves to be ill. My emotions were getting somewhat frazzled so I gritted my teeth and asked if they'd brought robes.

'Coy smiles from Media-Witch. Ooops, no, she'd forgotten them, so we'll have to work sky-clad … I looked at the others; the journalist looked hopeful; Adam looked nervous – and me? Well I just looked. One of those looks Granny would be proud of. I don't think so, sweetheart, not with all the draughts howling through our quaint country cottage. Everyday clothes will be fine.

'Now we've all heard 'nice' pagans saying that no one should ever enter the Circle when they're angry. Why the hell not? It's *my* space, anger produces oodles of energy and it's effortless, especially with someone stoking me up into the bargain. Anger's good, it's healthy and it's going to be perfect for healing, because from what I heard of our patient's problems, it's entirely self-inflicted and a desperate attempt to haul her husband out of Media-Witch's clutches via the good old tried-and-tested guilt trip. Oh, yes, I was raring to go. Let's let her have it.'

The beauty of this kind of healing spell is that everyone benefits (well, *nearly* everyone). The wife gets a jolt of pure anger that dissolves her negative passivity; in turn she puts a stop to her erring husband's chauffeuring Media-Witch about (Media-Witch doesn't have a car, so she can't inflict herself on any more kind, generous people living in out-of-the-way places); the witch's partner feels guilty about being flirted with and in turn treats his wife like a priceless object; while the witch herself basks in the glory ...

'The sheer pleasure of my projected triumph, manipulation and outright victory brought such a look of ecstasy to my face, that I glowed,' reported Pris modestly.

'Producing a pulsing battery of wonderful healing energy for Media-Witch to direct into the journalist for him to take home, I settled down like an old owl and let her take the stage. We set up a droning, insistent chant, I directed my energy into the journalist, Media-Witch invoked the Hornéd One into him. Hang on ... re-wind. What's all this, is this *absolutely* necessary?

'Too late. The journalist gave himself over completely and began by going rigid, fists clenched, breathing hard, face turning puce. His eyes blazed without focusing; slowly he began to rock. Lumbering unsteadily to his feet, that old Hornéd God energy was plainly present and just out of sheer badness I wound him up and up. I was buzzing; Adam was 'out of it' and I couldn't tell you about Media-Witch other than to say she was having the time of her life with her drum in the background.

'Suddenly, all this real magic became too much for the erstwhile novice and about fifteen stone of rampant man started crashing down on me. To be honest, I couldn't decide between assuming the pentagram position and bracing myself – or rolling out of the way, but I chose the latter as it required less effort. The ritual grounded, the drumming stopped and I was genuinely concerned that he seemed to be very slow in coming out of his trance. Eventually we managed to get him sitting up and talking, although all he could manage was, 'Bloody hell ... bloody hell ...''

Having got him to his feet, Media-Witch promptly announced they were leaving. Pris protested, insisting that he needed tea or coffee, as he wasn't properly grounded. The man wasn't fit to drive but the up-staged Media-Witch wasn't listening. Still groggy, the poor man was pushed out into the night without a word of thanks, or the chance to say goodnight.

The following day curiosity got the better of Pris and she rang to see how he was. Media-Witch dismissed her concerns casually and said that he'd been okay by the time he'd driven a few miles with the car window down.

'She did have one more thing to tell me, however,' said Pris between gritted teeth. 'She had the nerve to say that she thought mine and Adam's energies were too dark and that *we* should try some re-balancing magic. Wow, thanks. I'll bear it in mind when I'm asked to work with rank amateurs again.'

Funnily enough, nothing more was heard from Media-Witch after that but the pagan grapevine still hums with news and gossip. The journalist's wife is much better and he no longer trails around after Media-Witch – especially since she made a pig's ear of a very public magical working and slipped into obscurity. Even the Party Host doesn't bother with her now – probably because both of them discovered that the other was far too self-centred to promote anyone else other than themselves.

Perfect love and perfect trust – yep – that's what it's all about.

Castor & Pollux is not your ordinary run-of-the-mill occult shop. Guy runs the art gallery next door and the whole arrangement is an homage to minimalism. Gerry's side of the business has a small alcove kitted out with two comfortable white leather sofas and a non-stop supply of freshly-brewed coffee, so that anyone calling for a chat doesn't interfere with the smooth running of the business. Needless to say, we're often privy to the intriguing conversations that take place. One morning, Pris and I had called for a gossip, only to be confronted by two of the customers embroiled in a heated altercation over the fact that if getting it wrong, healing *can* cause harm.

'But of course it's okay to try and help people,' argued one earnest little thing we'd not seen before. 'Our guardian angels will make sure we don't do any harm.'

Annie, a feisty little red-headed shaman peered over the top of her gold-wire specs. 'You have to take responsibility for being a successful channel for healing energy and you can't abdicate that responsibility to an overworked guardian angel. In my experience of nearly fifty years, this may be true at the beginning of our healing careers but they have better things to do than bail you out if you make a cock-up. It would be nice to think that healing was always good and never did harm but that just isn't so.'

A few months earlier Pris and Adam had been coerced into helping out with what they understood to be a healing ritual for two members of Roger's group. When Pris called round to discuss the precise nature of the ritual, she discovered that it was a fertility rite for someone *none* of them had ever met. Needless to say, there were certain questions she wanted answering: like did the person in question know what was being done? Had their permission been obtained? Had all aspects of the problem been carefully thought out? Were the 'lucky' people involved prepared for an outcome that had not been planned, such as twins or triplets?

'Vanessa brushed aside my reservations with the answer that it would be perfectly alright because the Goddess would take care of it. And *that* was what was worrying me. The Powers That Be certainly do take care of things – and not always in the way we'd like,' said Pris. 'No matter what arguments I put forward, they were all answered with the same blasé indifference. Roger made me feel as though I was being deliberately difficult. My immediate reaction was to walk away and let them get on with it but I was more concerned for the folks on the receiving end of this little charade.'

Pris knew there was more to the ritual than the Gruesome Twosome were letting on, so she casually contrived to bump into Roger's wife in the coffee shop next market day. Not surprisingly, there's no love lost between Gwen and Vanessa, and Roger's wife is always more than willing to be a bit indiscreet about her husband's relationship with his High Priestess. It didn't take Pris long to discover that the couple for whom this ritual was being carried out, didn't know the first thing about it.

The request had come from the *mother-in-law* who desperately wanted a grandchild and resented her daughter-in-law having a promising career instead of staying at home to play house. The purpose of the ritual was for the unfortunate woman to become pregnant without her knowledge or consent! Okay, thought Pris, if you two are so cock-sure of yourselves, Adam and I will have to do a little magic of our own as we go along, since nothing's going to stop this ritual from going ahead. She knew that Roger and Vanessa wouldn't be familiar with the possibility of anyone participating in *two* magical rites at once, since she'd done it before on more than one occasion with their group and no one had ever noticed.

Basically this consists of leaving others to carry out the ritual in blissful ignorance while magically over-riding everything that is invoked and directing it elsewhere. It has to be said that whilst we feel no responsibility for the stupidity of others, we consider it to be morally wrong to carry out a magical working on behalf of a third party (in this case, the childless couple) who had neither been consulted nor consented. The knack of magically over-riding another's operation is to back off and assume the meek and mild attitude of someone who had been persuaded that something they doubted is now a good idea. This has the effect of throwing the others into a foolish state of 'perfect love and perfect trust' – which is a ridiculous attitude to have towards a fellow human anyway.

'So, having lulled Roger and Vanessa into a state of false security, I appeared to join in with the casting of the Circle. Sadly, I can't say the same for Adam, who made it blatantly clear that he disapproved of the whole thing. We did think it was a bit risky working with Hecate for a *fertility rite* but they were convinced that they knew it all, so we just let them get on with it.

'As fast as they called a Quarter Guardian, I dismissed them; which went completely unnoticed. That is, with the exception of the South, where Adam was stationed. As he turned to give the call, I had to suppress a laugh as I could tell that he wasn't calling the usual Guardian. The sudden burst of power felt fertile enough but I doubt it was who *they* thought it was. I saw the wicked gleam in Adam's eyes as he turned to face me and thought: 'Oh, hell, we're in for some fun now!'

'The Gruesome Twosome obviously thought everything was fine and wasted no time in leading the Chant. They were in their own little world and I don't think they noticed that my mind was elsewhere. All the time the Chant was going on, I was over-riding it with one of my own, something to the tune of: *'Hecate, Hecate, ignore this call. This is a balls-up, one and all …'* while Adam was clearly stoking up a bit of naughty work of his own.

'Eventually the Chant ground to a halt. Vanessa was breathless with excitement and her eyes sparkled unnaturally.

Neither had noticed I was drinking far and above my normal consumption of wine but it was quite deliberate. Vanessa's expression got sillier and she began behaving in an even more blatantly sexual manner than usual. She couldn't understand what was going on but after several unsuccessful attempts to seduce Adam, she turned her attentions on Roger. Vanessa wanted it, and she wanted it *now*. Adam and I got on with the wine, cakes and post-ritual cigarette while Roger obliged his highly-charged High Priestess. She didn't know what had hit her.'

Eventually Pris and Adam made their excuses and left even though Pris was bursting to go to the lavatory. As they walked to the car, Adam commented that the incense was a bit on the heavy side for a rite of that sort, and Pris confessed that she'd provided them with a nice bit of Saturnalian stuff to really get things going. At the end of the road, Pris lifted her skirt in the shadows and released the much-needed bodily function into the sewers. With that piddle went all the hard work of the evening; maybe a few rats would be especially fertile but that wouldn't matter over much. Adam later admitted that he'd thought it would be safer just to let the rite grind itself out in Vanessa, while leaving Pris to collect any magical remnants and piddle it way.

We can report that nothing happened after the rite – no pregnancies occurred – so no harm done. As far as our Coven was concerned, the evening was a resounding success; in Roger and Vanessa's opinion, it was an embarrassing failure they are careful never to mention. As Pris said: 'Perfect love and perfect trust, eh? Not if you're working with *real* witches, you don't!'

Perhaps I should explain that the way Adam and Pris work with outsiders bears no resemblance to the way we work *within* the Coven. Most outsiders go in for what Pris refers to as 'a bit of G&A role-playing' complete with Circle-casting and calling the Quarter Guardians, which is not how we do things at all. Neither do we have the pre-prescribed rituals that are learned and repeated by rote — but then you won't find our workings in any books.

It is always assumed that love spells are 'good' spells which harm none, but in fact they can be incredible selfish, destructive and sometimes, downright-wicked. What the books don't tell is that you, as the innocent dupe, can get the retribution dumped back three fold on you, if the facts haven't been thoroughly examined enough beforehand. One of Gerry's customers calls herself a 'feng shui healer' but she wasn't above asking for help when it suited. 'You're into this witchcraft stuff,' said the Healer. 'Can you do a love spell for me?'

It transpired that the recipient of these attentions was her sister's husband. Gerry pointed out that working magic to break up another person's relationship without their consent was tantamount to black magic. The Healer looked horrified and protested that all she wanted was a *love* spell. And anyway she didn't want her brother-in-law full time; she didn't want to break up her sister's marriage; she only wanted him to fall for her charms.

Gerry wasn't impressed. 'Since I knew this woman advises *her* customers on all manner of healing matters in which she invokes all manner of Christian saints and Oriental entities, I pointed out that a working of this nature could result in some very bad karma. She looked at me blankly before commenting that she'd worry about that in her next life. And these people call themselves healers; I wouldn't trust her to unblock a drain never mind act as a conduit for healing energy.'

This same woman also had the audacity to attempt to 'heal' a young man's homosexuality without his consent or any prior consultation. The reason being that a young woman friend fancied him and the Healer thought he would return the girl's interest if he were 'cured' of being gay!

There's also an increasingly growing number of people who read Tarot commercially but few know how to use the cards correctly as a magico-mystical device for themselves. The true purpose of the symbolism is to provide a focus for meditation, or as a mystical gateway to other planes. As such, the witch or magician's personal Tarot deck is considered to be a part of their magical equipment and therefore never to be tainted by being in contact with outside influences if it is to be used in ritual. Used correctly, each Tarot 'speaks' in a different way, which is why it is impossible to give a 'standard interpretation'.

Gerry finds this to be one of the most intriguing subjects for beginners, who often ask for a reading whenever they come into the shop. 'There are some who charge £40 a time for a bog-standard reading but it would be against my principles to do it, even though it would boost the takings quite nicely.'

And as Pris often says of the commercial readers: 'The greatest fallacy is that you have to have some psychic ability to be able to do it. You'd get the same results if you went out and bought a Tarot deck for yourself rather than pay a lot of money to someone else.'

Despite what some books and authorities may tell you, there is no such thing as a definitive meaning of any Tarot system – and no two books will agree on the exact use, layout or interpretation. Whatever system you use, the pictures or symbols are there simply to show you something that your deep mind already knows and is trying to communicate to you. What people find difficult to accept is that the future is not fixed. It is a series of probabilities that can be changed to bring them into line with your desires. The Tarot merely gives an indication of the likely outcome of situations *as they now stand*; which is why a routine textbook reading can hardly be deemed as valid. Neither should anyone try to be too clever with the reading since if you rely too much on intellect, you will certainly make the task far more complicated, and may miss the point altogether.

Another area that tends to flummox newcomers to Craft are the magical correspondences relating to the many herbs, plants and fragrances. Gerry is a most accomplished herbalist and holistic healer, who prepares and blends all his own herbs, oils and incenses. He often runs workshops for people wanting to learn more about the subject but who are not necessarily into Craft. Some of his more enthusiastic students, however, have found out the hard way that some very familiar plants can produce some extremely interesting side effects if you're not familiar with them. One group did some impromptu blending while Gerry was out of the way and quickly discovered that the indiscriminate gathering of garden plants can produce some rather strange reactions when the blend included opium poppy.

One of the most common problems is, however, psychic attack. It is a waste of time casting a circle of protection around your home that can be breached whenever your assailant phones to ask a favour. Grant it to be rid of them and you've effectively scuppered your own defences. What folk find hard to accept is that most psychic attacks are launched by those closest to them: family, a friend, a colleague or even a fellow covener. This is why the Coven has a jaundiced view of the popular 'perfect love, perfect trust' adage of modern Wicca – we've seen far too many who've provided psychic fast-food energy in perfect naiveté.

Protective wires *do* get crossed, however. 'How long does that milk bottle need to stay near the back gate?' asked Pris's son. His mother looked bemused until he brandished an impressive algae arrangement inside the glass.

'Nothing to do with me,' she said. 'It's obviously been there since you filled it with hot water to de-ice the car windscreen last winter!'

'Oh,' he replied. 'I thought it was one of your protective spell bottles.'

Nevertheless, he still relies on his mother's talents when necessary. He went for an interview in a smart suit and accessories, sporting briefcase and mobile phone – the perfect picture of the young executive. What the interviewer didn't see was the lucky stone, purple talisman and red string in his pocket.

He got the job but a few weeks later complained to his mother: 'The job's perfect but why did my boss have to be such a perfect bitch?'

'I covered *everything* you told me to,' she replied. 'You should be careful about what you ask for, you might just get exactly that!'

Our neighbours know what we are and apart from the odd request to Gerry in the pub for 'a bit o' something for me piles, love' nothing is ever mentioned about Craft or our part in it, except for some good-natured banter. Occasionally a visitor will breach these unwritten rules of etiquette but it rarely causes a problem. We're a tight-knit community and we take part in most of the social functions – even seasonal Church events.

At one party, Pris was accosted by a visitor from Belfast. 'I hear you dabble?'

Pris fixed her with a beady stare. 'I assured you I do more than dabble,' she replied.

'Can you do spell to get me daughter off the drugs?' the woman continued unabashed. 'And while you're at it, the house I live in brings nothing but bad luck. Every time I get on me feet, someone throws a spanner in the works.'

'Living where you do, I should be thanking the Old Ones that a spanner is the only thing that gets thrown,' was the reply.

Bramble Cottage is the last in the lane and over the past few months several elderly neighbours have died. As a mark of respect Pris went along to the funerals. At the last one a small, dapper chap kept nodding and winking at her over the buffet in the kitchen. Finally, when they were left alone he sidled over and murmured. 'Not you again! That's three of them down this year, perhaps I should start paying you commission. Let me know who's next, eh?' With another conspiratorial wink he was gone and Pris later discovered it was the local undertaker.

Pris and I were well and truly sealed inside our respective protective bubbles when we attended the full moon gathering of Roger's group on Granny's orders. Now if there's one thing I can beat the rest at hands down, it's the Cloak of Invisibility and tonight it was designer gear.

As soon as we walked into the room, I literally vanished from sight much to Pris's chagrin – since it meant she was the bait. In no time at all she'd been whisked off into a quiet corner by Alan Wicca, and his family saga continued without let or hindrance. I circulated around the room eavesdropping on snippets of the conversation each time I passed. It transpired that, in addition to his Norfolk connection, his Granny was also a *direct* descendant of Isobel Gowdie. Alan Wicca was the proud possessor of a copy of her Black Book, which he was offering to show privately to Pris, since she was obviously a lady of immense magical talent.

As anyone in Craft knows, the story of 'our Isobel' began in 1647 when she met 'a man in grey' in Auldearne church who put a mark on her and turned her into a witch. She was still active some fifteen years later until 1662, so she was knocking on for the time, yet in all that time she never had any children, so exactly how his Granny comes in is a mystery as Isobel was probably barren. Although Isobel confessed quite cheerfully, giving intimate details of her witchcraft and implicating others, she never mentions anything in the court records to do with keeping a Black Book. Her confessions were so expansive, lewd and offensive for Presbyterian Scotland that there is little doubt that she was executed as her trial was at the height of the witchcraft persecutions and her Black Book would have been produced as damning evidence. As Isobel talked herself to her death, she would have hardly kept quiet about the existence of such a book – even assuming she could read and write!

'Well,' I said, in the car going home. 'When do you get to see this wondrous tome?'

'There's a small problem,' replied Pris stifling a giggle.

'Apparently he lent it to a friend up in Scotland and he's waiting for her to *post* it back to him!'

I regret to say that we laughed so much we nearly drove off the road. Considering the rarity of books from 1662, it's strange how Alan Wicca would entrust his own unique and priceless copy to the vagaries of the Post Office.

Chapter Three

Sartorial Elegance

We come across many different people on our rich and colourful journey through life. Occasionally they even manage to infiltrate a close-knit group such as ours before their quirks and foibles begin to manifest.

Helena, our Mad Medium, has been a member of the Coven for years and has, in her time, been an extremely accomplished seer and diviner. Unfortunately, in her early days the Spiritualists got to her first and as a result, she was encouraged to let any visiting entity have its say, instead of confining the utterances to the weekly meetings. This state of affairs continued for a number of years until she suffered from a mental burn-out having completed her professional training and being at the beck and call of any psychic entity that felt like dropping in for a chat.

Guy and Gerry devoted a good deal of their time to teaching Helena how to control these unwanted interruptions and by and large she was eventually able to confine her psychic utterances to the Circle. Occasionally we would be treated to a normal conversation being interrupted by statements like: 'Does the initial 'F' mean anything to anyone?'

Those in the group would wait politely while Helena stared fixedly into space, listening intently. Then she'd shake her head and say: 'It was nothing,' and carry on talking as though nothing had happened. Unless Rupert was around and then the response would be: 'What a load of bollocks!' He has always thought Helena needed a swift boot in the bustle whenever she indulged in one of her impromptu psychic monologues, but the rest of us made allowances because of her first-rate powers.

'Things have gotten out of hand with Helena,' confided Gerry when Pris and I arrived at the shop, demanding coffee and conversation. 'One hates to say this about another Coven member, but I really think she's an incense stick short of a full pack.'

'Tell us something we don't know,' I answered.

'C'mon, Gerry,' coaxed Pris. 'There's more to this than the Mad Medium throwing one of her wobblies. We all know you go round the place like a thing possessed with incense and invocation after she's visited – banishing any lingering spiritual dross which she might have called in and then left behind. So what's wrong?'

Gerry smiled weakly. 'You'll think I'm daft ...'

'So, we think you're daft for being so nice to her,' I interrupted. *'What's wrong?'*

'She's started to invite herself round at all hours, mostly in the evening after we've closed for the day. Oh, bugger it ... she's throwing herself all over Guy at every opportunity. He's getting really fed up with it and says he'll leave the Coven if something isn't done about her and quickly.'

'Bottle the bitch,' advised Pris without any hesitation.

And I must confess I agreed.

What I've failed to mention before is that Gerry and Guy are a gay couple and Helena, like the rest of the members of the Coven, is fully aware of this. Although a large number of groups would have an apoplexy at the mere thought of a homosexual being admitted to a working group, the Coven doesn't have a problem. In fact, there are distinct advantages to working with gays, but as with anything else, it is a case of how well balanced they are within themselves.

From past experience, we know that a well-balanced gay person can quite easily integrate into an existing group as long as the other members can talk openly about gender energy. Coven workings have their fair share of 'camp' jokes but never stem from malice. And Rupert, who is the most macho of individuals, considers them to be highly valued witches, if only for the fact that Guy is a wonderful cook.

As far as the problem with Helena is concerned, it isn't the done thing to go around flinging yourself into the arms of a good-looking man who happens to be in a permanent relationship and a fellow Covener to boot. It transpired that in an attempt at blatant rudeness (since politeness had failed) Guy had turned on a recording of a Wagnerian opera to drown her out. A few minutes into the Overture and the Mad Medium started howling like a banshee from the depths of a rather energetic trance.

Rather alarmed by this state of affairs, the two men stared at each other, not knowing what to do next in case there *was* something seriously wrong. She lurched forward and as Guy tried to catch her, found himself enveloped in the grip of a rampant octopus. With Helena howling and Wagner giving it mambo, Gerry commented that it was almost like trying to prise her off Guy with a tyre lever when he realised it was a contrived performance.

'In the finish I thought 'bugger it' and emptied a pitcher of iced water over her head. Guy flounced off into the bedroom and I bundled her out into the car. But can you believe it, she didn't say a word! She sat in the passenger seat with water dripping down her neck and gossiped on about the roadworks in Market Street. When we got to her place, she thanked me for a lovely evening and climbed out of the car. So either she's barking mad or I am.'

I'm afraid we laughed but this sort of situation can seriously damage the working relationship of any coven, no matter how close the friendship. Furthermore Helena doesn't do that sort of thing at the hairdresser, and she doesn't do it at home in front of her mother (who *really* doesn't approve), and neither does she perform in front of her patients. She is a local health visitor who lives at home with a rather bossy and possessive mother so it could be just a classic case of repressed sexuality and frustration.

The three of us sat staring into the candle flickering inside the oil evaporator on the table. 'She's got to go,' I said as Dame of the Coven.

'You can't just throw her out, tempting as it might be,' said Pris.

'I'll get her moved on … no, I mean a new job or something,' said Gerry hastily as we both looked up.

'Will her mother let her go?' I asked.

'It will have to be a pretty big incentive,' added Pris doubtfully. 'That old mother's got claws like crampons.'

'Trust me,' said Gerry.

'Well, you'd better throw in a decent wardrobe while you're at it,' I muttered. 'No one will take her on the way she is. Our Gloucester Old Spot has more dress-sense than Helena.'

'And better taste, too,' added Pris, thinking of the bacon.

By common consent, the Coven dresses in black. Not because of any sinister or Gothic bent but purely and simply because this is the most practical way of dressing when working out of doors. On cold, wet November nights it is not a good idea to go trailing through the woods, or over the quarry, dressed like rejects from the Hellfire Club.

Instead we wear black trousers and sweaters that enable us to blend into the shadows and move quickly should any strangers approach. Our full-length, black hooded cloaks are carried in rucksacks and not worn unless it's bitterly cold or raining. And let me tell you, Pris and I each have a consecrated set of thermal underwear for winter working!

Sky-clad working isn't for us. This is not because we're prudish or unduly sensitive but because the weather in this climate is rarely conducive to romping around in the nude. There is nothing more off-putting that a shivering witchlet, covered in goose-bumps, desperately trying to get close enough to the fire without incinerating their pubes – while their backside turns blue. True, once the Circle is cast the cold recedes but it's not worth the risk of hypothermia for the tired witch or in those whose magical abilities aren't up to scratch.

There are those who claim that going 'sky-clad' means that there are no barriers between you and the natural energies with which you intend to work. I'm afraid we would respond that if clothing presents such an obstacle to magical energies, then something isn't right somewhere along the line. As with all Old Craft covens, there are times when ritual nudity is *de rigueur* – that is, require by etiquette or custom, and so there are rituals when we will perform *à la Aradia*: '*and as the sign that ye are truly free, ye shall be naked in your rites ...*'

Until we agreed on what Rupert refers to as 'going ninja', we all wore our own personal, but discreet, choice of robe and this is where Helena came into her own. One night she sported a billowing white chimeraic creation somewhat between a confirmation dress, a bridal gown and a nun's habit. We blamed it on the Spiritualist Church but it was bloody disconcerting to see a white nun looming up on the other side of the needfire, I can tell you! Not to mention the several near misses with the candles and her offering of a bottle of Blue Nun!

Even the more traditional Craft robes have their drawbacks. I well remember the night when Pris conducted the Autumn Equinox ritual with a bramble caught in the crack of her bum and a squashed slug decorating the back view of her robe in a tasteful surrealist design.

Not to mention my own mishap in being forced to borrow a robe from Gwen. We'd all been invited over to Roger's for a goodwill Lammas ritual (in the pre-Vanessa days) and having left my case open, discovered just as we were robing, that their cat had peed on mine. There was a hasty scuffling about and a spare robe smelling of something only marginally better than cat's pee was produced. Unfortunately the garment was designed for a six foot giant and I'm only marginally over five feet – and there was no spare cord.

I trailed into the coven-room looking like Dopey out of *Snow White and the Seven Dwarfs*. Pris went cross-eyed trying not to laugh, while everyone else ignored the spectacle. Moving around was preceded by a ballet-like sweep of the foot and all went well until we began the Spiral. Moving around the Circle I steadily climbed up the *inside* of the robe until my foot appeared out of the neck-hole. At this point, Pris collapsed in hysterics and the Circle ground to a halt; even normally taciturn Rupert excused himself to go to the bathroom.

Our turn came when Adam got stuck in the lining of his robe with his earring caught up in the stitching. It was an outdoor ritual and Pris had made some rather stunning, fully lined robes for him and herself. She appeared from behind the tree looking quite magnificent in the firelight – but where was Adam?

We waited as scuffling noises came from the shadows. Finally, there was *Psst!* **Pssst!** Pris disappeared to find Adam firmly wedged up the lining, trying to force his head through the sleeve. In attempting to extract himself, an earring had caught up in the fabric and he was flailing around like a ferret in a sack. That was the end of individuality and the onset of convenience.

If our own antics weren't enough to convince us that some form of standard ritual clothing was essential, then visiting another group clinched it. Having been asked if we'd any objection to working sky-clad, Joan decided to pay homage at the altar by kneeling and bowing her head to the earth. I was standing with Pris in the South at the time, having dodged around to avoid the smoke from the fire. All I can say is that I shall never be able to look upon the Qabalistic sign for the Sun ¤ in quite the same way again.

Despite our mishaps during ritual working, by common consent, we all look smartly turned out if we're going public for any reason. 'How can so many people who are all claiming to be 'expressing themselves' and 'following their own path', all land up looking like clones. And not only looking like clones but also sounding like cloned sheep,' growled Pris at one pub moot.

'The only hint at a difference in gender being that some are bearded and some are not. 'We're pagans,' they intone, 'we love the planet.' Love the planet! These wishy-washy tie-dyed sheep aren't even *on* the bloody planet.'

I decided it was a good time to pass on Harriet's latest bit of gossip. Since she's been cleverly out-manoeuvred by her coven's Magister into losing pole-position to a younger, more glamorous piece, she's feeling a little indiscreet. 'She has the magical aptitude of a gnat but all this pales into nothingness once she's peeled her kit off,' she reported. 'The women hover in the shadows hoping the fire won't cast an interesting mottled effect on their cellulite, while the men keep falling over each other because they can't take their eyes of the Strumpet.

'I don't think we've completed a coherent ritual since she arrived,' Harriet concluded.

My personal pet hate is pagan jewellery which is some of the most hideous I've ever encountered and whilst it's appreciated that not everyone can afford expensive items, why is it necessary to adorn every visible bit of flesh with occult symbolism? Pris reckons that the abundance of rings, earrings, necklaces, pendants, ankle chains and toe rings means that there's less to carry to a ritual in terms of drums and tambourines, since the jewellery provides the percussion and all the women have to do is move about a bit. That said, Pris used to wear a diamond nose-stud until the night she sneezed and the thing flew across the room and brained the cat.

Although it appears to have little significance in Wiccan circles, for us the staff, or stang, is one of the oldest icons of the Ol' Lad and can either be a decorated pitchfork or carved from the forked branch of a tree. Some use ash – we use alder or black-thorn. This is 'shod with iron' and usually adorned with an animal mask or skull. In Pris's case her individual beech staff sports a sheep's skull, affectionately known as Daisy – and often serves as the altar. One evening Pris was forced to borrow their son's small car as their own was at the garage for repair. It wasn't until they'd travelled some way that Adam realised that Daisy's 'head' was hanging over the rear passenger seat nodding and grinning away with every bump in the road. Several passing cars gave them some extremely strange looks until Adam got out and ignominiously covered the skull with a supermarket bag!

Alan Wicca's been putting himself about a bit and it was Gerry who was able to add the next part of his saga, since he'd been camped in the shop for over three hours. Guy kept wandering through from the gallery to scowl meaningfully, but this chap's hide is too thick to notice that he's out-stayed his welcome. Having left his Scottish ancestors behind, Gerry was treated to a monologue on Granny's links to the legendary (if not highly suspect) George Pickingill who died in 1909.

Being the good witch that he is, Gerry discovered that Alan Wicca was born in 1944 and *adopted*, which rather blew a hole in the Scottish connection but he declined to pursue the matter as to whether Granny was related by blood or *ink*. Being generous, however, we estimated that Granny was then about 45ish, which meant that old George was pushing a hundred when Granny joined his coven in her 20s. There are some wonderful tales surviving about old George but we reckoned the Wicca-man's Granny was about to beat 'em hands down. Especially when they got onto the Romany connection … and the New Forest …

Here we had an advantage.

Gordon's grandfather, Old Joe, had been gamekeeper to Rupert's father and grandfather. He was a natural man of the soil and, as far as we knew, the oldest surviving member of Old Craft in the locality – and he *had* known the New Forest witches during the war years. As far as he could remember, by the time his own son, Young Joe, was old enough to be brought into the

Craft, Rupert's step-Granny had been running things for several years. Which led us to another burning question: How old is Granny Jay?

'Dunno Missus, the old bugger looked like that when I were a lad and I's ninety-two next Candlemas.'

There's many an early morning caller who's been confronted by the terrible sight of Old Joe sitting on the outside lavatory with a shotgun across his knees. Unshaven, shod in a massive pair of boots and with his long-johns around his ankles, Old Joe takes his early morning exercise by taking pot-shots at the rooks and pigeons that invade his vegetable patch.

This early morning ritual is conducted in all weathers throughout the year, despite the fact that he has a perfectly good bathroom inside the cottage. We have the suspicion that this is the local baptism of fire for new health visitors who, unwarned by their colleagues about the apparition in the lavatory, fall into the trap of calling on the old boy at the crack of dawn before he disappears into the woods. Social Services have been trying to get him into an old folk's home for years, but he always manages to evade them. One bright myopic young thing suggested that his failing faculties could prove hazardous living alone in an isolated cottage.

Old Joe picked up the shotgun. 'See bird on yon fence, gel?'

The girl glanced in disbelief at a robin perched on the nearby trellis. There was the boom of the shotgun and a rook dropped from the fence on the far side of the paddock.

'Does that look like I can't see to get around?' the old man thundered as the social worker fled.

Whenever Old Joe brought game up to the kitchen, Rupert's mother had always offered a cup of tea. He hopped from one hobnailed boot to the other, juggling his cap and the cup and saucer as he performed his strange ritual dance on the flagstone floor. When he thought she wasn't looking he swiftly poured the tea from the cup and slurped it out of the saucer before bolting out of the door.

Although he's never seen without those massive boots, he's still as quiet as a cat when walking in the woods; even Young Joe swears about the old man 'creeping up' on him and scaring him witless.

Chapter Four

I Read It in a Book

Arm-chair witchery has a lot to answer for and it's time for folk to sling out the books which expound the dubious advantages of the popular pick-n-mix approach to magic before someone gets hurt. Those new to Craft have a great deal of difficulty in understanding that cross-Tradition working can produce some extremely unpleasant or unexpected results – details of which *don't* feature in the popular pagan press.

Like the witch-mum who, after packing the kids off to bed, settled herself down for a spot of gentle meditation by candle light, whilst taking a bath. One of the candles tipped over into the water and as our dedicated witch leaped up and bent over to retrieve it, she scorched her pudenda on another candle which gave a whole new meaning to the term Red Hot Mama.

Like the chap who invoked Isis is an area sacred to Brighde and wondered why the Celtic deity reacted strongly to the invasion of this foreign *bint*. Conflicting energies can cause sickness and disorientation because of the disruption of balance, so it is unwise to try to work with differing focuses of power in the same ritual.

Like the couple who conducted a fertility rite at the site of a Neolithic burial chamber and suffered a series of miscarriages as a result. They assumed because it was 'old' it would radiate beneficial magical properties.

Like the chap who claimed to an Old Craft Elder's face that he was from her own teaching tradition (he'd never worked with her or her coven) because he'd read something of hers in a magazine. The look on his face when someone explained to whom he was speaking was a sight to behold.

Like the woman who described herself as a healer but when

questioned about her working methods, explained that she'd *never* actually done any healing because she didn't want anyone to know she was a pagan.

Like the budding ritual magicians who invoked power into the triangle of conjuration placed *inside* the protective magic circle with themselves.

Like the unsuspecting who include Hecate in the welcoming chant for the Summer Solstice – the old girl's a bit of a party pooper and her dog is even more anti-social – best stick to solar deities and leave the Dark Ones for the darker nights and shadow working. Neither is it a good idea to schedule a 'love-spell' for All Hallows (Samhain), unless you're into necrophilia.

Harriet usually has plenty of her own tales to tell but the advent of the Strumpet surpasses all others at the moment, as they spend most coven meetings peeling her off the Magister. 'Rex has lost it,' she informed us. 'This lass can strip down to the buff in six seconds flat and has now taken to wearing an extremely large gold crucifix in Circle to ward off any evil that she feels emanating from me! If she wants the job that bad, she can have it.'

Jocelyn, another Lady of our acquaintance, reports the arrival of the Virgin Mandy who is apparently the cultivated dead ringer for the Xtian version. 'She stands there with a right-on serene expression, hair parted carefully in the centre, hands folded demurely over her neat light blue robe. She's a vegetarian who preaches love, compassion and universal kinship – to an Old Craft coven! And her totem's an owl. When one of the group asked if she was into swallowing live mice on the astral, she was nearly sick. I think she got off the bus at the wrong stop.'

Now whatever you read about witchcraft these days there is always the profusion of names to cope with and in modern Wicca, the Goddess is a rose by any other name, regardless of whether it's Celtic, Norse, Roman, Egyptian, Anglo-Saxon or

Greek. In Old Craft the deities are, more often than not, referred to simply as the Lass and the Ol' Lad. Newcomers are confused by this seemingly irreverent appellation but Old Crafters don't need all the extravagant trappings, ritual equipment and symbolism.

To paraphrase from one of Alan Richardson's books: all the images of gods and goddesses are products of our own making, which we use to give our minds something to focus on. The Lass and the Ol' Lad are good enough for us.

Alan Wicca's really getting into his stride and had them all spell-bound at the last pub moot. By this time in her career, his Granny's lineage was so impressive that she had been immediately accepted by the New Forest Covens. She was, apparently, great pals with Sybil Leek, Madeline Montalban, Monique Wilson *and* Dorothy Clutterbuck, who introduced her to Gerald Gardner. He, in turn, liked Granny so much that he insisted she spend her summers with him on the Isle of Man and she took little Alan with her each time.

Granny didn't believe in initiations – yet she slotted in quite happily with Gerald's gang and it's odd that Cecil Williamson, Doreen Valiente or Patricia Crowther never get a mention. (Perhaps now that Cecil and Doreen have gone to the 'Summerlands', they'll be featured in any future narrative!) Needless to say, the Wicca-man's Granny was naturally present at the huge gathering of witches who met to turn back the Germans during WWII so she managed to get about quite a bit.

All this *information* is readily available in book form to anyone but what is never pointed out is that in all realms of magic there are the Lesser and Greater Mysteries. The former are basic instructions for approaching a magical path but no matter how well read a person, they will never find any 'secret truths' in books. Even those written by well-known names in Craft will always stop short of revelation no matter what the publisher's blurb may promise. Those 'names' are fully aware that by revealing more than just the Lesser Mysteries would be breaking their oaths, not just to the Craft but to their fellow Initiates.

The Greater Mysteries themselves can only be understood by practical experience; they cannot be taught or expressed in words. It is often difficult for the beginner to accept that there is no secret formula which will help them avoid the hard work involved. It is also difficult for many to understand that formal initiation into one particular group or Tradition merely means the initiate has been accepted by that group or Tradition – *not Craft per se.* Neither does it automatically follow that the Greater Mysteries have been revealed to that Initiate. Books and teachers can only map out a few basic signposts; all they ever will be is the finger pointing the way in the Silence that follows.

Because of the plethora of rubbish that is passed off as Craft by a large number of pagan writers, Pris was persuaded to join the team as Agony Aunt for a pagan newsletter to 'tell it like it is'. The problem with most of the letter writers is that they've learned their witchcraft from books and when they get conflicting information from different authors, they don't have the *practical* experience to differentiate between modern Wicca and traditional Old Craft.

Admittedly there have been one or two who have benefited from a guiding hand but by and large, the content of the letters hardly stimulate the intellect – or the sympathy for that matter. We were sitting at the kitchen table sorting through some of the letters and becoming increasingly despondent at the number from people who obviously just wanted someone to write to. The agony was in the repetitive saga of manifested 'things' that were lurking around in hundreds of bedrooms up and down the country.

'This is contagious over-active imagination,' groaned Pris. 'What on earth can I say?'

Rupert, who'd been leaning against the Aga drinking his

coffee, rinsed the mug under the tap and put it in the dishwasher. 'Tell 'em to pack it in and get a life,' he said, walking out of the kitchen.

Pris stared at his retreating back for a moment. '*That*,' she said, 'is probably the most sensible bit of advice I could give any of them.'

Whatever you may read about 'harming none', make no mistake about it, witches really do look after their own. Recently it was necessary for the Coven to call upon that 'Higher Law' we believe in to protect those in the service of the Old 'Uns.

Late one evening Pris was driving past Granny's lane when a motorbike pulled out in front of her, causing her to swerve into the ditch. At the third attempt she managed to reverse the car out of the mud and, swearing under her breath to teach the two young thugs a lesson, she started for home. Suddenly she was aware of a cold chill in the pit of her stomach. Granny's lane came to a dead end and the two youths had a reputation for terrorising the young and the elderly. She backed up and made her way carefully down the track.

The icy grip refused to go away and before getting out of the car, Pris put through a call to the Farm. Light was streaming out of the kitchen door and huddled on the step was Granny, her head lying in a large pool of blood, with Baggins standing over her, his eyes wild with fear. By the time I got there, Pris was pinned up against the wall by the irate goat, who would not allow her to touch his helpless owner.

'Get this bloody animal off me,' said Pris between gritted teeth as I lugged the brute away and fastened his chain.

'He's frightened,' I said simply.

'*He's* frightened *me*,' she replied rolling up her sleeves and bending over Granny. 'It's a nasty head wound and the best thing we can do is try and get her indoors so we've got light.'

Between us we managed to lift Granny through the door and

onto the rickety old sofa, which is normally occupied by the dog. 'I think she should go to …' I was about to say 'hospital' when Granny's eyes flickered open.

'*Please,*' she whispered hoarsely. 'Don't send me to hospital … get Gerry, he'll know what to do. *Please,* Gabrielle … *don't let them take me …*' For the first time in her life, Granny was scared of something, and seeing the old girl reduced to such a pitiful state made me angry. Pris put a call through to Gerry.

'Who did this?' I asked.

'Those two yobbos who Rupert threatened to shoot last month when he caught them chasing the horses with a motorbike. You know the police won't do anything and most people are too afraid to report them,' replied Pris.

'We don't need to involve the police over this,' I said sharply.

Pris glanced up just as Gerry swept into the room with his medicine bag of herbs, creams and salves and ordered us out of the way. 'Head wounds always bleed a lot,' he said cheerfully, 'but as long as there's no shock or concussion we don't need a doctor, if that's what Granny wants. We'd better stay here the night.'

Pris and I looked around the kitchen that was in an even worse state than usual due to everyone paddling about in the blood and the copious amount of goat droppings that littered the stone floor. There was a broken window and shattered glass. Gerry took charge and started directing operations by mobile so that our families knew where we were.

He was also adamant that Granny shouldn't spend the night downstairs. The flat he and Guy have above the gallery is a hymn to good taste but he didn't bat a carefully brushed eyelash at the muck and devastation. Neither did he wince as the knee of his beautifully tailored trousers came into contact with a pile of goat shit. Pris and I were despatched to investigate the bedroom and to our surprise, found the upstairs rooms immaculate. Wooden floors covered with an impressive collection of Persian rugs in faded blues and russets; the furniture old but highly polished and everywhere smelling of lavender.

'Bloody hell,' said Pris, 'Who would have believed it?'

Between us we managed to manhandle Granny upstairs and while Gerry did his stuff, Pris and I cleaned the kitchen floor much to the annoyance of the dog and the cat, whose nightly routine was being thoroughly upset. The offending wax coat was crumpled on the floor and we eyed it and the Rayburn longingly before resisting the temptation to burn it.

Eventually Gerry reappeared with Granny's version of events. Apparently, earlier that afternoon, the youths had chased a young girl down the lane on their motorbike. Hearing her scream, Granny rushed out brandishing her besom as it was the closest thing to hand and clouted the one who'd grabbed hold of the girl. He leaped back on the bike and, as the driver spun it around, kicked out at the girl, sending her flying. Granny picked her up and offered a homemade lemonade into which she'd sneaked a few drops of her own 'rescue remedy' before carefully washing and dressing the injured arm.

It transpired that Rachel was staying with her uncle and aunt, the Kelligans, while her parents sorted out their divorce. They're 'incomers' and already crossed swords with Granny over the activities of Baggins, who'd ruined their chances of entering the local flower show earlier in the year. Understandably, Rachel was afraid to walk home so Granny escorted her and, having heard their niece's side of the story, Granny was offered a cup of tea. It transpires that the boys make a habit of riding over their land through a gap in the fencing, and race down the steep paths into the old quarry where they go rabbiting.

After dark Granny heard the sound of the motorbike, followed by the crash of splintering glass as a brick came hurtling through the window. Rushing outside she was deliberately hit on the head; the last thing she remembered was Baggins charging her assailant and knocking him flying.

By this time in the narrative, Adam had driven over to mend the broken kitchen window and, taking a good look around, noticed the tyre marks from the bike and the number plate, obviously torn off in their haste to get away. There was no doubt as to the identity of the culprits but by the time the social workers had their say, there'd be little done by way of corrective sentencing. We knew what needed to be done; this was women's work for which we don't need to involve the men.

At midnight, Pris and I made our way down to the group of ancient apple trees where, for years, Granny has gone to work her own special magic. No candles, no wine, no paraphernalia were needed because we immediately felt the magic of the place and we wasted no time in calling upon the Old One who watches. Clouds cut across the sky. There was no moon and only the odd star to be seen as the wind howled and gusted, first this way and that, making the ancient trees creak and groan. Pris's voice blended with the howling wind; her words snatched away by the night.

Here, yesterday, a terrible deed was done … come forth from hills and dales to take revenge upon those who sought to harm your priestess and Witch … And from your realms I summon the great spirit of Bazalmaicha, who shall rend the veil of time to walk again in this world. For this night, and this night only shall you enter our world and you shall seek out the evil ones who did this deed. And you shall rent torment upon them and they shall bleed, and their blood and foulness shall be your bargain … Having done your work shall you return to your realms, to dwell in quiet until such time as you are called again … Bazalmaicha, Bazalmaicha, Bazalmaicha, Bazalmaicha …

The wind howled even louder and the chant power increased until it reached a climax. Suddenly a large bird screamed and shot through the middle of the Circle and out into the night. The chanting stopped and after a few moments' silence we dropped down on the grass to recover. Without either of us speaking we left the orchard to make our way back to the cottage. Pris searched in the cupboards for the best drink in the house, pouring a little on the step in libation. By dawn, Granny was all for getting up and, while Pris and Gerry helped her to dress, I walked down to the orchard with a plate of scraps for the birds. To quote Crowley: So mote it be.

Rachel's uncle was also about bright and early to fix the gap in the fencing. He told Pris later there was a large rook that seemed to be watching him and when he stopped for a bacon sandwich, he threw the bird a crust. The bird remained close by and inexplicably he found himself talking to it, explaining why he was mending the fence, especially since the poor old lady (!) had been attacked. As he finished his repairs the bird flew off but remained circling the quarry. Not being a countryman, he wondered whether there was anything significant about its behaviour.

The youths were also about bright and early. Obviously they noticed the number plate was missing and realised it would incriminate them if it had been found near the cottage. There were too many people about to risk riding down the lane but Adam heard them as he was repairing the window.

The motorbike was heard idling about for most of the day but it was dusk before the youths decided to cut across the Kelligan's land and approach the cottage from the fields. No doubt laughing about how easy it had been to flatten the old witch, they sped across the open ground and in the half-light failed to notice the fence has been mended. Tyre tracks in the damp grass showed that at the last moment the rider tried to brake but he later claimed that a rook swooped off a fence post and into his face, causing him to swerve. The bike went from under them and they sailed over the fence, down into the quarry.

Now it just happens that Pris's totem is a rook ...

Later that week in the Fox & Hounds, we heard the rest of the story from one of the regulars whose brother-in-law's cousin's wife was one of the ambulance crew who fetched them out.

Fortunately (or unfortunately) for them, some irresponsible farmer had dumped half a dozen *very* dead sheep over the rim of the quarry and these rotting animals broke their fall. The impact caused the bloated carcasses to burst open and the youths were covered with rotting intestines and maggots – not to mention the stench.

'Patrick Kelligan heard them screaming their heads off and went to investigate,' said our informant. 'He couldn't do anything to help because the smell turned his stomach and there was this big black rook feasting on the maggots. The best he could do was call the emergency services.

'The stink was so overpowering that the police and the paramedics were reluctant to do anything and even suggested the lads took 'emselves to hospital. In the finish, they wrapped 'em in bin liners but it still took days before they could get rid of the smell in the ambulance. From what I can gather, there was copious amounts of vomit from all directions.'

The youths were discharged from hospital after a few days with only minor breaks and bruises but every time they appeared in the town they were followed by cries of 'Baa … baaa … baaaaaa.'

'Okay,' said Pris with a shudder. 'Whose perverted mind came up with the rotting sheep?'

Chapter Five

Coven Etiquette

Each coven or group has its own rules and regulations but even here there's always room for laughter. Jocelyn (or Josh as she's affectionately known for the reason she doesn't 'josh' i.e. joke when it comes to serious coven matters) reports the advent of the Bum-bag Witch on the pagan scene.

'Everyone thought she was pregnant when she turned up in the circle wearing a robe with an interesting little bulge. It later transpired that she was unwilling to be parted from her cigarettes and lighter and, at one stage, even walked *out* of the closed circle to light a fag from a candle. According to those who were present, it was most disconcerting to have her ferreting around under her robe via some side pocket arrangement throughout the working.'

With Bum-bag's negative energies in the circle there probably wasn't any real power-raising going on, anyway. Nevertheless it is extremely dangerous for those actively engaged in Circle work should the Circle be breached – for whatever reason. At best, it may be the unintentional dispersal of energy needed for a spell working. At worst, it could admit malevolent or negative energies – after all, it's not called a 'protective circle' for nothing.

Pris recalls a similar situation that happened to her when she was a witchlet. She and another neophyte had been taken to a very atmospheric part of a wood for a path-working exercise. Everything had gone well until the neophyte, seeing the fire had burned very low, had unthinkingly walked out of the Circle to fetch more wood. Their mentor had shouted at him to stop but before he could react the Circle had been breached. There was no mistaking the cold, malevolent energy that entered and even the experienced members of the group were hard pressed to remain calm as they closed down the operation. Talking about it today, all these years later, can still send a cold shiver down Pris's back.

When it comes to breaches of etiquette, our lurcher is blessed with an extremely long, intrusive nose, which he always insists in burying between ladies' thighs.

'How else can he get to know you,' said Pris in his defence.

'Well, I suppose he could always lick your behind,' I snapped, annoyed at my authority being undermined.

'There's too much of that sort of thing going on in the pagan community already!' she retorted.

Dogs, of course, are not impressed by that sort of thing. If you get to thinking you're a person of some influence, just try ordering someone else's dog around and see where it gets you. Dogs like to know where they stand in the pack and providing the perimeters are firmly set, they allow nothing to interfere with the system or confusion sets in. So it is with members of Old Craft …

For us the 'Man's' function is to fulfil the letter of the law and administer justice according to Coven law *when it is asked for*. To the Man and the Dame of the Coven, all members owe absolute allegiance, while to the Man or rather, the law he represents, they owe duty. The dual function of the Man and the Dame is what it has always been: to oversee the training of new members up to certain standards, develop any hidden or latent powers they may have, and to encourage the acceptance of truth as opposed to the illusion which often clouds much of what passes for occult teaching.

Traditionally speaking, the Man was looked upon as the human embodiment of the sacrificial god who, at the end of a seven-year cycle, was required to shed his blood, or that of a living representative of the totem animal of the group. Today, this form of sacrifice is no longer demanded; the Man has relinquished his 'divine king' overtones and in many covens much of his authority has passed to the Dame, or 'Lady' as some prefer.

As far as the Coven is concerned, however, the Man retains

this traditional role as the one who makes the sacrifice of dedicating himself to the group. His pact is made in the manner he sees as fitting to the position he holds and is renewable every seven years; this is a private rite carried out in the form of a solemn and binding oath and is part of the Greater Male Mysteries. If the pact be sealed in blood, *it will be his own*, not that of some other poor creature — and Rupert is very much a man of honour and tradition.

The Dame assumes the responsibility for the management of the Coven and, in our case, conducts operations with the assistance of the Coven's proculators. Like her Man, she has reached her position by being elected and remains there for as long as she is willing to do so – renewing her oath every seven years, although in some groups the Dame must relinquish her position once she is no longer fertile. She directs all Coven activities and within the sacred area her word is Law – which is why Rupert hasn't been bothered with details about Helena's attempts at disrupting the domestic harmony at *chez* Castor & Pollux, or Granny's recent problems with the malodorous bikers.

Depending on the number of people involved, the Coven comprises three levels of members: full Initiates and, (for want of a better description) acolytes and neophytes. A neophyte is required to serve for a year and a day before being formally accepted by the Coven. In the case of those who have not reached 28 years of age, their position as an acolyte can be a long one.

Initiates must be fully capable and experienced enough to assume any position in a temporary capacity; which is why Pris and Adam often get hauled out to act as relief shepherds to Roger's flock at Granny's insistence. (I wish we could get away from the subject of sheep.) Since his own initiates managed to set fire to the coven room the last time they were left to fend for themselves, he daren't leave them unsupervised! Every time, Adam swears he won't be roped in again, but Granny has a most persuasive nature – it's called fear!

We're in Castor & Pollux. 'There!' said Gerry triumphantly, sticking a 'Genuine Witch's Honey' label on the last jar of Pris's stock.

'He'll be asking us for 'crone's water' next,' muttered Pris as we moved over to the alcove to join Madeleine for a session of coffee and gossip. And a quiet letch at Guy, who really is one of the most beautiful men I've ever come across.

'What a waste!' Pris always mutters.

Before Gerry could join us, a young woman came into the shop and the temperature fell noticeably. Now Gerry can be a trifle waspish – but never to his customers. To them he's one of the warmest, most laid-back of people, so we were intrigued to discover what could bring about such a chilly response. Unperturbed, the young woman giggled and simpered around for a bit and, as she left, called back over her shoulder, 'I swear on the Goddess that I'll bring them in next week. I promise.'

Gerry sat down heavily, obviously out of sorts. 'Silly bitch. Doesn't she realise that taking the Goddess's name in vain like that could result in some very nasty kick-backs?'

'Probably never even thought about it. Isn't that the woman who's supposed to be making robes for you?' asked Pris.

'That's the one,' replied Gerry. 'I've had everything from a personal promise, to a vow, to an oath sworn on the Goddess but nothing ever materialises – if you'll excuse the pun.'

'Promises, vows and oaths are taken at various points in a witch's life and become more and more binding as the years go by,' I said sniffily. 'If she can't tell the difference now, then it's evident that she can't be trusted on any level in the future.'

'I'm not sure that *I* understand the difference,' said Madeleine.

'A promise is a *personal* undertaking to do something,' I said, 'and should it be broken, you've only let yourself down in the eyes of others. A vow is a solemn pledge which is often made *before* deity and one which places an obligation on the one making the vow upon formal acceptance into a Coven – such as you made at the time of your Dedication. An oath is a direct appeal *to* deity in witness of the truth of a statement. It calls into effect the very punishments or consequences *you* said *you* would bear if that oath were ever broken. This is the sort of oath you and Robert will be asked take at your Initiation.'

Those new to Craft often balk at a coven's insistence on them making a solemn oath not to reveal to anyone the rites that are carried out within a coven or sacred area, irrespective of the nature of the working. The oath is also designed to protect other members of the group who do not want their identities to be made known to outsiders through careless talk.

On the other hand, we have heard of witchlets being asked to take the most bizarre of oaths without understanding what is being demanded of them. To bind themselves by a promise is the best anyone should expect from a neophyte with little more than a scant introduction to the Lesser Mysteries. However, if a neophyte is not willing to undertake this pledge, then they should seriously question their desire to be accepted into a formal coven.

Few people realise the actual importance of the witch's knife. The knife, blade or athame is an essential part of any witch's regalia and throughout history, there has always been a knife on the altar of the gods, regardless of culture. It is therefore always a point of much amusement when a witchlet produces either some pathetic blunt instrument or worse – a knife with a blade carved from wood. One chap turned up with an African carved paper knife to use as his ritual blade with absolutely no thought that wood was a 'natural' product that would produce completely different, if not conflicting energies, to the traditional metal one within the Circle.

The sacred knife, from any culture, is a consecrated embodiment of the elements. Metal from the earth is forged in the fire; the fire is fed by air from the bellows and the metal is cooled by water; the spirit or Will of the creator (or owner) imbues the knife with its sacred purpose. A witch's knife acts as the tool that directs that Will in the form of magical energy; on a practical level it is used to 'draw' the Circle – and to simply cut things. For many, particularly in Wicca, their knife is the black-handled athame while others prefer to use a knife that feels 'right' for them. In many cases this will be a second-hand blade that has been cleansed of all its previous history and re-consecrated by the new owner for their use alone.

Because the knife is looked upon as an extension of an individual's spirit, an oath sworn on the knife is deemed unbreakable. But should any covener commit such perjury then s/he would be banished from the group and the knife blade ritually broken. In many Traditions it is acknowledged that no blade should be drawn and returned to its sheath without being blooded although today most witches would forgo this particular observance.

The subject of the witch's knife was the subject for discussion at one of Pris's moots and who should be there but our old friend, the Wicca-man, who wasted no time in wowing the assembled crowd with his connections. What was even more puzzling was that his Granny's old chum, George Pickingill, wouldn't have any metal in the Circle according to legend; yet according to the latest instalment, she was thrilled to bits when Gerald passed his athame on to little Alan.

'Ooh,' breathed one young thing. 'Could you bring it to show us?'

The Wicca-man turned a benevolent smile on the simple child. 'I'm afraid not at the moment. I've lent it to a friend of mine in Scotland.'

Pris snorted at his cavalier attitude to such priceless relics. 'Perhaps you could get her to post it back to you when she sends the Black Book.'

For a few moments he held her glance and then turned away

to talk to another of the group. But in that second, Pris had penetrated his soul and she didn't like what she'd seen. 'That bugger's dangerous,' she whispered to Adam, who'd been watching the exchange. From time to time, the Wicca-man shot malevolent glances in Pris's direction and she couldn't ignore the violent under currents that radiated across the room in her direction.

The gloves were finally off.

The gloves were also coming off at Castor & Pollux. Guy had been treated to another of the Mad Medium's exhibitions but this time it was in the courtyard behind the flat while he was busy spraying the roses. Spying him through the bathroom window, Helena had slipped down into the garden and advanced on the unsuspecting gallery owner. *'The portents …'* she shrieked, her eyes rolling around like marbles in a glass jar. *'The portents … listen to the portents!'* Guy, startled out of his reverie, leapt backwards in surprise just as Helena, acting true to form, threw herself forward into his arms – and missed.

'What the hell's going on?' asked Gerry as a furious Guy strode passed. 'Where's Helena?'

'Lying on the flagstones with her head in the fish pond,' he retorted as the door slammed behind him.

We were all in agreement that this state of affairs couldn't continue; after all, it was Helena who'd broken the faith with her fellow coveners. It was obvious that she would continue to use her self-induced trances as an excuse to drape herself all over Guy, despite my having told her to control herself. Although in the case of an Initiate doing deliberate harm to another member of the group, the traditional punishment is banishment, it was decided that we would ease her out gradually using magical means. Gerry and Guy were given permission to perform whatever ritual they saw fit but with as little hurt as possible.

Another serious breach of coven etiquette that requires instant banishment is to disclose the 'secret teachings' to outsiders, particularly non-Crafters. One of Jocelyn's students, known as 'New Forest Gump' had been cultivating his own sense of importance by bragging to fellow-mooters about Jocelyn's witch-power.

'The lad is a stranger to the word discretion,' sighed Josh. 'He bounces from witch to witch, playing off one set of teachings against another. The fact that the information comes from completely different Traditions makes no difference. All we get is, 'You told me X and so-and-so told me Y, so which one is right?'

'There's no concept of the fact that magically there can be more than one 'truth'. Neither does he see anything wrong in discussing our affairs with other people. The general philosophy seems to be, 'We're all pagans, so we should all get along and not be fussed with all this secrecy.' He just doesn't understand that you could drive a Scammel between Old Craft and modern Wicca and still not touch either side.'

In all honesty, New Forest Gump probably will never see himself as being disloyal to Jocelyn – he hasn't grasped the need for our privacy and 'rules' no matter how many times this is explained to him. From the Coven's point of view, he wouldn't be allowed anywhere near our members even on a social level because we have no desire to be 'name-dropped' around the county.

'It's bad enough being exposed to some of Granny's foundlings,' groaned Pris, 'without being Gumped into the bargain.'

Chapter Six

Sabbats and Celebration

Regardless of Tradition, most witches celebrate the four Great Sabbats in the wheel of the year – although many in Old Craft observe them according to the 'old Julian calendar' some ten days later. In modern Wicca it has become the norm for the festivals of the year to be designated by their Celtic names but this is not necessarily the case in Old Craft. Many old-time witches worked a 'double-blind' by using the names the Church had imposed over the older festivals.

The Coven tends to work at the 'natural' times of the year at the solstices and equinoxes. We celebrate 'may-time' when the may (hawthorn) is in flower and the harvest supper comes when the last of the produce has been gathered in – not by any formal date on the calendar. Nevertheless, Pris and Adam have seen their fair share of pagan celebration over the years ...

Imbolc or Candlemas

In the early days, before Pris and Adam joined the Coven, they belonged to a large group from the West Country. Although they worked Old Craft, the Magister was a bit of a showman who insisted on holding public rituals for the four Great Sabbats. These would be held on some blasted heath or woodland clearing with up to fifty people joining in the celebration.

The crowd waited in silence as the Magister made propitiation to the deity of the occasion and held aloft the Great Book for the blessing. He turned away from the altar and swept his eyes over the circle of people, before singling out Pris. With an imperious gesture he pointed to her and commanded her to 'step forward to serve as the Maiden of the Light'.

All pink and flattered at being chosen, the young Pris walked towards the altar where a huge candle was thrust into her hand. With his Lady standing close by and also holding a candle, the Magister placed his hand on Pris's head and murmured softly. 'Right you two, keep up with me and make sure the light falls on my notes. I've forgotten to bring my glasses and I can't see a bloody thing in the dark without them.'

Spring Equinox

Having been invited to participate in a large 'open meeting' for the Spring Festival, Pris and Adam were asked, as guests of honour, to help the organisers offer the cakes and ale around the huge Circle following the ritual. Those whom they hadn't met before quietly introduced themselves to the organisers. The party made its way slowly around the Circle and eventually came to a woman, whose arm stuck out at a strange angle.

She smiled warmly, accepted the cup and as she leaned forward whispered, 'I hope it was alright to bring Arnold, only he wasn't actually invited.' The organisers glanced at the chap next to her and smiled in welcome. The chap looked a bit blank but it was assumed that he wasn't used to ritual and that it was all a bit too much for him to take in.

The little party moved and eventually the time came to close down the Circle to give people the chance to mill around and catch up on the news. Suddenly the woman with the 'bad arm' came rushing up to the organiser. Breathless and with her eyes sparkling, she gushed her thanks for the lovely experience 'especially as Arnold had had such a lovely time'.

'Oh, look,' she cried, 'he's moving … he likes you all.' Her arm was still extended and from her hand dangled a plaited, multi-coloured cord with some wooden pegs inserted in it. Pris and Co looked at this object, they looked at each other, they looked at her. She smiled blandly – yes, this was Arnold!

Slowly Pris and Company edged away, heading for the nearest holly bush before collapsing with laughter. 'Somehow,' said Pris, 'we managed to keep it together until we'd said our goodbyes. With a gentle push in another direction, we managed to steer her back to the Spiritualist Church. After all, *they'd* apparently 'helped' her find Arnold in the first place – and the Church has the nerve to claim that witches are dangerous!'

Beltaine, May Eve or Roodmas

The 30th April fell at the Dark of the Moon when Pris and Adam found themselves taking Madeleine and Robert to their first ritual away from the Coven as guests of a couple who'd recently hived off from Roger's group. 'They're extremely powerful,' he'd told Pris, 'but they haven't managed to form much of a group yet. Can you go along and give them a bit of support?'

The venue was a dark, dank wood situated in a deep ravine; approaching the site was not easy and the atmosphere was somewhat subdued due to the concentration necessary to negotiate the difficult pathway while carrying several heavy bags. Eventually they all arrived at the clearing and the guests busied themselves with their own preparations while their hosts directed operations with the rest of the group.

Pris had questioned the absence of a besom at the outset but her query had been casually dismissed by those officiating on the grounds of it being 'just one more thing to carry'. So, despite the site being contaminated with unknown energies of total strangers, no cleansing of the ritual area was carried out.

With some misgivings, Pris's group quietly changed into their robes in the shadows as the officiating High Priest attempted to light the Beltaine fire. It was obvious that few preparations had been made and the damp wood that had lain all winter struggled into life, smoking heavily and, at times, almost dying out completely. Although only a guest, Robert coaxed it into flame and without further ado the High Priest announced that the gods to be invoked would be Pan and Demeter!

Pris caught the look of uncertainty in Madeleine's eyes and

smiled what she hoped was a look of reassurance but she was having serious doubts about proceeding with the ritual. There was a distinct atmosphere of apprehension but this was either blatantly ignored by the officiating couple – or they possibly never even sensed it because the members of their own group didn't seem in the least concerned.

The High Priest raised his athame on high and opening with the familiar words, stepped away from the altar as though to walk the boundaries of the Circle. After two paces he turned and drew a Circle in the air – which effectively only included *himself* – before replacing the athame on the altar.

Next it was the turn of the High Priestess, who blessed the water and salt, which she took around the Circle, sprinkling and blessing the earth – on the *inside* of the Circle which again excluded those taking part in the ritual. Under the shadows of cloaks and hoods it was impossible to read their expressions but the vibrations emanating from Madeleine and Robert were now verging on panic. Pris could detect a faint blue light surrounding the couple that showed that they had, by now, automatically cast their own personal protection as they'd been taught to do as part of their own Coven training.

The moments passed in awkward silence as the High Priest and Priestess fumbled at the altar searching for the incense, followed by a muttered curse as the High Priest tripped over the copper thurible, scattering glowing charcoal everywhere. It was only by Adam's quick thinking that it was retrieved and the ritual lurched on.

The four guests had been allocated the quarters to call, despite two of them having little experience of Circle work outside their own group. Yet even to the complete novices, it was apparent that their calls were not being answered. Vainly they waited, patiently trying to fulfil their duties, both clearly sad and embarrassed by what they felt was *their* failure.

Still their hosts blundered on; arms raised they proceeded to call upon Pan and Demeter. Both Madeleine and Robert said afterwards that their spines had crawled and that they had felt chilled and numb. Adam, as Officer of the North, having a direct view of the altar, swore to witnessing the High Priestess sprout a magnificent beard and moustache! She and her partner must have been satisfied, however, because at this point they began dashing around the Circle, linking hands and calling all to join in the Dance of the Mill.

A chant was started and everyone joined in; on and on; faster and faster, unending. The dancers stumbled, the chant broke down and fragmented, and still no sign came from the High Priestess. When one elderly member of the group nearly fell into the fire, the dancers ground unsteadily to a halt. Everyone looked around. Surely now the power would be directed? But no – the Circle had been breached and the High Priest and Priestess wandered back to the altar.

The wine and cakes were hastily blessed and the Circle (such as it was) closed. Not choosing to realise their guests were visibly disappointed, the hosts continued chatting gaily with their group – even commenting on how well things had gone. Once everyone had changed back into everyday clothing and the pitiful fire had fizzled out on its own accord, the assembly made its way back to the parked cars.

'It wasn't until two days later that we learned what happened,' said Pris as she handed Rupert a cup of coffee. 'Even though we were there as invited guests, they all roared off into the night and left us to find our own way out of the wood. From what we can gather, within moments of them disappearing from sight, they skidded on the muddy road and smashed into one another. Three of them landed up in hospital.

'On the way back home, all four of us confirmed that as soon as we realised we'd been left out of the Circle, we mentally cast out own protective barriers because once raised, the power needed to go somewhere. Had all that undirected energy found its mark? I mean, you can't build power like that and then leave it careering about wildly and uncontrolled or directed. What do you think?'

'The world's gone mad,' answered Rupert grimly. 'I think all magical and social contact should be withdrawn. They're not of our Tradition and it was only supposed to be a goodwill gesture. If they want to celebrate Beltaine in England with volatile god-power at the Dark of the Moon, with an inverted Circle that protects no one but themselves, then they will eventually kill someone. If they aren't willing to accept the responsibility for their actions then we cannot afford to associate with them and put our people at risk.'

'Where do they come from?' I asked.

'They originally hived off from Roger's group some four years ago and moved out of the area. They've since returned and recruited new members,' said Pris.

Rupert's mouth was set in an even grimmer line. He doesn't like amateur bungling in anything. 'It wasn't without good reason that the Mysteries were kept 'hidden'. The handling of magic is not something to be taken lightly, and the appointing of Priests and Priestesses should not be handed out quite so casually.

'Perhaps it's a good time to take a good hard look at the social and political structure of the Craft. People are always talking about bringing back the 'Old Ways' but unless something is done to re-instate some discipline into Craft, it will degenerate further out of all proportion. I'll talk to Roger about it tomorrow ...'

'Oh dear!' I thought. 'Another family feud in the offing ... Happy Beltaine!'

Mid Summer and Summer Solstice

Despite the fiasco at Beltaine and the fact that the brothers hadn't spoken since Roger's verbal trouncing by Rupert, we tried to heal the rift by accepting Gwen's invitation to a summer solstice garden party. No rituals, no play-acting, no drama queens camping up Craft – just an extended family get together involving the members of the two groups. The weather was absolutely glorious and Gwen's beautifully kept garden was the ideal spot to relax with a long, cold drink under the shade of the old apple trees.

Roger's group is always a little in awe of our lot, mainly because, apart from Granny Jay, they only usually see Pris and Adam. They know Gerry and Guy of course, because everyone shops at Castor & Pollux, but Rupert and I have as little to do with them as possible. This isn't because we're elitist, it's because we prefer to remain true to Old Craft and not have it cluttered up with all these foreign deities and oriental imports. Given free choice in the matter, Pris and Adam wouldn't get involved in half the farces they do, if it wasn't for Granny's insistence on knowing what's going on. And as we've said elsewhere, she's still a force to be reckoned with.

By the time the sun was sinking in the west, Vanessa was more than the worse for wear and determined to regain centre stage even though she was a (deeply resented) guest in Gwen's home. As the candle lamps were lit along the edges of the lawn, she announced that there was going to be a surprise to round off the solstice celebrations.

Madeleine and Robert were called into the circle of light and Vanessa grandly announced that as a special surprise she had decided to hand-fast them! The look of abject horror on their faces conveyed the message; their stunned silence spoke volumes. An awkward silence hung in the air before Vanessa asked if 'anyone else wanted doing'?

Furiously, Rupert grabbed hold of Roger by the scruff of his neck and frog-marched him into the bushes. Pris raised an eyebrow at me to ask if we should intervene but I shook my head. I don't interfere in family discussions and besides, Granny looked pleased at the possibility of Roger's athame being inserted where the solstice sun doesn't shine.

Lughnasad or Lammas

This is normally the traditional time for the contemplation of the past year's work and thanksgiving for whatever has been achieved. It's also the time for cutting and harvesting and that was the ultimatum Gwen gave Roger over Vanessa. Her behaviour was becoming an embarrassment, and not just within Craft. The vicar found himself in the uncomfortable position of having to explain his sister's strange *ménage à trois* to the bishop. According to Granny, two couples had already left the group because not only couldn't the High Priestess keep her hands of the booze, she couldn't keep her hands off the other male members either. Pun intended!

I was busily bottling fruit when Granny came into the kitchen. This was the first time she'd been in the house since Rupert banned her over the incident with the Aga but Rupert wasn't around, so I made coffee and we sat down at the table. There was a long silence but as she obviously wanted to talk, I waited for her to begin.

'You realise that without a word of a lie, Roger can lay claim to being an hereditary witch?' I nodded and she continued. 'He has never been instructed in any of the ways of Old Craft but by token of his blood, I can't deny him even though I think he's a bloody fool.' Again I nodded. 'Because of Vanessa's behaviour, Roger is going to find himself in serious trouble before long. She's out of control.'

Vanessa had been caught in *flagrante delicto* with a couple of local lads in the woods. Fortunately for all of us, those doing the catching were also local men and the story didn't pass very far beyond the saloon bar of the Fox and Hounds. Her indiscretions were nothing to do with Old Craft or Wicca but that wouldn't matter a bit to the tabloid newspapers and that was right where she was heading. These things happen from time to time but we were more concerned about the 'in-comers' moving into the area: people who knew nothing of local characters and customs, and who would sell their own grandmothers for five minutes of glory in the media spotlight and a fat cheque.

'She's got to go,' I heard myself saying for the second time in as many months.

'Roger doesn't see it that way. He's still besotted with her and says he doesn't believe the stories. He thinks she's just a flirt.'

'Then do whatever needs to be done,' I said formally.

Granny stared hard at me without blinking for a moment and then with a satisfied nod, she got up and left the kitchen. I was left to contemplate the dregs of cold coffee. Some might ask what gives us the right to interfere in other people's lives but our methods are all about maintaining a sense of balance and harmony. Helena's behaviour over Guy threatened the harmony of the Coven and the domestic harmony in his relationship with Gerry; Vanessa's antics could have much more serious and far wider reaching repercussions. Not only was she openly breaking up Gwen's marriage and jeopardising the vicar's career; more seriously she was drawing 'outside' attention to the fact that there were several active covens in the community and none of us had a desire to be the focus of a prolonged bout of media exposure.

Later that night Gerry and Guy performed a banishing ritual (*sans* references to sheep) at the site of the old quarry. Although the site hasn't been worked for well over a hundred years, few people venture there after dark; largely due to the rumour that the place is haunted. For generations it's been a special place and we suspect that it was a tale put about by our forebears to keep folk away from the quarry when it's being used for ritual purposes. There's even a small cave hidden by the bracken that we use if the weather's bad and we still feel the need to be out of doors.

Gerry and Guy were heading for the alder thicket when they caught sight of several figures cavorting round a fire near where they'd intended working. Creeping nearer they saw that a group of unfamiliar people had pitched camp and there was the unmistakable smell of a spliff on the night air. Now, we don't like uninvited strangers on our patch, particularly when they're doing drugs.

Gerry was all for calling Rupert on his mobile but Guy had a different idea. Wound up over Helena and ready for action he pulled on his hooded cloak and stole softly towards the clearing. He'd been standing silently in the shadows for some minutes before anyone noticed him. Lifting his face a fraction, the flickering light from the fire must have caught the barest outline of his fine features hidden by the cowl, giving it a cadaverous appearance. There was a short, stifled scream. Guy raised an arm and with pale finger pointing, indicated that they should leave. Obviously no one was going to argue with this unexpected spectre and, to a man, the whole group leapt to their feet, wheeling like a flock of starlings before disappearing into the darkness.

It was obvious that the ritual was in tatters and that no earthly purpose would be served by attempting to carry it out. Picking up their belongings, they were about to leave the quarry when they heard a pitiful whine coming from the trees. Tied to a trunk they found a scruffy, long-haired lurcher who had been forgotten in the panic. This was the story we heard a couple of weeks later when Madelaine, Pris and myself called into the shop.

'We told the police we'd found him tied up in the woods and that we'd keep him until he was claimed. That was a fortnight ago and no one's come for him, so he's legally ours now,' said Guy, stroking the dog's ears. 'I look on him as our karmic debt, because if it hadn't been for those people being there, who knows what we might have wished on Helena that night.'

'So you haven't done anything about her then?' asked Pris,

feeding the dog part of her biscuit.

Gerry launched into a long and involved spiel about a preparation involving faeces, rose petals and a fig wrapped in long strands of black synthetic hair. Unfortunately there's nothing to rival a gay male in terms of over-kill when it comes to spell casting – not even Pris.

'I'm not sure I understand,' whispered Madelaine when Guy was called through to the gallery and Gerry decamped for more coffee. 'Why did they use …'

'Don't ask,' I said, 'You really *don't* want to go down that road.'

Pris wasn't at all impressed. 'I'd have just bottled the bitch!' she retorted.

Autumn Equinox

It wasn't difficult to persuade everyone to gather for the equivalent of a pagan harvest festival supper. We'd cleaned out the large stone barn for the purpose and again, unwillingly but at Granny's insistence, extended the invitation to Roger's group for the occasion. She doesn't usually concern herself with such social niceties – which raised a considerable amount of suspicion on our part, especially when she requested that Vanessa be allowed to perform the ritual of passing around the welcome cup.

'Bloody hell, it's neat scotch,' whispered Pris. 'Granny's totem animal should be the *Grouse* rather than a goat!'

As Vanessa made a slow progression around the large circle of guests, Philly followed behind with the pitcher Granny had handed to her to top up the chalice. After each guest took a sip, Vanessa received the cup back and took a huge swallow. By the time she'd completed half of the circle she was unsteady on her feet and began sliding her hand over the groin of the male guests as they took the chalice. It was by now common knowledge that she would tweak the genitals of any passing male and appeared to think it was the prerogative of a High Priestess to feel up any male members of the group. (Oh dear, it's that pun again.)

'I hope she doesn't try that on with Rupert,' I muttered to Pris.

'I do,' she replied, 'and so does Granny,' she added shrewdly.

Rupert's a dear old-fashioned thing who doesn't tolerate any breach of etiquette, either magically or socially and I couldn't believe that Vanessa would be foolish enough to pull one of her stunts on him. She'd been well-oiled when she arrived but after doing three-quarters of a lap of the guests, she must have drunk nearly a bottle of neat scotch. And she couldn't hold her booze! There were two more males to go and as Vanessa offered the chalice to the next male guest, his wife's expression hardened as she repeated the now familiar gesture.

Then it was Rupert's turn.

His cold blue eyes bored into hers but Vanessa was much too far gone to notice or care. Her hands reached out and groped ... and in a second it was all over. Rupert picked up one of the large buckets filled with water that had been placed there as a fire precaution and promptly emptied it over Vanessa's head.

The carefully coiffured hair collapsed and make-up slid down her face, streaking it with rivers of mascara. I know she had it coming but I couldn't help feeling sorry for the pitiful creature. The expressions on the faces of the rest of the guests, however, showed that none of them shared my sentiments. Retribution had come swiftly and been seen to come.

Later that evening, after most of the guests had gone, a small group of us sat around discussing the evening. Once Vanessa had been carted off by Roger and Granny, the rest of the party went with a swing, as everyone joined in the spirit of the harvest celebration. There was a tangible lightness to the atmosphere that we've not usually felt when we've been with Roger's group before. The guests relaxed and enjoyed themselves and, what was even more important, talked to each other.

'All in all, it turned out to be a very productive evening,' said Guy.

'Don't you think you over-reacted a bit?' I asked Rupert.

'No, I don't. I certainly wasn't going to have that infernal woman fiddling about with my balls. My body language should have told her to back off.'

'She was too far gone to notice,' said Adam.

'Anyway it had the desired effect,' said Pris.

'Two of the couples have asked if they can join the Coven,' said Gerry.

'It wasn't done for effect,' snapped Rupert, 'and I don't want any of Roger's luvenliters in the Coven. We've enough troubles of our own at the moment, without their defection adding to the brouhaha.'

'Daddy, you were wonderful,' interrupted Philly. 'Everyone thought you were great, the way you just took over and carried on as if nothing had happened.'

Rupert bridled with pleasure at this breathless approval from his daughter and Richard rolled his eyes heavenward. Good girl, I thought, you've learned well. These macho types only need a bit of careful handling and you can get anything out of 'em. Whichever way you looked at it, Vanessa had reaped what she'd sown and that was all there was to it; when I discovered that she'd tried her hand with my son, even my sympathies began to wane.

Samhain or Hallowe'en

Jocelyn runs her mob with a rod of iron but she's not above relating a good tale, even if it's against herself. She's often accused of keeping her group on too tight a leash but bitter experience has shown that even the 'grown-ups' can't always be trusted to conduct a seasonal ritual with dignity and common sense.

One Samhain, when she was unable to conduct affairs because of ill-health, the rest of the coven assured her that they would carry out the observance in a secluded garden belonging to one of the group's parents. Feeling that some discreet supervision on home territory was better than letting them run loose in the woods, she agreed. The fire was duly set but obviously one erstwhile witchlet decided that as the Old Girl wasn't about, the damp kindling could do with a helping hand, and poured petrol onto the wood. The fire ignited. So did the trail of spilt petrol leading to the can ...

Since the cap had not been replaced, the next thing they heard was an impressive belch of Magical Catalyst as the contents of the can burst into life. With his robe hitched up over his thighs and with a bare-footed kick that would have earned him a place with the British Lions, one lad booted the flaming can into touch whereupon it promptly landed in an ornamental pond. The remaining contents spilled out onto the water and the first Josh knew of the debacle was when the phone raised her from her sick bed to announce:

'You better get round here. Your lot have just set fire to my bloody fish pond!'

Yule and Winter Solstice

With Philly and Richard home for the holidays, we decided on a private family party with Pris, Adam, Gerry and Guy. Since Gerry can't resist organising us all, he decided that we would have a toga bash for Saturnalia – which meant that everyone was issued with a clean white sheet and the sitting room re-arranged to accommodate a low-lying table and piles of cushions. Guy took charge of the kitchen and with two dogs watching every move, conjured up an impressive Roman feast.

There we all were, draped around in a tableau of ancient decadence when the front doorbell went.

'Damn,' I said. 'Ignore it.'

'It could be Robert and Madelaine back early.'

'They'd ring first.'

Philly jumped up to answer the door and the next thing we

knew the Vicar was striding into the room, rubbing his hands in glee. 'Oh, I say. A fancy dress party. What fun!'

We've had our serious doubts about this chap for years; Rupert reckons he's a closet pagan. Unfortunately his wife's ambitious, hence the summons from the bishop to explain his position over the Roger-Gwen-Vanessa ménage even though it was nothing to do with him. It didn't take a lot of persuading to get him to join us, complete with toga although we'd run out of single sheets and his skinny frame was bundled up in a double. We'd passed a pleasant hour, enjoying some excellent food and wine when the door suddenly flew open and an imperious voice boomed across the room.

'Simon, get out of this house immediately! How dare you … you …'

The Vicar leapt to his feet liked a startled cartoon character but unfortunately, true to comic strip form, his toga didn't follow him. Philly found she'd been sitting on the excess material and as the Vicar headed for the ceiling, the sheet unravelled leaving him standing there in his vest, baggy underpants and socks – with suspenders still attached. If the sight of her husband lying there enjoying himself between two voluptuous woman (Pris and Philly) had enraged Mrs Vicar, then his semi-naked state elevated her to even greater heights of frenzy.

'You … you … heathen … pagans, all of you!'

And with this most accurate of parting shots, Mrs Vicar grabbed hold of her unfortunate spouse and dragged him out of the house without waiting for an explanation, or even giving him the chance to retrieve his clothes. To add insult to injury, the night was clear and frosty and she'd forgotten where she'd put the car keys. The Vicar's car keys were still with his clothes inside the house and she'd slammed the door behind her. Amid the confusion, the cricket club carol singers arrived on our doorstep to perform, only to find the half naked, half-frozen Vicar had beaten them to it. With barely controlled laughter, the club secretary offered to drive them home while the remaining mobiles spread The Word.

We decided that in order to show some support and solidarity with the Vicar, we'd all put in an appearance at the carol service and enjoy a good sing. His wife went a bit pinched round the mouth when we all trooped into the church and the Vicar went out of his way not to make eye contact with any of us. As we were leaving after the service, however, Pris was on the receiving end of a rather cheery, conspiratorial wink.

Chapter Seven

Pub Moots

The one subject that causes the greatest shock to newcomers at pub moots is the fact that *all* Coven members are omnivorous – that is: all-devouring, feeding on anything available. When the neo-pagan arrives in our midst, they're only too anxious to assure us that they are vegetarian and simply *adore* animals – which is why it's not a good idea to have Rupert around at such gatherings. Pagans, in general, view farmers as bloody-thirsty butchers who will massacre anything for pleasure or profit. These sentiments are usually dealt with by a verbal blast from both barrels, followed by a thunderous silence. If they're really lucky they may get the tirade about keeping small caged animals and birds as pets, or confining dogs and cats in flats, but we try to keep the warring factions separate and avoid bloodshed.

What most people forget is that 'hunting' in all its forms is what country culture's based upon – including the Wild Hunt. Long ago when our hunter/gatherer ancestors formed themselves into communities they made a pact with the animal kingdom. Most still carry it out with respect although, of course, there are always exceptions. The majority of landowners of our acquaintance, do more for preserving the countryside than any conservation agency, for the simple reason that their bond is one of the blood. Most of them have spilled a great deal of their own on the land as part of that working relationship. Old Joe knows more about living off the land than the entire department of the Meat & Livestock Commission and he's managed to live to the ripe old age of 90 by regularly going out and catching his own Sunday dinner.

Country people don't claim they have any particular monopoly on spiritual enlightenment but to quote Charles de

Lint: *'I still think our relationship with the natural world has much to offer as a kind of touchstone for others to form their own pacts with the earth. We are just people with our own ways, our own beliefs – nothing more, nothing less.'*

For the student of human behaviour, however, the pagan pub moot can be a fascinating experience. There are usually two categories that the newcomers fall into – either the over-the-top witchy-pagan-Goth or the plain jeans 'n' jumper (with pristine trainers) and no make-up or jewellery in sight – especially wedding rings.

'They are organised,' explained Pris, 'either by people who like the sound of their own voice or a simpering wet who keeps saying, 'Isn't this nice, us being here together. Thank you all for coming. There's a litter-day in the local woods next Sunday. Bin bags, rubber gloves and sticks will be provided and it would be lovely to see you all there.'

'The conversation consists of neutral topics, including moots past, present and future, the merits of *EastEnders* over *Emmerdale*, and how much everyone hates their job. Anything, in fact, that has nothing whatsoever, in any way shape or form, to do with Craft, which means that Adam is frequently wearing one of his two favourite moot expressions – abject boredom and abject boredom with disapproval.

'They also go to extraordinary lengths to steer clear of anything to do with magic,' she continued. 'One woman said she didn't exactly *practice* but she did like walking in the woods with her dog. They may mention angels and fairies and sooner or later, the talk will get around to animals they feel empathy with – like dolphins, unicorns and wolves – which they wear about their person in the form of sweat-shirts from the WWF catalogue.'

It never ceases to amaze me that the most timid of 'vegi-vors' (as Rupert calls them) are the ones whose so-called totem animals are predators. Traditionally a totem animal is one whose shape a witch can assume when the occasion arises. This means that the witch whose totem is an owl, *becomes* the owl. She or he needs to understand how the bird's mind works in seeking out its prey, or to feel the sudden sensation of the swoop and the adrenalin rush at the kill.

Back in my young days as a witchlet, I can remember being totally perplexed by the fact that a highly respected local Magister (who was also a farmer and Master of Foxhounds) had the fox as his totem animal. Curiosity got the better of good manners and I had to ask why. His response was that he 'knew' the animal both as a verminous, indiscriminate killer and as a highly intelligent adversary – in short: respect. He swore he could shapeshift into a fox and cause his *own* hounds a merry dance just for the thrill of the chase. He thought and felt like a fox. He *became* the fox.

'Don't forget that wild animals don't die peacefully of old age in their beds,' he'd said. 'For the fox to die a *natural* death is to do so through disease or starvation since it has no natural predators. When my time comes, I'll turn m'self into a fox and die by my own hounds. Quick and easy like.'

Several years later the Magister was diagnosed as having cancer. According to his Lady, who nursed him through those last weeks, he constantly referred to a large dog-fox that came and sat on the lawn outside his window. Knowing that he would never ride to hounds again, she arranged for the first hunt of the season to meet at their house and pass round the stirrup cup for the last time, although the old huntsman barely had the strength to walk outside.

The following morning, his unmarked body was found some nine miles from the house; the muddy ground nearby was covered with paw prints which were identified as foxhounds despite the fact that there had been no hounds in that area on the previous day. Coincidence? I rather think not.

Another popular pub moot irritation is the general use of

'Blessed Be' in the form of a greeting to all and sundry, regardless of the Path or Tradition. It is not unknown for a letter to be signed in this manner, regardless of whether the recipient is known to have Craft connections or not. Traditionally, the Wiccan 'Blessed Be ...' should only be used by one Initiate to another, and some will tell you that it should only be bestowed by members of the priesthood to another Initiate.

Today it is used amongst pagans in the same manner as the colloquial Italian *ciao,* which can be used to mean both 'hello' and 'goodbye'. Newcomers often look askance when a member of the Coven refuses to return their greeting. A traditional witch is more likely to use 'Merry meet' as an abbreviation of *'Merry meet and merry part, and merry meet again.'* We just say 'Hello'.

There are several regular moots in the area and although Pris generally exercises a firm control over the proceedings, Janet and Jack's presence can always induce a cold, sinking feeling in the pit of her stomach. Janet is a chain-smoking, beer-drinking matron, who talks in a loud, penetrating voice generously punctuated with 'Naaa', 'Ger'orff' and 'An' I bleedin' well told 'er'.

The more she drinks, the louder and more ribald she gets. Any sentence uttered by another member of the group that can be found to contain anything remotely resembling a double entendre is immediately translated into junior school lavatorial humour. Consequently, as the night wears on those in the group become more and more terrified to speak. The rest of the pub gradually gets quieter and quieter as they become riveted with gruesome fascination by Janet's behaviour.

9.30: Three pints down

'Get another in, darlin', will yer?' Drains half her pint and wipes her mouth on the back of her hand. 'I've got a throat like a nun's gusset.'

Jack smiles proudly at his witty wife and trots off to the bar where he lounges with shirt agape to reveal chest-hair that would be the envy of a grizzly bear, with an enormous gold pentagram nestling coyly amongst the foliage.

10.30: Five pints down

'I've 'ad a really good night, luv and if you play yer cards right, you'll be in fer one an' all.'

Jack smiles proudly at his witty wife and trots off to the lavatory. Upon his return Janet reaches (or lurches) towards his groin … 'You've been a long time, luv … Hope you didn't leave it out in the cold for too long 'cos I want summat left fer me to 'op onto later.'

Jack smiles proudly at his witty, adoring wife.

11.45: Group asked politely by landlord to leave – *now*

Having downed two swift gins, Janet is undeterred. 'Who fancies whacking up a quick Circle an' 'avin' a go at bringing up the Ol' Horny One?' There's a blank response but Janet is well into her stride. At the top of her voice and waving an arm, she spills her third gin, she addressed the rest of the pub. 'Cos I'm a third degree 'igh Priestess of t'Ol' Uns, I'll have you know. Mine's the body of the Mother an' I've got these to prove it!' She whips up her jumper to display an ample bosom that ripples like blanc-mange.

The remaining females in the pub get jammed in the door to the ladies' toilet as they rush to check their make-up, while the remaining men look bemused. Jack smiles weakly and says: 'Calm down a bit love, let's get you home to bed.' A bad mistake to which Janet responds in an animated slur.

'Ooooh … that's the best offer I've 'ad all night. We're going to invoke t'Ol' Lad after all and I could do with a good dicking from Ol' Horny.' Jack hurries her out to the car park, bundles her into the car and leaves in a cloud of exhaust fumes.

With the exception of Roger's group, Alan Wicca has found it impossible to gain an introduction to any of the Old Craft covens in the area and so his performances have been restricted to local pub moots. Unfortunately, this also gives him access to the young, the naive and the gullible who, understandably, hang on every word. As Granny pointed out in the beginning, his appearance gives the impression of credibility and they have no reason to doubt any of his claims. Except that no Old Crafter would dream of revealing, publicly or in print, details about their antecedents in order to impress or gain admittance to a group.

There's no pretence, however, in his antipathy towards Pris and Adam because they now allow him no quarter. 'All hereditary witches are always born with certain inherited abilities fully developed,' he told one young girl.

'And what would they be, Alan?' challenged Pris over his shoulder.

'All witches are highly intuitive and emotionally sensitive …' he confided to another.

'That must have been a real bummer of a handicap when you were in the SAS,' said Adam.

Now that he's run through his repertoire, he's very careful not to divulge any checkable personal details about his Granny other than to occasionally quote her odd words of wisdom but he now claims to have controlled 13 covens in the 1980s. By the 1990s this number had increased to 130 including those across Europe and yet no one in Old Craft (or even in new Craft either for that matter) has heard of him. Neither does he ever produce anyone to verify his stories, obviously working on the assumption that if the dead can't lie, they can't pose a threat to the truth coming out, either.

Chapter Eight

Ancestry and Antecedents

As I've said before, according to tradition, the only one sure way of identifying a true witch is to judge them by their works and by their silence – unless there is a need to speak out. More often than not, however, those who lay title to impressive pedigrees can't back up their claims with magical ability.

Several years ago, one such claimant began writing articles in pagan magazines that purported to be based on the teachings of a very well-known witch who'd been dead for a couple of years, and claiming to be a Third Degree of their lineage. Never mind that this particular late witch didn't use the 'degree' system, the magical illiteracy screamed off the page and those who knew the deceased extremely well knew that the impostor hadn't got a clue what those teachings would have entailed. As we've explained elsewhere, *anyone* can have access to the basic Lesser Mysteries but making a false claim to knowledge of the Greater Mysteries will always end in tears.

Media-Witch hasn't been the only one to accuse members of the Coven of being too 'dark'. It is a common occurrence for those Old Craft covens that refuse 'entry on demand' to be labelled as being 'black' or 'dark'. In reality this 'dark' aspect is merely the occult term for the fourth face of the goddess; the period when the moon's face is in total darkness and primordial energies hold sway. It is as natural as the cycle of the moon when she remains hidden for three days and Old Crafters are trained to work with these energies as part of their training in the Greater Mysteries. There is much written about the maiden-mother-crone symbology, but few seem to venture into the uncharted waters of this primordial darkness.

The fourth face of the goddess is that of the creator-destroyer embodied in the powerful deities such as Kali, Lilith, Tiamat and Hecate. These Great Mother figures are just as much part of the Wiccan mythos as they are of any other Path and so *all* Wiccan goddess rituals are, by their very nature, left-hand path workings. From what I can see, much of this misunderstanding can be traced to pagan publications that attempt to eliminate the god-force from both the magical and spiritual practice. The erroneous but popular modern concept that pagan worship is essentially female orientated and that the male energies can be suppressed, or cast out all together, is extremely damaging and corrosive – not to mention short-sighted.

A considerable amount of modern pagan worship stems from the adoption of an ancient fertility/nature cult on a purely *mundane* level. The Goddess is seen as the Great Mother of all things, a symbolic representation of the Earth and Nature. Yet in *ye olden tymes* the Goddess was prayed to for the continuance of plenty, a high yield of crops and livestock to keep the tribe/clan/family fed through the harsh months of winter. All this fertility, of course, meant that the Goddess herself had to be fertilised – by the God, and often he paid for this with his life by becoming the sacrifice for his people.

According to Granny's report after the Vanessa debacle, Roger had claimed that he was resentful of the way the Coven excluded him from what he considered to be his birthright. Although his mother, Elizabeth, hadn't been a witch (she was pretty but far too stupid, commented his grandmother), he still felt that he should be given recognition as the rightful heir to his grandmother's teaching. He wanted to be admitted to the Coven – and it would be extremely difficult to refuse him entry, even at neophyte level.

'He always was a lying, conniving little sod,' she concluded, 'so I don't believe a word of it.'

All this left us in a rather difficult position. Roger was magically inept but he was family – sort of. Added to this, two couples from his group had already expressed a desire to join us although this could be viewed as 'poaching'. We'd not followed up after the autumn equinox but on two separate occasions they'd gone into Castor & Pollux to ask Gerry whether it would be possible.

Several others had decamped as a result of Vanessa's behaviour, which left a handful who, according to Granny, only went along for the dressing up. Finally after a full Coven meeting we compromised by inviting Roger and the others to join a teaching group, ostensibly to enable them to get to grips with our different way of working. In reality, it would keep them away from the Coven until we were sure their sentiments were genuine.

'It won't last,' I said to Rupert as we snuggled down under the duvet.

'Of course, it won't,' he responded. 'Roger will never be fit to be initiated into Old Craft while his arse points downwards.'

'But if he *thinks* he can, it will remove the stigma of him not being acceptable in Granny's eyes to become Magister. He'll try and find a way ... Rupert ...?'

'I've got other things on my mind other than my step-brother's insecurities,' he said meaningfully. And I must admit, his idea was *much* more interesting.

We didn't have long to wait. Pris arrived looking white and shaky the next morning while Rupert and I were having coffee in the kitchen.

To cut a long story short, Roger, wasn't satisfied with having been accepted into the Coven's teaching group. He had called at the cottage while Adam was out and proposed that Pris leave us and set up as 'High Priestess' of her own group, since she was obviously wasted where she was. With her abilities, he'd told her, 'they' could attract a lot of people who were just dying to get into Craft. If Rupert was too short-sighted to see that she would make a much better HPS (he still hadn't got to grips with our ways!) than me, then he was a fool.

With her own coven she would blossom (Pris, *blossom*? Heaven forbid!), although where Adam came into all this, Pris never found out. He'd always admired her. 'Fancied her rotten,' he'd added just before he pounced. His hand slid up her skirt but before he could reach knicker level, she'd fended him off with a soup ladle.

I poured her a strong coffee, to which Rupert added a generous slug of *Famous Grouse*.

'Goddess knows how he'll explain that black eye,' she said, the colour coming back to her cheeks.

'Shouldn't worry about it,' said Rupert pleasantly, 'I'm sure he'll think of a good story.'

Alan Wicca's story had *finally* begun to raise eyebrows. Even the most naïve of people began to suspect that his family history smacked of over-kill and started to consult the library books. How come, they started to ask, if Gerald Gardner bought the Mill on the Isle of Man in 1950 and Granny, having been introduced to him by old Mother Clutterbuck *and* taken part in the famous WWII ritual in 1940, Granny doesn't get an invite for another six years by which time little Alan was 12 years old. Odd that, what with Granny and Gerald being *so* close.

The Wicca-man claims to have Gerald's athame, pointed out another, yet he never mentions Monique Wilson who was Gerald's last High Priestess and who inherited his estate. Apart from anything else, Gerald was an old fraud with bogus qualifications to boot, so why would any *genuine* hereditary witch like Granny want anything to do with him? Neither does Granny ever mention Donna, Gerald's wife; and why didn't she talk about Cecil Williamson? After all, Gerald purchased the Mill from him and Cecil put up the memorial nearby. He called all the southern witches to the Mill – but why not Granny – who didn't go until 1956?

By this time, the books were out and everyone was becoming

an expert on the life and times of Gerald Gardner. The pub moots were buzzing with indignation. Funny that Doreen Valiente got in touch with Gerald via Cecil Williamson in 1952 and swiftly got into working with him and Daffo – yet the Wicca-man never mentions Doreen who split from Gerald in 1957. How convenient. And wouldn't you think, observed another, in 1956 witch-hunting was revived through the press resulting in national hysteria; if you'd have been Granny would you have revealed all the secrets of a 'hereditary' coven to a 12-year-old boy? And surely this well-travelled, well-connected child would have been introduced at the some of the Mill gatherings?

The list of questions was growing longer …

The pagan or occult community is extremely incestuous. When it comes to gossip, what many folk don't realise is that those who've been actively involved in magical shenanigans for any length of time, get to know who's doing what to whom very quickly. What newcomers don't understand is that the old timers don't come bounding over to introduce themselves and deliver chapter and verse about their magical pedigree.

It's rather the opposite, in fact, but it takes no time at all for news from the North of England to reach the South. Even goings on in the remotest corner of Wales can be served up as hot gossip over supper in less time than it takes to roast the chicken. It's also normal procedure to check up on anyone moving onto our patch and so Pris and Adam were quickly despatched to investigate the new occult shop that had opened in a nearby town.

Their *modus operandi* was to appear hesitant and curious – rather like a middle-aged couple who'd popped in out of the rain, while on their way to Marks & Spencer. For a couple of ex-Goths this must be quite an achievement. Adam's even been approached with the 'something for the weekend, sir' routine while waiting with a bored expression for his wife to examine every item in the shop.

Hecate's Fountain (yes, they've obviously read Kenny Grant) is set in a thriving street leading down to the harbour. The window displays are faultless and the place seems inviting enough ... until you enter under the watchful eye of the staff. 'You get the distinct impression of being silently appraised,' reported Pris. 'You browse quietly for a few moments, then something manifests behind you which makes you whip round. One of the staff is lurking, eying you up and offering to help. Somehow they manage to give the impression of saying, 'I can see that you don't know what you're doing, so I shall give you the benefit of my vast experience, whether you want it or not', even though they've only said, 'May I help you?'

'I was choosing a book on herbs for Madeleine, trying to read the blurb, while this creature babbled away but against your will you have to look at the thing. Without fail they are male, aged about twenty, with long, greasy hair – mostly black but they do keep one ginger specimen. They are always chestless wonders, with poor complexions and revolting hands. Usually sporting the distinctive ensemble of faded black jeans, scruffy trainers and the obligatory pagan T-shirt which invariably has some silly slogan on it like 'Born Again Satanist' with images of blood dripping down it ...'

'Well, we thought it was blood,' interrupted Adam, 'but on second thoughts decided that it could be the remains of a bacon sandwich with tomato ketchup which had been hastily stuffed under the counter as we walked in.'

'There is a vague waft of patchouli surrounding them (or it could just be mildew),' continued Pris, 'and they can't wait to show you how much they know and how little you do. If these tactics fail, as they are inclined to do, the boss himself appears and goes for the shock treatment: 'A lot of people nowadays are beginning to explore these old ways ... Of course, newcomers don't *really* understand how herbs were used ... Now over here we have a *very* interesting book ...' He nudges and winks in what must be intended to be a 'meaningful' way and leans even closer. 'I know of a sex magician who swears by this one'. By this time Adam was looking a little tense, and going that worrying white colour around the mouth. He hadn't spoken so far and that could be counted as a blessing.

'Tight lipped we said a cool 'good afternoon' before escaping out into the street. Once round the corner we had to stop because you can't go into hysterics and walk normally for some reason known only to Mother Nature. Would we go back? You bet your arse we will, we haven't had such a good laugh in ages!'

Chapter Nine

The Pagan Camp

We didn't intend to host a pagan summer camp but the request coincided with the local Arthurian re-enactment society's letter asking if we would be prepared to make a small field available for a medieval fair. Pris reckoned that since most pagans didn't know the difference between Celtic fact and fiction, they'd probably all have a very nice time. In the end, we agreed to a weekend providing that both parties agreed to clear up every scrap of litter when the event was over.

The Arthurians were going to be responsible for the 'jousting arena' and supplying the canvas 'pavilions' for the local traders; the pagans were going to supply the entertainment and maintain a tight control over the camp. The pagans got to construct the fire-pit; the Arthurians were in charge of the lavatories. In all fairness, the organisers for the pagan side of things were competent and not frightened of hard work.

The only problem, they explained, was that they wanted to make the needfire from the nine sacred woods – they knew which they were on paper, but they couldn't identify them in the wild! So, would Rupert a) give them permission to collect the wood, and b) help them locate it? A little work party bounced off across the fields on the tractor and trailer. There was a small wood that had been badly hit by the recent storms, and it was Rupert's intention that they would clear some of the fallen trees among which were ash, birch and pine. By the time the trailer returned to the campsite, the fire pit had been dug and the huge logs were unloaded to form the base for the needfire.

Rupert also knew that the Vicar was keen to cut some of the lower branches on the yew trees in the churchyard and that was their next port of call. A couple of the lads tried to do the 'you won't get me in a churchyard' bit but Rupert pointed out that the yews had been there longer than the church and that it was probably an old pagan site anyhow. The hazel, willow and hawthorn were less plentiful but a supply of rowan was provided by a neighbour who had lost his tree to the storms.

'Why can't we take this lot?' asked one lad, pointing at a pile of fallen branches that had been stacked in the corner of the field.

'It's elder,' replied Rupert.

'Yeah, so?'

'To burn ellen-wood without first asking permission from the spirit of the tree could be inviting disaster. No self-respecting countryman will burn it on a domestic fire and that's what the camp is, to all intents and purposes. Would you want to risk it?'

'Hey, man, you're *really* into this stuff, aren't you?'

'Aren't you?'

'Yeah, of course but I didn't know all this stuff about trees. I mean, trees are great but I didn't know they were all different. Where did you learn about it?'

'Oh, I just read a couple of books, here and there,' replied Rupert.

We know from experience that basic wood-lore is sadly lacking among most pagans even though the vast majority claim to follow some strange form of pseudo-Nature worship. We have several sacred sites hidden deep in the woods and all of us could find our way there and back blindfolded if necessary. We also know that after dark the woods take on a completely different perspective.

This is why it is not wise to attempt to set up an outdoor meeting on unfamiliar territory and expect everyone to arrive there without a hitch once twilight has passed. One group found what they thought was a perfect spot for a Midsummer meeting whilst out for a picnic but when they tried to find their way back to it after dark, they quickly found themselves lost. In the ensuing panic, the group fragmented and the woods echoed with the cries of lost souls. Eventually, they all managed to meet up again and the High Priest announced in rather miffed tones that they'd better get on with it, unless they wanted to be there all night! He raised his arms to invoke deity … and disappeared. There was silence, followed by a splash and a scream that rent the night air. Apparently, when they'd regrouped at a different location to the original site, they'd failed to notice in the darkness that the ground fell steeply away from a raised plateau. The High Priest had stepped back into nothingness and landed up in the brook at the bottom.

The camp was filling up with a varied assortment of humanity and their dogs, which gave rise to a bit of alarm. A pack of excitable dogs would cause havoc if they got in among the sheep and so there were a few hasty phone calls to move the flock to the furthest point on the farm. The afternoon was hot but there were still those cocooned in bike-leathers. Not to mention plenty of tie-dyed women and chaps in combat gear; a bus-load of Guinevere's, a brace or two of chaos magicians, dozens of half-naked children wearing rubber boots and a pair of middle aged men with curtains wrapped around their waists, and wigs made of wool with stag horns on top. There's a lot of curtain-wearing in pagan circles, it would appear.

The fire was due to be lit at 6 o' clock prompt, following the customary opening ceremony. Pris, who'd had some experience of these things, objects strongly (and quite rightly, I think) to joining in a circle and mixing energies with total strangers, and thought she'd keep out of the way until it was all over. Rupert said he couldn't be bothered with 'all that load of bollocks' which was just as well, since the organisers called down the blessing on the camp 'in perfect love and perfect trust' which would have really put Old Craft cats among the pagan pigeons. Purely by co-incidence, I'd arranged to meet Josh at the station and got back in time to find Rupert and Pris complete with binoculars, observing the ceremony from an upstairs window.

By the time the complete Coven and its guests arrived on the scene, several of us suitably fortified with *Famous Grouse*, the camp was in full swing. There was a phalanx of swaddled bodies firmly ensconced by the fire, seated like feudal kings on plastic chairs and wrapped in blankets despite the fact that it was a *very* warm evening. As the fire took its hold on the large logs at the base, the heat became almost unbearable but none of them moved. We waited with morbid fascination to see if the chairs would melt.

By the time the sun was dropping down behind the trees, the folk band had everyone's feet tapping but unfortunately the quality of entertainment wasn't to last. 'The trouble is,' said one of the organisers glumly. 'People volunteer their services and you don't like to refuse. They like their moment in the spot-light.'

She was referring to the rather appalling story-teller who'd been monopolising the fireside for the past three quarters of an hour and he wasn't the only one who'd lost the plot. A verbal punch-up had started when someone had told him to belt up; a middle-aged woman had remonstrated over the lack of manners and the story-teller was drowned out by the shouting.

'Well, he's had nearly an hour,' replied Adam, 'and no one's got a clue what he's on about.'

'He said he was a professional story-teller,' said the girl miserably.

'Never assume that a horse is sound until you've taken it over the jumps yourself,' said Rupert.

'Ehh?'

'Never mind. I think your story-teller's about to be burned alive,' replied Rupert with a grin as the story-teller was seized and lifted aloft by four burly chaps. He was last seen being carried off into the darkness and, as far as I know, was never heard of again. The folk-band returned, the harmony of the camp was restored and we wandered back to the house for a nightcap. After midnight, Rupert walked up to the campsite to make sure the fire was being property tended and found there were still a few people about fussing over a Wiccan Elder.

Apparently she'd settled down for a quiet five minutes by the bonfire after everyone else had retired for the night. Sometime later her partner went out to look for her and found her still sitting there with a daft expression on her face and a definite list to starboard. Rupert sniffed and looked among the ashes, only to discover that some idiot had placed laurel on the fire and she was in the middle of a trip!

The following day dawned bright and fair. By mid-morning the medieval fair had attracted visitors from all over the County and the booths were doing a roaring trade. 'I've had to send Guy and Adam back for another load of stock,' beamed Gerry, wiping his face with a silk handkerchief. 'At this rate there won't be a thing left in the shop.'

Rupert was in charge of the ox-roast, having donated one of our beef cattle and being ably assisted by the chap from the previous day's wood detail. Although nothing was said aloud, this was *our* sacrifice to the Old 'Uns in the hope that they would see fit to cast a kindly eye over the proceedings. There were the 'vegi-vors' who complained about the smell of roasting meat but they were in the minority.

We know our own fields and we privately walk our own boundaries in the springtime to ask a blessing on the land and livestock. So it came as a bit of a surprise when a woman asked if she could speak to Rupert about the farm.

'Why?' I asked. 'He's a bit tied up at the moment.'

'I'm a Wiccan High Priestess and I wanted to ask whether he would like me to bless the land for him.'

I'm afraid I looked at her with blank astonishment for a moment before annoyance at her presumption took over. 'Not on *my* patch you don't,' I snapped. 'We're quite capable of carrying out our own rituals, thank you very much.'

'Ooooooh!' said Pris as we walked away. 'That's the first time

I've ever heard you lose your cool. You should have let her ask Rupert, she'd probably be barbecued along with the ox.'

'I'm sorry, but these people make me mad. They don't stop to think for one moment that anyone else might be quietly going about their own business without the need to make a complete arse of themselves. She hadn't got a clue what we use the land for, or what we grow on it. Probably thinks all you have to do is stand at the farm gate and wave your arms about.'

Pris raised an eyebrow. She was obviously thinking about the time when she and I blessed the cornfields and nearly came down with pneumonia. She was about to make some comment when she was distracted. 'Over there, by that tepee. Isn't that Helena?'

It *was* Helena hanging on every word uttered by a tall, androgyny, whose beautifully painted sign stated that s/he was both artist and bee-keeper. We couldn't resist getting a closer look and under the cover of the crowd, we casually worked our way over to the tepee. We'd never seen Helena so animated and she was flirting like mad, even though we still couldn't decide whether the object of her attraction was male or female. We sloped off to find Gerry and report.

My attention was caught for a moment by Granny in deep conversation with the young girl she'd rescued from the bikers and by this time, I'd lost Pris in the crowd. Having been waylaid several times, when I finally caught up with her by the ox-roast, she was puffed up with indignation. Apparently she'd been accosted by Gwen who'd roundly accused her of leading Roger on, having obviously believed his version of the soup ladle.

'What did you expect?' said Rupert, putting an arm around her shoulders. 'We knew he'd tell a good story about how'd he'd got that black eye.'

'Yes, you shameless hussy,' I added since Gwen had nabbed me after stalking off in indignation. 'You wanted to become his High Priestess and when he rejected you, you hit him in temper! I've been warned to be on my guard because you'll be after

Rupert next. I know these things – Gwen's just told me. And she's going to be his High Priestess now Vanessa's gone.'

'They'll both wish Vanessa was back when I'm done.'

'Pris!' Rupert assumed his Man-act mode. 'Let it go. Roger's convinced Gwen and there's nothing needs doing about it. It gives us good reason to break off all contact whether Granny likes it or not. Most of the trouble we've had over the past year has been caused by that group, so let's just draw a line under it and get on with our own affairs.'

'They'll have difficulty reforming the coven anyhow,' I added. I'd just been talking to one of the couples who'd come over into our teaching group and they had no intention of continuing to work with Roger and Gwen. They'd seen the light, as it were. 'We'll keep them on the outside for a while until we're sure they're genuine and so there'll be no question of poaching.'

'Roger's only left with the dressing up brigade, if these four wish to remain with us,' coaxed Rupert. 'No one will believe what they're saying. People know him *too* well.'

Rupert went back to his ox-roast and we ambled over to the fortune teller's tent where Josh was giving the Arthurian soothsayer some grief. We decided to leave them to it in case a meaningful relationship was forming. Pris still looked thoroughly miserable until Rupert's disciple came trotting over carrying an extremely large drum.

'Hey, can we drop in for a spot of drumming and meditation later?'

The wicked gleam came back in her eye. 'I'm afraid we don't go in for *that* sort of thing,' she whispered huskily.

'What's your thing then?'

She leaned closer. '*Real* witchy things.'

I had to turn away as the chap gulped nervously and his Adam's apple travelled the whole length of his throat and back again. When I turned around he was standing there like a confused puppy, wanting to know more but afraid to ask the questions. He and Rupert had been joined at the hip for most of the morning so I could only assume that, despite appearances, the chap wasn't a complete moron or Rupert would have pitched him on the fire. My old Man's a good Craft teacher when there's a receptive pupil; it's fools he won't suffer.

'What a strange young man,' muttered Pris as we walked away.

'Rupert seems to have taken him under his wing, for some reason. I just hope he doesn't mention the drumming.'

Drumming is rapidly becoming the main bone of contention at many pagan camps. At one event the drummers drowned out the voice of the story-teller; they drummed past the 11 o'clock curfew; they drummed incessantly all through the following day. They were asked to stop – they were told to stop and – finally, they were evicted from the camp amongst much ill feeling. It was their 'right' to be there, despite the fact that they had failed to observe the pre-stated camp rules.

This 'right' reflects the attitude of a growing number of people who see paganism and many aspects of Wicca as a sort of cop-out in much the same way as that offered by the hippy movement back in the '60s. In fact, to paraphrase and update a comment made by Robert Cochrane from that time, paganism has become a funk-hole in which those who have not been successful in solving various personal problems may hide.

Unfortunately, few bother to study true Craft, turning surly and resentful when it's pointed out that what they are doing is ill-informed or an outright travesty of what they're pretending to be. Often you'll find Old Crafters positively reviled for not accepting new-comers on face value or welcoming them into the fold as equals.

'In a parody of the words of the blessed Raven,' I said quoting my favourite author, 'the modern pagan slogan is rapidly becoming: If I can't, you mustn't; and even if I don't want to, you still mustn't, in case, unknown to me, I'm missing out on something. This is not because I want to understand but can't – I don't give a damn about that – but because someone else might understand and take pleasure in the knowledge, and the neo-pagan movement couldn't possibly allow that.'

'Wish I was as clever as you, Brian,' said Pris, now re-fortified with a double *Grouse*. 'Sorry I was a pain in the arse back there, but Gwen really upset me. I always thought she quite liked me.'

'Got nothing to do with it. This is all about face-saving. Roger saves his marriage; Gwen gets to play High Priestess; Gwen's brother makes his peace with the Bishop and Gwen's sister-in-law carries on with her ambition to be married to a high-ranking clergyman. Gwen has a position of respect and Roger doesn't have to worry about being divorced – for the time being that is!'

By late afternoon the medieval fair was over, as was (or so we'd heard) Alan Wicca's time on our patch. The gossip wasn't long in circulating that he'd been seen hastily loading the car and leaving his rented cottage. This sudden departure had been precipitated by an unexpected visit early that morning by a farmer the size of a Charolais bull and the accusation that the Wicca-man had tried to force his attentions on the man's 16-year-old daughter. The farmer got angry; the Wicca-man got thumped and a neighbour got worried and called the police.

It transpired that this was not the first incident of its kind and, true to form, Alan Wicca had folded his tent and stole away while the rest of the town was enjoying itself at the fair. No doubt he'll take the stories of Isobel, George and Gerald with him and will, in time, resurface elsewhere with an attempt to ingratiate himself into another pagan community.

The camp fire was replenished with logs and the remains of the ox-roast distributed among the needy by Rupert's disciple, acting as official sorcerer's apprentice. The Arthurians returned bearing beer and the Battle of the Songs was enjoined. When the songs ran out there was a camp story-teller's challenge – which included the one about the chap who stood outside his tent during a violent thunderstorm, his sword pointing (perhaps a little unwisely) towards the heavens as the thunder rolled and the lightning flashed. *'Odin!'* he bellowed. A shuffling figure in a sou'wester lumbered past. *'Wrong god!'* it hissed. *'Oh, shit,'* came the response. *'THOR!'*

Gerry, however, was more fascinated by the goings on in the artist-cum-bee keeper's tepee and was now on his fourth circle of inspection. 'I'm sure it's Helena in there,' he whispered.

'And if it is, she's being shagged senseless,' replied Guy who was trying to deflect his partner's absorption with the strange noises filtering through the canvas.

'So much for rose petals and a fig wrapped in long strands of black synthetic hair,' said Pris.

Gerry pretended to be offended. 'Sex, love, attraction and Minnehaha. It's all there!'

'Perhaps you tripped over the rug when you directed the spell,' teased Rupert. 'Lesbian shenanigans in a tepee is *not* what you had in mind. You're not that devious.'

We'd long since retired to bed but the drummers, no doubt invigorated by the beer and the success of the day, were still going strong.

'I'm going up there,' muttered Rupert.

No sooner had he swung a leg out of bed than there was the unmistakable and deafening roar from the twin barrels of a shotgun, which sent the large colony of rooks into hysterics. When the birds settled down again there was a blanket silence over the camp.

The sound of footsteps on the gravel outside had Rupert hanging out of the window in a flash. 'It's all right,' came Gordon's voice from the garden, 'it's only Grandad after the drummers.'

'Well, at least it's shut them up,' he said getting back into bed.

'If you suddenly encountered Old Joe out in the woods in his long johns and hobnail boots, brandishing a shot gun, wouldn't you flee for your life,' I answered.

People began to drift away from the camp after the closing ceremony – which I studiously avoided by volunteering to drive Josh back to the station. From his vantage point at the upstairs window, Rupert declared it was safe to return to the field now that all the 'perfect love and perfect trust' had been got out of the way. The field had been cleared of every scrap of rubbish and, apart from the fire pit that was still smouldering, we wouldn't have known a camp had been there over the weekend. The procession of motorbikes, cars, dogs, kids and hikers filed away down the lane.

Rupert's disciple came up to shake hands with tears in his eyes. 'What can I say, man. It's been great. I mean ... you *know* things. I mean, *really* know things ...' All the time pumping Rupert's hand vigorously.

Rupert kept his arm stuck out rigidly at an angle for fear that the young man would kiss him. 'Well ... er, glad you enjoyed it. Perhaps we'll see you again next year.'

'You mean we *can* come back? Hey, that's great.' And he ran off yelling. 'We're coming back next year. Hey, next year, here ...' A few people turned and waved in response.

'I thought you weren't going to make a habit of this,' I said as we walked back up the field to the smoking fire pit.

'I wasn't but the re-enactment group want to do a repeat, the town's in favour, and we can't find fault with the happy campers. If there's only one who goes away with the essence of genuine knowledge, it's been worth it ...' He broke off and nodded at the charcoal embers.

There in the centre were the charred remains of a very large drum.

Chapter Ten

HPS or High Priest(ess) Syndrome

As I've pointed out before, we must remember that 'grades' or 'degrees' are only valid between one particular group or tradition and the god and goddess to which they are dedicated; other groups work differently and will not automatically accept or recognise them. The ranks of 'High Priest' and High Priestess' are modern appellations dating from the 1960s to denote those witches who have attained their Third Degree. This was originally the highest rank in Gardnerian covens but is fast becoming the norm in many other groups. Among Old Crafters (such as members of the Coven) these terms are unknown.

In Gardnerian groups, attaining the Third Degree was usually looked on as a preliminary to, and essential for, any couple who were going to 'hive off', i.e. leave their mother coven and start their own group. Equally in Gardnerian groups, people did not usually take their Third Degree until it was necessary for them to hive off: when, for example, the original group had grown too large; or if the couple were moving away from the area and wished to start their own group in their new location.

One such couple turned up at a pub moot with a view to inviting any interested parties to fall in under their leadership. They were called Harry and Pam but introduced themselves as ... Great Tor and Tinkling Moon-stream ... to which Adam muttered that it sounded like a childish euphemism for bathroom functions!'

Harry and Pam had just attained their Third Degree before moving into the area and were enthusiastic, nay desperate, to have their own group and to hold their first 'solo' ritual. No one else volunteered and so at Granny's prompting (she likes to know who's moving onto our patch), Pris reluctantly agreed that she and Adam would join them for a midsummer celebration.

'The invitation hung over our heads like a lead shroud,' she said, curled up in the corner of Gerry's sofa like a large, sleek cat. 'Adam was pacing about and grumbling that I should develop PMT and get us out of it. Anyway I offered him a large *Grouse* and smiled that soothing smile we all develop when social niceties have forced us into accepting an invitation to something that no one else in their right minds would attend.

'I made myself scarce to pack the bag: robes, cords, matches, home-made bread, boiled bacon and a decent bottle of red. As we were guests we shouldn't have needed anything else and after all, our hosts were running the show but old habits die hard. They were newly qualified and rarin' to go. They just wanted an opportunity to show us how well they could cope. 'It'll be fine,' I said passing Adam in the hall but the only response was an even blacker scowl. He was very, *very* quiet.'

The drive to the woods was executed in double quick time with Adam taking hairpin bends in an exciting fashion. To the accompaniment of much tutting and slamming of car doors, they were greeted in a suspiciously animated fashion by Harry and Pam.

Bottles of supermarket lager were pushed into their hands and a wobbly tape of '70s hits warbled in the background. Pam was enthusing about the fantastic secret grove they'd discovered; a place of great power and the assurance that the 'Old Ones' never fail to show up. Pris tried to keep this foremost in her mind as another bottle of lager was pressed into her hands.

Pam seemed to be sinking them a bit fast, so Pris quickly suggested they made a start, discreetly emptying the bottle under a bush. Adam remained quiet. Undeterred, Pris chattered on about nothing and refused another bottle of witch-pee on the grounds that her ulcer was playing up. Unfortunately it was true but she consoled herself with the hope that the Circle energies would sort it out. Harry stood waiting. He was packed and organised like Sherpa Tenzing, torch in hand to guide them through the darkened woods.

'Have we got everything?' asked Pam.

Harry looked smug. 'It's all packed, it's been packed since last week.'

Pam beamed. 'Oooh, he's *so* clever. Do you know he's made all the candles himself, and blended the incense, and written us a brilliant ritual; as well as cooking a huge casserole of *chilli con carne* ...' Pris's heart sunk as her ulcer grumbled in dread.

Harry beamed. 'Ah ... ha ... but Pam's made all the plonk herself. It's still a bit cloudy but it tastes okay. Only one of them cheapo kits but don't worry, there's absolutely loads of it, isn't there, love?'

Pam giggled a bit unsteadily. 'Oh yes, it's quite quaffable. In fact, I tried two or three glasses earlier before we set off.'

Pris glanced at Adam who was glowering at her. She couldn't actually *see* him glowering but she'd a nasty feeling he was. When you're a crone you sort of sense these things – it's called bitter experience!

After a mad scramble down an embankment that would have daunted the Vikings, they arrived at the grove. It was a bit squelchy underfoot but Pam assured them that it was wonderfully fertile because the river was just behind them, conveniently to the West.

'It's all so perfect,' chirped Harry. Pris muttered she was sure it was – unless you happen to be terrified of slinky, slow running, deep, dark rivers sneaking about behind you – which she is! 'And you're in the West,' Harry continued as her heart sunk lower.

Fortunately Adam knows her fears and gallantly offered to take the West so that Pris could take the South, but Pam had metamorphosed into Tinkling Moon-stream and was having none of it. Manfully taking a huge swig out of Pris's lovely Canadian red, and thumping the cork back into the bottle, she launched into her role.

'Oh, no ... No ... You can't swap places. You'll muddle us up. Harry spent all last night writing this ritual and I can't let you mix up his parts.'

Pris gave Pam a look that Granny would be proud out and thought to herself that she'd got absolutely no interest in doing anything whatsoever with Harry's parts. Okay, West it was then. She pinched Adam's bum on the sly and he grinned. That's better. He was obviously starting to suspect that there could be something in the way of fun to be had and her heart lifted a bit. Without a hitch (for once) a reasonable fire was lit and after ten minutes of rummaging and muttering, a large stone was crammed with everything the modern Witch could possible want on an Altar. The rite was about to begin ...

Without further ado, Tinkling Moon-stream whipped off all her kit and donned her cord, with Great Tor rapidly following suit. 'We thought we'd work sky-clad tonight,' she gaily trilled, causally testing the full chalice again.

Adam and Pris fixed the smiles. 'Fine,' they responded with the secret witch-word for 'shit!' Neither of them were thrilled at the prospect, but they were damned if they'd admit it and risk being thought prudish. After all, as witches they'd a certain reputation to maintain and prudishness doesn't come into it!

'As you know, we're not prudish but it was more a case of *squeamish*,' continued Pris. 'Now I don't mind slugs and snails and rotting foliage sticking to my robe, but sticking to other parts of my anatomy is a definite turn off. However, we were merely guests so when in Rome, etc ... We stepped away from the firelight and tried to get all our clothes to fit into the bag. Adam was propping our boots up in a tree, when we heard ...'

'Aaargh ...' A yelp issued from Tinkling Moon-stream. 'Bloody leeches ... Harry ... Get that one off the frigging Altar!'

Poor TMS needed another hefty swig to calm her as Great Tor deftly flicked the hideous thing with his athame and it landed a few feet away with a little thud. He assured Pris that the place was full of them, a sure sign that the old wise healers would have loved the place, and would certainly have gathered a few to take home. Course they would!

'Now we're all staunch believers in authenticity but leeches …. we weren't there for a healing rite, for Goddess sake! Along with head lice and one bath a year at Imbolc, it's a tradition I could cheerfully let slip,' groaned Pris at the memory.

'Great Tor gently shoved everyone into their respective stations, with me firmly in the West, and handed out large sheets of paper. Everyone's part was highlighted in glowing green and, according to Adam, those were the only highlights that night! My stomach growled as we settled ourselves and I felt the need to apologise, blaming the old ulcer, which sulked but shut up.'

Silence … the rite began. Silence … More silence. No one moved. Still silence.

Adam and Pris waited politely, faces impassive, thinking 'Wow, these two must really be raising some power'. Suddenly Great Tor elbowed his Lady who nearly lost her balance.

'*Light the candle*,' he hissed out of the corner of his mouth and TMS fumbled for the matches. Striking one, it fizzled sadly and failed to spark … another … and another. Muttered curses (poor TMS needed a drink) as she quickly went through the whole box. Great Tor turned apologetically and called softly, 'Has either of you got a lighter?'

Adam turned and reached out behind the tree where their clothes were safe from marauding wildlife and Pris swears he was about to light a cigarette but resisted the impulse. By this time, TMS was swaying a little unsteadily around the fire which was beginning to die down.

'*Mashes* damp,' she slurred.

Behind their backs, Adam built up the fire mainly to keep them warm in that cold, dank place but arms akimbo, candles blazing, neither Great Tor nor TMS seemed to notice. So with two middle-aged bottoms glowing in the fire light, the rite finally began. TMS cast the Circle. It was a bit egg-shaped due to her avoiding the spot where the leech had landed but in some circles they say intention is everything.

The Quarter Guardians were called. TMS took East; she likes East because she's great at Scrabble so it must be appropriate!

Great Tor approached her from the Altar, holding out a stumpy yellow candle. She accepted it gratefully with a smile and waited. Great Tor dashed back to the Altar and returned with a lit candle. TMS held her candle to the flame; the soft wax melted, dripping onto the Altar candle, effectively extinguishing it. The fire smoked heavily and Pris held her breath for more reasons than one as Great Tor trundled back to the Altar yet again, this time bringing the lighter.

Together they huddled and stooped, muttering, fumbling ...
'Hold it this way ...'

'It's gone out' ... until eventually Great Tor took charge and insisted that TMS take the Altar candle.

'Your wick's too short,' hissed his Lady.

Great Tor got a trifle huffy and returned to his place by the Altar to sulk as TMS invoked the East. Arms half up, she stamped her foot like a bad-tempered ewe, making cellulite ripple gently as she called in a grisly whisper: 'Oh Great *Sylpsh* of Air, we call thee to this *conshecwated plaish*, to *witnesh* our rites and protect all what stand *wivvin.*' Planting the candle soundly on a flat stone at her feet, she turned to face Pris, smiling. Behind her the candle slowly toppled over but continued to burn.

Then it was Adam's turn. He was desperately trying to keep his face straight as Great Tor advanced toward him bearing his symbol of the South. A renegade muscle jerked at the corner of his mouth while accepting the limp joss stick that wobbled crazily as it was lit. His glance caught Pris's eye as he turned to call the South and mentally she screamed at him: 'Don't you dare!'

'As we all know, there's more than a bit of devilment in Adam, who works exceptionally well in the South,' grinned Pris. 'Unfortunately it's *what* he works *with* that's the problem. Great sense of humour some of his entities, and so much to go at in that particular Circle. Oh dear, I thought, grounding myself thoroughly and telling *it* (whatever *it* was) to piss off.'

Adam looked dangerously animated. TMS looked impressed. Great Tor adjusted his cord and rummaged around on the Altar. Pris took a deep breath because it was her turn. Suddenly through the smoke Great Tor was standing in front of her, holding out a blue Milk of Magnesia bottle. She smiled, how kind of him.

'No, it's okay,' she whispered, patting her stomach. 'It's settled down now.'

But he insisted, shoving the bottle into her hands. Firmly she pushed it back, looking questioningly at him. Again the Milk of Magnesia bottle was forced upon her with an insistent hiss.

'It's the moon-blessed water for the West!'

Pris looked away. 'Ooops, er … sorry.'

Feeling incredibly foolish clutching a plastic container for an indigestion remedy, she turned to pretend to invoke the West. There was no way she was insulting *her* Guardians by inviting them to this current fiasco. Great Tor loomed behind her. 'Put it on the stone,' he muttered, obviously convinced that she and Adam were rank amateurs at this lark. Following orders, Pris placed the bottle on the stone whereupon it promptly fell over and glugged sadly into the mud.

Now it was time for some real action and their intrepid High Priestess instructed them to read from the scripts. Gazing skyward she intoned:

Great Forest Lord on Summer's Night
I call thee to bless this rite
Your lady waits in utmost glee
Oh Hornéd One I welcome thee.

Gazing adoringly at TMS, the High Priest replied in a flat

monotone:

Beloved lady of the Night
I welcome thee to this our rite
Dancing gaily through the trees
On bended knee I welcome thee

They hugged and kissed, Great Tor having considerable difficulty extracting himself from TMS's ardent grasp. Hell's teeth, though Pris, what has Adam conjured? Eventually, with a little shove that sent TMS cannoning into an oak tree, Great Tor turned to give Adam a meaningful look, prompting him to do his bit. Out of the corner of her eye, Pris caught TMS having a crafty swig to steady herself.

Adam's eyes glinted as he advanced to take Pris's hand and looked all too deeply into her eyes. He called to her soul, and she responded, locked in a tense moment of Oneness – until the brief spell was shattered.

'No ... no ... that's not in the script!'

Poor TMS needed another quick drink to settle her. Great Tor, also unsettled, nervously insisted on hauling them all around the bonfire. He set off like a long-dog and it was all they could do not to fall into the fire. His voice boomed out:

Hecate, Hecate, grant us a boon
Dancing under silvery moon
Hecate, Hecate, grant our plea
As we do will so mote it be!'

Before anyone could attempt to pick up the chant, it was brought to an abrupt halt and they all cannoned into each other. Pris was furious since they'd had no prior notice of any intended spells and to invoke *Hecate* for midsummer ... where on earth were these people coming from? What was the purpose of all this?

As they all stood around puffing and recovering their breath, TMS looked bleakly at Pris and Adam and shrugged. 'Erm .., *hash* anyone got anything they want doing?'

This was met with total silence and weakly she looked to Great Tor for help. He looked every bit as lost as she was but bravely he tried to keep the momentum going. 'Come on folks, lovely big cones of power going to waste … There must be something …' he trailed off sadly.

Adam and Pris looked at each other and firmly shook their heads. Enough was enough.

'Oh well, we'll just have to have the feast then,' shrugged Great Tor. TMS was all in favour of that and after a fashion the feast was blessed.

They'd obviously been reading some more Wiccan literature, because Great Tor suddenly took it into his head to kneel naked (middle-aged, paunch and wearing nothing but his cord) in front of the Altar with his back to the rest of them. He leant forward to kiss the earth, displaying what appeared to be two hard-boiled eggs in a Persil bag. What made this display so unnerving was the fact that his testicles were scraping the ground perilously close to where the unfortunate leech had landed.

'Now that's what I call putting your faith in the Goddess,' said Pris. 'Poor Adam went quite pale and vowed on the spot to become a Satanist because at least they get to wear a black leather thong.'

By this time, there was only half the wine left in the Chalice, so it had to be topped up with home-made plonk. Pris watched Adam's eyes water as he took a tiny sip; holding her breath she forced a mouthful down, apologising to her ulcer. Her pronouncement was that the dribbly drops that always lurk in the bottom of the lavatory brush holder would probably have tasted better. Their hosts didn't seem to notice and managed to make quite a dint in it.

'Three hours had dragged by,' concluded Pris. 'And I was so hungry that even luke warm *chilli con carne* didn't trouble me. I accidentally forgot to contribute the boiled bacon, so the following day I took half of it over to Granny and told her the tale. No doubt she'll stamp her stick at the next meeting and rant about 'improving standards' – and we quite agree – after all, things can't get much worse.

'*Can* they?'

Epilogue

The stories related in this volume of *Coarse Witchcraft* have happened to experienced practitioners who are confident enough in their own magical abilities to be able to say 'I made a mistake'. We all make those mistakes – the fun lies in sharing them. And as the late Bob Clay-Egerton once remarked, he'd got 50 years magical experience under his belt and he still occasionally made a prat of himself!

The members of the Coven are all genuine magical practitioners within Old Craft. The Coven really does exist and the events recorded in *Coarse Witchcraft: Craft Working*, have happened to both ourselves, and to those of our acquaintance, over a short period of time. We hope, however, this book will amuse the reader, but also stand as a warning to those who wish to discover more about the Craft, so that they steer clear of the charlatans, the poseurs, the magically ignorant and the spiritually inept.

But wouldn't the Craft be boring if every spell working came out perfectly? It is a fact of life that, like everything else in this world, magic is something that needs to be worked at, experimented with and adapted to suit each individual's requirements. Although there are certain magical laws that need to be observed, personal magic leads the neophyte on their own voyage of discovery that is both exciting and mind-expanding.

Remember that outward appearance isn't anything to go by. And that the insignificant little chap or woman sitting quietly on the edge of a group, may be much more powerful than the long-haired idiot wearing a pentagram the size of the Isle of Wight. Never be afraid to ask questions – and if you don't receive a response it is probably because the High Priest or Priestess doesn't know the answer. Don't be fooled by the rebuke that you're not ready to learn something; or that certain information is only available to Initiates. Any Priest or Priestess, Magister or Lady, worth their salt should be able to give an explanation without revealing anything of a private or personal nature.

So you've tried to find us on the map? Well ... we will admit that St Thomas on the Poke is fictitious but then we value *our* privacy. We chose St Thomas because he was the only sensible one of the disciples who demanded proof and refused to accept things at face value. In Old Craft his wisdom would have been applauded.

The Twelve dance on high. Amen
The Whole on High hath part in our dancing. Amen
Whoso danceth not knoweth not what comes to pass. Amen.

PART TWO: CARRY ON CRAFTING

RUPERT PERCY AND GABRIELLE SIDONIE

Prologue

Since the publication of *Coarse Witchcraft: Craft Working*, the Coven has undergone several changes. The major difference is that, much to Granny's chagrin, Adam and Pris have refused to attend any more of her arranged Circle workings involving strangers, no matter how tantalising the prospect of gossip. Once their experiences had been committed to print, they decided that never mind the lunatic performances of the hosts, their *own* credibility was being seriously compromised by being seen to be taking part in such travesties of Craft.

But the best laid plans of mice and witches ...

By and large the Coven remains pretty much the same, although our working numbers are down to a handful due to the loss of Helena, our mad medium, who ran off with a lesbian lover, and the absence of our son and daughter, Richard and Philly, being away at college. Madeleine and Robert are still staunch members although Robert's job has taken them abroad for three years. Gordon still puts in an appearance but he's courting a girl from the next village, so he spends most of his time over there, once he's finished at the stables. We have to let them all go ... so that eventually they come back.

Besides myself and my wife, Gabrielle, that leaves Pris and Adam, Gerry and Guy (who run Castor & Pollux, the local occult shop) and, of course, Granny, who is itching to interfere with Gordon's relationship and draw him back into the fold: especially as the girlfriend happens to be the daughter of a Pentecostal lay-preacher. My half-brother and I are no longer on speaking terms, and the teaching coven has disbanded – much to our relief – when they realised how much work and commitment was expected from each of them.

On a more positive note, several books about what we believe (rather than what we do) have been, or are about to be written. As a result, St Thomas on the Poke is becoming the literary centre of the pagan world and never before has the kitchen table witnessed such in-depth discussions of what should, and should definitely *not*, be included in everyone's next *magnum opus*. Needless to say, there are no great secrets revealed in any of our titles but *A Witch's Treasury for Hearth & Garden* and *Equine Magical Lore* do give a whiff of the 'real stuff', as one highly respected occult author put it.

Rupert Percy

All Hallows

'So if I were to join in one of these witchcraft rituals, would I have to run up and down with a lighted taper in my arse, singing the *Hallelujah Chorus*?' The question was patronising and more than a little offensive, even if it wasn't on camera.

Rupert fixed the interviewer with a steely look before responding in his best, clipped public-school tone: 'You could if you wanted to, old boy, but it wouldn't add anything constructive to the proceedings.'

With that, he climbed into the Land Rover and drove off, leaving the television crew staring after him, open-mouthed, while the public relations girl looked as though she was about to burst into tears. I *had* warned them well in advance not to ask daft questions but obviously the media genius with the Beckham mentality had decided to busk it – and this was the result. So there they stood in the middle of a field, on a damp October morning – a complete production team, whose star performer had just buggered off! And no amount of coaxing was going to get him back.

Needless to say, it was a couple of weeks away from Hallowe'en, and this was an attempt to inject something 'topical but spooky' into the early evening *Country-Style* programme. Rupert had only agreed to take part because he'd been led to believe it related directly to his new book, *Equine Magical Lore* and he was expecting to talk about traditional British 'horse whispering' and natural animal cures. (He can wax quite lyrical about pig oil and sulphur, which he considers to be a cure for most things. I once caught him eyeing the children speculatively when they were small and suffering from measles!) He was *not* prepared to talk about Old Craft, on or off camera, with a moron who was just trying to provoke some good television.

As we've said many times before, the problem is that the media doesn't want to portray witches as sane and rational adults with jobs and family responsibilities. They *want* weird (as opposed to *wyrd*) and will try any trick to manoeuvre their victim into doing, or saying, something stupid so the nation can snigger behind its collective hand, convinced that we're all mentally defective. Unfortunately, there are a handful of so-called magical practitioners who *will* perform this kind of stunt for five minutes of fame but they are only representative of those whose roots were grafted after the popular surge of occultism in the 1970s.

Having finally managed to soothe Rupert's affronted pride, and attempted to persuade the production crew that camping out in the greenhouse wasn't a good idea, most of the morning had gone. Judging by the amount of frantic mobile telephone activity – conspicuous in a stable yard by the discordant assortment of electronic ringtones – they had obviously been told not to return to base without a result. For some time we amused ourselves by watching from the upstairs windows as they circled the house, trying to conceal themselves among the bushes and shrubs, waiting to pounce. The publicity girl, now thoroughly sodden, had tried banging on the door a couple of times, but Rupert was not for turning. It was going to be a long day, but the dog was keeping them on the move, and finding it all immense fun.

Periodically, someone would mooch past the kitchen window, sporting what appeared to be a dead ferret on the end of a pole. I was reliably informed by my son (who telephoned in the middle of this hiatus), that it was a microphone and part of the sound equipment, but out here in the country, you can never be quite sure. We know of one local lad who managed to sell the same dead fox to a television production team on three consecutive days, by keeping it in the freezer overnight and fluffing up the fur each morning with his mother's hair-dryer. And they say country folk are thick … he earned £100 for that roadkill!

Anyway, Rupert refused to leave the kitchen while the media

circus was still lurking about, and just as we were sitting down to an early lunch, in came Pris, spitting feathers. 'I'll murder the bugger!' she kept saying, until Rupert's special blend of strong coffee laced with *Famous Grouse* worked its magical calming effect; not to mention feeding her a cheese and pickle sandwich, the size of which would have felled a healthy Rottweiler.

At first we thought poor old Adam was coming in for some flack but it was much more serious than mere marital dispute. A stranger had ridden into town and, compounding sacrilege with blasphemy, had announced to all and sundry that he came from the very same Old Craft tradition that had spawned Pris. Now we have ways and means of recognising our 'own', as it were, and this pretender was not giving out any of the signals that would have endorsed his claim.

In all honesty, Pris's old teacher was a bit of a colourful character with some most peculiar working methods – which may account for some of Pris's strange habits – but his magical approach was certainly unique. As she'd said on many occasions in response to prior bogus claims to her lineage: 'He might have been a scurrilous old bugger, but he was *our* scurrilous old bugger!'

This type of claiming 'kinship' is, unfortunately, no longer a rarity, especially as the schism between contemporary Wicca and the Gardnerian-based traditions is widening all the time. Those older traditions that have formal, initiatory training and an established hierarchical system now wish to distance themselves from this eclectic free-for-all that typifies 21st century paganism, by referring to themselves as 'traditional' Craft.

For those of British Old Craft, however, the gulf between modern paganism and our ways could *never* have been reconciled. As we frequently point out, there's nothing altruistic about Old Craft, which retains its tribal mentality and does not wish to take on the responsibility for global problems that occur outside its own sphere of operations. We tend to work on the guiding and hallowed principle of looking after our own ... full stop!

All this convenient pagan colour-coding has resulted in more and more folk coming forward to claim antecedents for themselves, to which they are not entitled. As a rule they allow around five years from the death of one of these Old Souls and if no one else appears to lay claim to the tradition, they publicly proclaim themselves to be the inheritors of the old wisdom of the dear departed. Even if the closest they've ever been is bumping into one at a pagan camp; holding a couple of telephone conversations of a pseudo-magical nature; or being involved in the same public ritual as *'the Name'*. Old Crafters are notoriously secretive and this form of *lèse-majesté* is the only thing that will bring 'em out of the woodwork to defend their corner. There's many a pretender who has been faced down by an affronted Old Crafter ... and it's not a pretty sight!

'So who is this chap?' I asked, when Pris had cooled down enough to talk coherently and wiped the smear of home-made chutney from her cheek.

'He's just taken over as relief manager of the Duck & Ferret in the next village, and called into Castor & Pollux, to introduce himself as a traditional witch. Of course Gerry kept quiet while he rattled off his pedigree but he wasted no time in getting on the phone to me to check him out once the chap was off the premises.'

Gerry has elevated the art of keeping 'closeted' to an art form and will rarely give anything away about his own background, magical or personal. There are still those pagan groups who have difficulties accepting homosexuals in their midst, but this reveals more about their magical abilities than their personal prejudices. Our 'boys' are valued members of the Coven and no one can prise information out of unsuspecting customers like our Gerry.

'And there's no way he *could* be one of your erstwhile band?' said Rupert, attempting to prevent any knee-jerk reactions involving hexing, bottling or spit-roasting, or a combination of all three.

'Nope. I did my own checking. The Old Man never formally initiated the person who this chap claims initiated *him*, and I *can* prove that. It's like one of us claiming initiatory links with the New Forest lot simply because we live within spitting distance of the forest and Granny having had some spurious connection with them in days gone by. No, I got my facts right *before* I lost my temper.'

'Anything we can use publicly?' I asked, knowing that some of their strange ways might raise an eyebrow or two in some circles. And some things *are* most definitely best kept hidden.

Pris fiddled with her spoon for a moment or two and then a grin started to play at the corners of her mouth. 'Do you remember some years ago, when the Old Man *accidentally* revealed that bogus rite to a chap who was so desperate to join the coven, and wouldn't take 'no' for an answer? ...'

' ... Then an article subsequently appeared in a highly respected pagan magazine, claiming to be revealing a secret rite from an authentic tradition, and written by one of their revered Elders?' It pays to have a long memory.

'Yup. As you know, there were some extremely stupid, tell-tale words inserted in the chant and now this chap has claimed that knowing them *proves* he's genuine! Of course he can't reveal the whole thing, it being secret and all that ...' she laughed again. 'We couldn't believe it when the rite appeared in print because it was complete and utter garbage but now it's doing the rounds as his passport to Old Craft.'

'Is it the same chap who wrote the article?'

'Judging from Gerry's description I'd say not, but he's certainly picked it up from somewhere.'

'So what's his name?' asked Rupert.

'He's calling himself Arthur Kinsman but he's no kinsman of *mine*.'

'Well, you know what they say, Pris,' replied Rupert with a

gleam in his eye. 'Half a kinsman is better than none.' We all burst out laughing and the tension was immediately diffused but 'arfa Kinsman it would remain.

Although we turned it into a joke amongst ourselves, kinship is something that genuine practitioners do take *very* seriously, although the rites and oaths they take to cement those bonds have long been the source of mockery (i.e. the Freemasons) or fear (Old Craft and the Magical Orders). Because of the symbolic threat implied by certain aspects of the rites, it is automatically assumed by outsiders to mean death should the oath be broken, or if an initiate attempts to leave the group. And because these warnings are couched in purple prose, the implications can appear extremely alarming, if not down-right frightening to the inexperienced. This may have been necessary when occult practice was deemed heretical and carried its own death penalty but in today's magical circles the implications are much more subtle.

Perhaps this is best described by Uncle Aleister himself, who explained that any oath taken within an esoteric order is deemed sacred and, because magical punishment always fits the crime, it is inadvisable to betray the group, or any individual fellow member, without expecting some kick-back. The understanding of this is all part of the Initiatory experience but the esoteric meaning is much more significant. When the Initiate takes the oath, it is to *themselves* as well as to the group, and usually involves making certain statements on, or by, the deity in which they believe. Subsequently, anyone breaking such an oath is blaspheming only themselves and 'having switched on the current of disloyalty [he] would have found disloyalty damaging him again and again until he had succeeded in destroying himself.'

Spooky stuff, I agree, but it *is* All Hallows and magical law has a way of running its own course. Those who publicly blaspheme it by claiming spurious connections to that which they have no entitlement are insulting those who *do* keep the faith; what they don't realise is they also risk the 'most frightful dangers to life, liberty and reason' that they are drawing down upon *themselves*. The repercussions are as *natural* as a lightning strike and this is probably the complex origin of the modern, dumbed-down version of the 'law of three-fold return'.

A couple of days later, the four of us were sitting around talking about our own All Hallows rite and how we were going to observe it. It's always a source of mirth for us when so-called pagans talk about 'celebrating' Samhain, since death and the honouring of the ancestors is hardly a *celebratory* occasion. After all, would any sane adult think of 'celebrating' the anniversary of September 11th or Remembrance Day with games and frivolity?

Nevertheless, it is always a problem when running a working coven to try and think of something different to try that will continually push the boundaries of our own abilities. It also magically challenges everyone in the group when there is some ultimate goal to aim for, and in our own Coven we have always tried to maintain a tangible contact with the shades of previous generations of witches, from whom we draw our inspiration and understanding.

We were in the middle of our discussion when Granny turned up and I could hardly leaving her standing on the doorstep, when the rest of us were sitting cosy and warm around the coffee pot. So I invited her in, despite Rupert banning her from the house on account of her rather distinctive and pungent personal odour.

In all fairness, this has improved quite dramatically since the demise of her rather decrepit sheepdog and the kidnapping of her vile old tomcat; the latter being lured away for a couple of days and surgically altered by a well-meaning cat charity. We suspect the neighbours finally got fed up with it spraying in their rather expensive Amdega conservatory, and under the pretence of it being a stray, handed it over for a clandestine de-balling!

Granny wasn't best pleased but even with all her magical skills it wasn't possible to retrieve the severed testicles from the vet's incinerator.

Rupert scowled meaningfully and I sat her down at the furthest point from the Aga, just in case she started to ferment in the heat. Without any preamble she pressed home her attack in her usual forthright matter. 'What are you going to do about this Kinsman fella?'

'Nothing.' Rupert has always resented the way his own father was coerced into marrying Granny Jay's daughter, and so allows her no quarter when it comes to Coven business. It had long since ceased to surprise us as to how Granny always managed to be one step ahead of any gossip or drama unfolding.

'Young Pris can't be expected to defend her own corner without some sort of back up,' she continued. 'Young' Pris managed to look both innocent and amused, while Adam was developing his customary 'rabbit faces stoat' expression that characterises his reaction to any close proximity to Granny. Both chose to remain silent and let battle commence.

'She won't have to,' said Rupert stiffly, 'but nothing will be gained by going off half-cocked. Sooner or later he'll make a fool of himself – they always do.'

'Ay, they do as that,' said Granny, taking a hefty slug of overly sweetened tea. 'Do you remember that little madam who claimed to have inherited my teaching? Gave her the shock of her life when she discovered I wasn't dead and that I was standing right behind her … and had heard *every* word.'

There are those who might be forgiven for thinking Granny *was* dead on the grounds that nothing living could smell that bad, but we let it pass. The real villain of the piece in the odour stakes is the large Bagot goat she allows to walk in and out of the cottage as it chooses. As a result, the stench of billy goat pervades everything, but Granny remains oblivious to her neighbours jostling for an up-wind position whenever conversation is unavoidable.

Her bright blue eyes watched Rupert closely from under her battered waxed hat.

'What are you going to do about Gordon?'

'Nothing.' As far as Rupert's concerned, Granny surrendered her authority when she decided to step down as Dame, and so refuses to accept any interference despite her still being an argumentative, meddlesome old crone. Nevertheless, we now knew the real reason behind her visit.

'The boy will come to harm, if he's left to his own devices. He's besotted with that girl. The parents are making out they don't mind him following the Old Ways but as soon as the ring's on her finger it will be a different kettle of fish all together, you mark my words! I've heard it said that she's been told 'You just get him wed, my girl, your father will see to his spiritual needs'.'

We all perked up over this bit of news and wondered who would be delegated to magically sock it to the Holy Rollers but Rupert had other ideas. 'If that's the Path he *wants* to follow, we can't stop him. I agree with you that it would be a tragic waste but we don't have the right to interfere … even if we personally believe him to be misguided, he must make his own choice.'

Granny looked mutinous and the words 'over my dead body' hung unspoken in the air but she swallowed her chagrin and joined in the All Hallows discussion. None of us were fooled for a moment but this kind of moral dilemma is a double-edged sword and the rest of us could identify with both Rupert and Granny, on either side of the argument. On the other hand, this particularly virulent brand of evangelism with its spiritual healing and 'speaking in tongues' is highly contagious and none of us (including Rupert) were convinced by Granny's seemingly demure acceptance.

To throw a smokescreen over the subject, she started with one of her stories. 'We can *all* make mistakes over inaction,' she said meaningfully. 'During the last war, our coven had taken a battering and was magically under-manned, but they were troubled times and the All Hallows rite needed to be observed. One cold November night a small group of us gathered in the woods and the working area was prepared in the Old Way, and although I had my doubts about one of the group, I said nothing. The particular rite we were working was a familiar one for most of us, and previous generations had probably felt much the same stirrings around their backs, as the Old Words rose and fell in their rhythmic chant.

'As we slowly began to circle together, there was an air of expectancy. Nothing was spoken, and not even a meaningful glance passed between us, but we all knew 'something' was brewing. The air almost crackled with magic. At the appropriate time, the chanting stopped, and each stood or knelt, gazing into the cauldron that now seemed huge enough to swallow the world.'

Granny can be quite poetic when talking about the old days and we hung on every word, even though we knew there would be a sting in the tail. 'From the corner of my eye, I noticed a shadowy, cowled figure walking the perimeter of our circle. It was tall and graceful, and in no way threatening; no blood-splattered spectre as we might have expected, given the times in which we were living. Everyone held their breath, for this was the moment we had worked so hard towards for such a long time. I sensed the recognition, and though I did not know exactly which of our Ancestors had answered the call, I was certain that it was one who was very familiar with the old rite. Stealing a sideways glance, I saw that the others were also awe-struck by its closeness. Time stood still, and we experienced that thrill of enjoying a mutually magical moment, and my mind was in a whirl. Could we hold the contact — should we interact with our visitor? Not least of all I thought: 'What the hell do we do now!'

'We were saved (if that's the right way of putting it) from making any decision about how to carry on, because suddenly the moment was shattered by the woman, whose place that night I'd previously doubted, leaping to her feet. She whirled round and without further thought, soundly banished the Wise One from our midst. Without thanks or warning, the poor soul was literarily hurled into nothingness, to vanish into the night.

'The smug creature beamed at us saying, 'Well, that showed the bugger!' and for all the world I think she was expecting to be congratulated. I was too disorientated and angry to speak, but others asked what on earth she thought she was doing? She explained in a patronising tone, that didn't we know we should be careful about beings encountered on the other planes? She did not feel that it had been invited, so she had banished it as soon as she saw it! Which begs the question of how much she ever understood about what we were about.

'The gathering was closed down in a sombre tone, and a serious discussion followed. The outcome being that the woman was asked to leave the group, her offence to the Ancestors being so great as to leave us all feeling guilty. As Dame of the group, I felt that I had failed; both in having said nothing about my doubts over her ability, and in my protection of those who had gone before us. To this day, I have never again made such a contact during any group working.

'For me, hard lessons were learned that night, and the hardest one was in accepting that we cannot keep people as members of a coven simply on the basis of friendship.

I had had my doubts about her understanding on many occasions, but out of a desire to remain friends with the member who had introduced her, I hadn't had the common sense to suggest that she may not be working in total harmony with us. It can be all too easy to lose friends and incur criticism when we undertake to walk the path of the Man or Dame. Many people have an overwhelming desire to hold those titles, but how many are truly worthy of them?'

Picking up her mug, she fixed Rupert with a pointed stare

over the china rim. A muscle twitched at the corner of his mouth but he decided not to respond to her goading. This issue was not going to go away and while Gordon was perfectly free to make his own decisions, there was still the underlying concern about what he might reveal about the Coven *if* he were to fall completely under the spell of the Pentecostals.

All Hallows marks the end of the Old Year and from now until the Winter Solstice is a period of Nature marking time. The constellation of Orion is visible again in the east, after his sojourn in the southern hemisphere. The hunter has returned to watch over his sleeping consort until the spring; when she awakes he will slip below the horizon until he is recalled again in time for the Hunter's Moon. For us as a working group, this is a time of extremely potent magical energy and the rites we perform as the old year slips towards the new, are the ones that will take 12 moons to come to fruition.

Winter Solstice

It never ceases to amaze me how pre-occupied the pagan community at large becomes over other people's Traditions. Since the publication of the first *Coarse Witchcraft*, we find the Coven being discussed and speculated over in numerous Internet chatrooms. Complete strangers have apparently tried to find out who we are, and where we live, and each little nugget of information is posted up in an attempt to give the poster more occult-cred than the rest.

Guy and Gerry have been forced to replace those tell-tale white sofas in Castor & Pollux in order to throw people off the scent – although they do sell our books in the shop. There have been debates over whether we are hereditary (we've *never* said we were); whether we are a channel for more sinister purposes (interesting but most certainly inaccurate); and whether we actually exist at all (oh, we do, we most assuredly do!).

Under the guise of some idiotic 'net-name' – which usually goes through the entire Celtic pantheon with depressing regularity, or something equally bizarre – like Gwenfrewi Tanglepussy – the armchair pagans exercise their right to pontificate and disseminate their views on *our* authenticity and working methods. Our son, Richard, who keeps us informed about the surfing shenanigans, will often reveal himself as a member of the Coven and offer to answer any of their more specific questions. Having suddenly manifested in their midst, however, he usually finds himself alone in the echoing vaults of cyberspace! Personally, the rest of us can't be bothered, although on a tip-off from Richard, Adam will often appear as a 'demon king' in one of the chat rooms and stir up trouble just for the sheer hell of it – until he's kicked out.

The dictionary definition of a witch is one regarded as having supernatural or magical power and knowledge, but I'd rather go along with our old friend, the late Evan John Jones's often-quoted view: 'If one who claims to be a witch can perform the tasks of witchcraft, i.e. summon the spirits and they come, can divine with rod, fingers and birds. If they can also claim the right to the omens and have them; have the power to call, heal and curse and above all, can tell the maze and cross the Lethe, then you have a witch.'

For us, we also take Hotspur's stance in *Henry IV* when Glendower boasts: *'I can call spirits from the vasty deep,'* and Hotspur replies, *'Why so can I, or so can any man; But will they come, when you do call for them?'* In other words, we're really not that interested in what other people claim for themselves, except when they bring their false claims onto our turf and attempt to use them to gain access to our Coven. Call your spirits by all means, but we will demand a personal introduction.

We finally got to meet 'arfa Kinsman through an unexpected twist of fate, which was to trigger some old, and not very pleasant memories all the way around. In the winter, one of our fields is set aside for the annual point-to-point meetings, which generally start in the New Year, with the proceeds going to the upkeep of the local hunt's hounds and horses. Rupert used to ride in the races but age *has* wearied him, and he now prefers to put our son's horses through their paces, and act as a fence judge on race days. The manager of the Duck & Ferret traditionally organises the beer tent.

He was busy rubbing down one of the horses after riding out, when a shiny 4x4 pulled into the yard and out climbed a stranger, advancing on him with an outstretched hand.

'Hello there, Rupert,' he greeted. 'I'd been hoping to run into you around the village but haven't bumped into you or your good lady in order to talk about the bar for the point-to-point meeting. Still, nothing like bearding the lion in his den, eh?'

The bearded lion managed to out-fumble the stranger and, not having a clue who this hail-fellow-well-met chappie was, avoided shaking his hand. 'Quite ... erm ... Not my area of responsibility, so I'm afraid you've come to the wrong person.'

'Well, yes, I realise that but I'm a great friend of Jackie Pratt,' continued the beaming stranger. 'She told me to look you up if I was ever in the area. Wonderful little witch, is our Jackie.'

Rupert was feeling totally bemused by this quick shift from beer tents to besoms, until Pris, unable to control her curiosity any longer, sidled up and enlightened him. 'The pustuler postulant!' she hissed in his ear, referring to the named person's unfortunate skin complaint.

If Kinsman (for that's who it was) noticed the hardening of Rupert's expression, he gave no indication and turned his beaming attention on Pris who had, fortunately for us all, already recognised him from Gerry's description. 'And you must be Pris. Jackie's told me how you always used to ride together. In fact, she's told me lots of stories about you all.'

'I bet she has,' retorted Pris, as Rupert hastily excused himself and disappeared into the house. 'What's she doing with herself, these days?'

'Oh, you know …'

'No, I *don't* know. Suppose you tell me?'

'Jackie told me all about the Coven,' he replied, lowering his voice, as if frightened of the horses overhearing. 'I'd just like a piece of the action. I went into that occult shop in the town, but the couple of daisies running it wouldn't know a besom from a burin. I mean the local pagan scene hardly stretches the old magical reflexes, does it?'

'I wouldn't know,' she answered. 'I don't have a lot to do with it.'

'Oh, *come on!*' There was a hint of aggressiveness in the tone but Pris cut him short.

'If you'll excuse me, we are very busy.' She had no intention of engaging in a verbal brawl in the stable yard and quickly followed Rupert's exit into the house. We always prefer to bide our time.

'Was it something you said?' asked Rupert, pouring her a coffee, to the sound of a 4x4 burning rubber across the cobbles.

'No. I don't have all my facts yet in order to challenge his claims because Kirsten hasn't got back to me. It's the fact that Pratt-face is somehow involved with him that freaks me out. By the gods, I loathe that woman. She caused so much trouble ...'

'And is still doing so, by all accounts,' I added, having been watching the goings-on from the safety of the kitchen window and trying to avoid falling over the dog, whose purpose in life seems to be focussed solely on getting in the way.

It's a funny thing, but in Craft it seems as though things that some folk would prefer to remain firmly besomed under the carpet, have an embarrassing habit of eventually rising to the surface. Nowadays, there is nothing that people such as 'arfa Kinsman like doing, more than 'name-dropping', but when Jackie Pratt's name had popped into the conversation, old and unwelcome memories had begun to stir in all our minds.

Jackie Pratt. The 'pustular postulant' and erstwhile competition rival of Pris's West Country schooldays, who had spotted her riding one of our horses at a local event while on holiday many years later, and assumed, quite wrongly, that Pris worked for us. She'd asked around and discovered that not only was the family one of the largest landowners in the area, but that we were well-known for our Old Craft associations. It was certainly a heady combination and it wasn't too long before Jackie Pratt was hanging around the yard whenever Pris appeared, and badgering Rupert to let her help with the horses, or talk to her about his Craft interests. As it happened, Rupert had taken an instant dislike to her and wasn't about to let her near either.

It wasn't until we were sitting together having coffee one morning, that Pris finally came clean about what had been going on in our midst for some months. It seemed that the Craft 'scene' had a new heiress to the throne, a new witch-queen – large in mouth and bosom, and generous to a fault with her affections (if the sly winks and bawdy comments made by the lads during one of Adam's rollicking rugby supporters' trips were anything to go by.)

'Adam's second-hand description rang a bell but the tintinnab-ulation wouldn't allow me to 'name that tune'. A couple of days after I had ridden Max in the show, I bumped into her in town, quite by chance. A complete stranger suddenly enveloped me in an alarming bear hug and exclaimed (to my horror), that she knew me of old. Perhaps the riding hat in my car had triggered her memory, but it soon transpired that as 'girls' we used to compete in the same local Pony Club events. Without further ado, she was soon waxing lyrical about her standing as head-girl in a prestigious yard, which was nothing less than impressive, considering that some of the best names in show-jumping were there.

'Having finally made a bolt for it, I remembered that I *did* know who she was, and the memory was not a happy one. As you know, when you do the Pony Club circuit, you get to see the same horse boxes, and the same people over and over again. I now clearly recalled the shabby old box, with a badly turned-out crew and, without putting too finer a point on it, most of the competitors had raised an eyebrow over the condition of the ponies as well.

'For my part, I was a keen 15-year-old intent on a career working with horses and I'd been up since the crack of dawn, plaiting manes and tails. Getting togged up in my best jacket, tack polished to perfection, I was feeling pretty confident that I was in with a good chance of being in the ribbons. Like any competitor, my friend and I started to take note of who might give us a run for our money. One figure in the collecting ring was attracting a few stares. It was one of the team from the shabby horsebox. The rider was hatless (you could be in those days), jacketless and wearing a T-shirt; the under-weight mare was clearly unhappy and things were not going well.

'Jackie Pratt was being urged to make more use of the whip and feeling desperately sorry for the pony, I edged closer, fully intent on attracting the attention of the steward. Finally with much shouting of *'Gerrrrrrrron ya bugger!'* and copious use of the whip, the mare did a standing jump over the practice pole before galloping wildly back towards the entrance. Pratt-face, flushed and clearly very angry, leaped off and the mare was swiftly taken out of sight behind the box. Before I could do or say anything, my number was called and it was my round.

When Jackie Pratt's number was called, the mare and rider emerged and shot straight through to the ring without a backward glance. The pair had a dismal round and what the mare didn't knock down, she either trashed or avoided, and once again the red-faced rider and pony disappeared. And not long afterwards, so did the box. Rumour had it that one of the officials had been seen talking to the man in charge – and that was the last I ever saw of them.

'Imagine my horror when I realised that this person, who was now supposedly in charge of some very expensive, and much loved competition animals, was the same bad tempered teenager who had given that poor pony a very hard time. The past has a habit of catching us out, and throughout her alleged magical training she obviously hasn't come across the old maxim – 'Know thyself'. If we can't know ourselves, it's always wise to bear in mind that others might have better insights.'

Since Jackie Pratt had been refused entry into the Coven and left the area in high dudgeon (but not before spreading a lot of highly malicious rumours), none of us had thought about her in years, but we were about to be reminded by more than just a bit of casual name-dropping ...

For the Coven, the Winter Solstice is a sacred time of the year and we always try to observe the rebirth of the Sun in a fitting way. An old friend of Pris's (from way back when she was a witchlet, and from those same origins that Kinsman claimed were his!) had come to visit and the plan was for them to take her to one of our working sites for an open air ritual, since she's been city-bound for many years. Meeting Kirsten off the train immediately raised some doubts as to the wisdom of the exercise because the intervening years had turned her into a fine strapping woman but (in her own words) not exactly built for speed trials.

Unfortunately, once Pris has the bit between her teeth, it's not that easy to deflect her from the path and she decided to carry on with the original plan. Being cautious types, the Coven has its gatherings in places that are not easily accessible, which usually means finding our way through woods, slithering down an embankment and crossing a fast running stream before scrambling up another bank to negotiate a tall stile. The site selected for this particular event is one favoured by Pris and Adam for more personal rituals but it also involves an additional trek across two large fields flanked by high hedges.

'Kirsten had found it hard going but it was a beautifully clear, crisp night and we were making our way back across the fields after the working,' said Pris, as we sat in our usual place around the kitchen table trying to organise our own Solstice observance. 'It had been a good one and all three of us were in good spirits as we left the darkness of the woods and climbed over the stile. As you know, when you're cold, tired and a little under the *Grouse*, not to mention carrying bags of robes, etc., that last walk across those fields can be a bit of a drag.'

Under normal circumstances, Adam (who is a bit younger and fitter than the rest of us) goes striding ahead so that he reaches the car first, in order to get the engine running and the heater going full pelt. Pris, who hates the cold, gasps and grumbles loud enough to be heard three fields away, is determined to be back in front of a roaring fire as quickly as possible, and is never usually very far behind. On this particular night, Kirsten – whom Pris remembered as being an accomplished witch with nerves of steel – trudged slowly by her side.

'I was feeling pretty chilled out in all senses of the word. An owl began screeching and, as I looked up, I noticed the stars seemed incredibly close and beautiful. Pausing to gaze at the heavens, I pointed out Cassiopeia and the Great Bear to Kirsten. Getting no reply, I glanced around only to see her a fair way up the field, and going like a train. It crossed my mind that perhaps she was on a personal fitness thing again … Adam was well out of sight, but the night was beautiful and for once I was content to meander.

'After a few minutes' steady walking, the owl called again, and once more I stopped in my tracks to gaze up at the skies. The stars were putting on quite a show from one of the meteor showers (I forget which) …'

'The Ursids,' interrupted Rupert.

'Granted … and I clearly saw the shadow of the owl as she swooped into an oak tree. I paused and marvelled at all this natural beauty and counted my blessings at having access to such a place where the night held no fears for me,' Pris continued. 'The last stile was in sight. I could see the car lights and Kirsten waving wildly – and I remember feeling sorry that they had to spoil such perfection with their impatience. The cattle were grazing in the next field and the air was so pure that I could smell them. The owl called again but the sound of the car horn rudely interrupted my reverie. I climbed the last stile as Adam pulled up alongside and gesticulated for me to hurry up and get into the car. What was wrong with these two? The night was perfect, the magic had been there in the woods, the owl was hunting, the stars were brilliant. Who would be in such a rush to leave it all behind? With one last glance at the stars, I pulled off my boots and got into the car.

'Two faces peered intently at me, but for a moment neither of them spoke until Adam broke the silence. 'Are you stark staring mad?' he asked. I gaped at him in astonishment as Kirsten butted in: 'Pris, that was either incredibly brave, or incredibly stupid!'

As you know, it isn't often that I'm lost for words but this unexpected verbal battering threw me completely. Blankly I looked from one to the other, hoping that one of them would enlighten me as to what they were prattling on about, and was beginning to wonder what might have been in the altar wine.'

In exasperation Adam had apparently slapped the steering wheel, then taking a deep breath, began to address his wife as though she were the village idiot. With exaggerated patience, he explained that as they had climbed out of the woods and into the field, he had spotted the very large and distinctive shape of Joseph, our prize Charolais bull in the corner, under the shadow of the trees. Knowing Joseph to be a temperamental animal and not wishing to attract too much attention to their presence, he resisted calling to warn the women and had, instead just got on with the job of getting up those fields as fast as he could. And who says the age of chivalry is dead?

Pris and Kristen had been too busy laughing about which of them was the most likely to fall over this particularly awkward stile to notice any bull, and it was not until Pris stopped to gaze at the stars that Kirsten had turned and noticed him. She assumed that as she lived and worked in the country, Pris would not be unduly worried about the fact that a *very* large Charolais bull was standing about four feet behind her. As she had huffed and puffed her way up the field, with occasional looks back over her shoulder, all she could do was marvel at her friend's unspoken empathy with the animal.

'With relish she described how Joseph, pale and ghostly loitering, had doggedly plodded along behind me as I toiled up the field,' said Pris. 'And each time I stopped to gaze, he had stopped with the same four feet between us, waiting patiently (thank the gods!) until I set off again. All this was a complete revelation to me! And to think how blissfully unaware I was of him being there. I still shudder to think what would have happened if I'd spotted him, but it's a pretty safe bet that I would not have noticed Cassiopeia, and I would *not* have been the last to the car!'

It was also on the way home that night, Pris thought she recognised a familiar face peering out from the hedgerow, as the car sped past. 'That looked like Granny,' she said to Adam.

'Don't talk daft,' he said, making no attempt to slow down. 'What on earth would the old girl being doing out here at this time of night. It's miles from her place.' *But it's not miles from Gordon's girlfriend's place*, Pris had thought to herself as she recalled the glint in Granny's eye over the rim of her coffee mug just before All Hallows. But Kirsten was in the car and she didn't pursue the matter.

The Winter Solstice is an ancient celebratory rite although some of the other Traditions consider this tide (from now until the Vernal Equinox) to be one of the most dangerous for any active magical work. To be honest, we have always found it to be one of the best and would prefer to be outside under a clear winter sky working a rite, than waiting for the long summer nights. The Hunter is still visible in the sky and there is also an air of celebration and festivity about the season as we acknowledge the Old Lad in his role as the 'holly king'.

Candlemas

'Right! Thanks for the warning, Gerry,' I said, switching off the phone. 'Storm warning,' I said to Pris, who glanced up from the estate agent's particulars she'd received that morning. 'Rupert has just savaged one of Gerry's customers.'

'What on earth was he doing in the shop?' she asked. 'He normally avoids the place like the plague because of the morons he claims inhabit the place.'

'He was doing Gordon's egg-run. Apparently some woman was asking for a statue of the Triple Moon Goddess, and two-dozen newly-laid eggs almost got scrambled on the spot. Before Gerry could head him off at the pass, he'd asked where she'd got *that* damned silly idea from, and she'd replied she'd read about it in a book.'

According to the phone-in version, while Gerry was desperately hacking his way through a jungle of wind chimes and vaulting over their lurcher to intervene, Rupert had asked between gritted teeth, what the hell the woman thought the 'goddess' did during the dark quarter of the moon's phase. No doubt expecting the 'perfect love' of universal paganism, the unfortunate creature was confronted by some raving egg-man wearing Wellington boots and a ratting-hat. Gerry managed to relieve him of the eggs and, with both hands free, Rupert began to remonstrate over the fantasy image of the goddess promulgated in pagan art and publishing. His parting shot had been: 'You would not want to encounter the *real* goddess, *believe me!*', which had sent a cold shiver down Gerry's back, never mind the effect on the poor woman who stood staring open-mouthed at the retreating figure.

'Not like Rupert to be so theatrical,' said Pris. 'He doesn't usually give *anything* away.'

It's not easy to explain how we view the 'goddess' but Rupert's closing gambit wasn't far short of the mark. Old Craft is not a religion *per se* and so the focus for female energy in terms of magical working is seen as a seasonal manifestation, or abstract personification, of a potent Nature energy that influences the growing and the harvest. For us the 'goddess' would indeed be a terrible sight to behold and she is kept from mortal view by her protector and guardian, the 'god', who roams the fields and woodland ready to spring to her defence should any stray too close.

In ancient Egypt there was a temple inscription dedicated to the hunter-warrior goddess Neith at Sais which said: *'I am all that has been, that is, and that will be. No mortal has yet been able to lift the veil which covers me.'* This is probably the closest we can get to describing our ways, and why we feel that the fantasy caricatures of pagan art that show young, glamorous lasses with flowing tresses is such a travesty. The 'goddess' in all her majesty is more likely to appear as Kali, than Nicole Kidman.

It probably also goes a long way to explain why Old Craft is more male oriented, simply because we raise 'Horned God energy' in order to connect and procreate magically with the 'Lass' *through* him. In modern Wicca, the 'Old Lad' has almost been dispensed with completely in favour of a feminine-cloned chimera that is both barren and illusionary when it comes to harnessing natural magical energies. Perhaps this is why Wicca has come to represent a purely devotional expression of the pagan ethos, which is nearer to Christianity than it is to traditional witchcraft.

Kirsten had phoned Pris after her visit and gone through the archive to check on whether 'arfa Kinsman had ever been a member of their old Order. Pris, not being very good with paperwork and accounts, had miraculously ducked out of inheriting it all when their old Magister had retired and the responsibility had fallen to Kirsten. A few days later she had pulled out a grubby folder that showed Kinsman's application to join the

Order, having made all sorts of bogus claims to his antecedents – and that was ten years earlier.

'Thank the gods, the old man *never* threw anything out,' said Pris, shuffling through the photocopies. 'He carried out a thorough investigation at the time, and not one of Kinsman's claims held up when the right people were contacted. Look, dates, names, places … and not one of them would authenticate his background.'

'He's getting to be a real pain,' I said reading through the papers. 'Wherever I go, he seems to turn up. What's so interesting about us that *everyone* wants to join our Coven? After all, we're now down to just 'Three Studs and a Tart'.'

This was the name our team was entered under in the local team-chasing event, and it was here that Kinsman had snuck up on me again while I was busy setting up the picnic in the back of the Land Rover. Team-chasing is one of those rural past-times that the Health & Safety brigade haven't yet managed to interfere with. Rupert, Gordon, Richard and Pris were over with the horses, champing at the bit and waiting for their turn over the jumps, while Adam and Philly were in the beer tent keeping out of the way in case they were roped in for something.

Then they were off, riding against the clock, with only the times of the first three in the team counting. One Stud and the Tart took the fences with ease, but the other Two Studs collided and Rupert was pitched into the gorse hedge. He landed headfirst, with just his black boots sticking out.

'He's fine,' called one of the organisers scurrying past. 'Just got some thorns in his backside.' It has been said that the spirit of Agincourt lives on in team-chasing.

'Hubby riding today, I see, Mrs P.' There was an obvious gleam of satisfaction in Kinsman's eye, no doubt caused by Rupert's unceremonious unseating. 'He should be more careful, that sort of accident can prove fatal at his age.'

There was something about the way he'd said it, that made my flesh crawl. Over the past few years, Rupert had been 'dropped' on several occasions and it had been one of these incidents that had forced him to give up riding point-to-point completely. Kinsman walked away, but not before I'd glimpsed another smug smile of satisfaction. The old psychic alarms bells weren't just ringing, they were belting out the *Halleluiah Chorus*!

Suffering nothing but a badly bruised shoulder, Rupert was confined to the kitchen for a few days and decided to spend the time cleaning some of the old tack that had been hanging around for years. Pris and Adam arrived with the details of their new business venture – although Adam was less than excited about becoming the proud owner of a three-storey Victorian mill building, with dodgy drains. The asking price had been cheap because it had been leased out in small sections to about thirty local antique dealers, all with cast-iron contracts to boot. There was a run-down 'caff', which Pris intended to turn into an up-market café, where 'ladies who lunch' could go to spend a few hours and also, hopefully, several hundred pounds.

'It's going to be called 'The Witch's Kitchen' and when it's been decorated, and with that old black range leaded up, it will be really smart. And instead of putting up the rents, I'm to receive a percentage of all sales.'

'*But what are you going to do about catering?*' From the tone of his voice, it was obviously a question Adam had asked on numerous occasions and, as yet, gleaned no satisfaction from his wife's response. 'I mean, you can produce a pretty mean casserole and Sunday roast, but you're not exactly adventurous in *that* department, are you, love? 'Ladies who lunch' aren't going to want your *only* two specialities of the day on a permanent basis.'

Pris scowled, partly miffed by this lack of domestic solidarity and partly because the dog was resting its head in her crotch in the hopes of receiving the remains of her sandwich.

'Why not round up some of the local farmers' wives who do

the Farmers' Market, that way you'll be able to offer home-produced … damn!'

'What is it?' I asked. Rupert had been saddle-soaping a saddle that had belonged to an old favourite of his, and had not used it since the horse had been put down some years before. It was a heavy, old-fashioned saddle and he'd been working soap into the under-side.

'I've cut my finger on something sharp … wait, it's a piece of card wedged under the tree!' He worried at it with his fingernail and finally extracted a carefully folded piece of paper 'What the …?'

'It's a fetish,' said Adam slowly, as Rupert unfolded the paper to reveal a simple esoteric design.

'But what's it doing in *that* saddle?' I asked. 'It hasn't been used for years.'

A familiar hiss escaped from Pris. 'And who had their hands on that saddle last? Bloody Jackie Pratt! Don't you remember, she was always hanging around the yard about the time Weyland had to be shot? The saddle was all muddy and none of us wanted to clean it because it was all too upsetting. She volunteered to take it home with her, and she kept it for weeks.'

'Yes,' replied Rupert, 'and I actually had to go and retrieve it myself.'

I suddenly remembered the smug expressed on Kinsman's face and wondered if the fetish-placer had told him about the old charm. What she hadn't known was that the saddle hadn't been used again, and had been kept in the loft above the tack room ever since … but it was near enough to send out its malevolent impulses to anyone who spent a lot of time in that building. Was this Jackie Pratt's attempt at revenge for not being allowed in to our personal and magical lives?

'What are you going to do?' Pris and I asked in unison.

Rupert carried on polishing the leather without answering, but we all knew the score. He would bide his time but the malice would be returned to its sender.

With the question of the fetish still in my mind, I was surprised when, some days later, Gordon cornered me in the kitchen garden and asked if he could talk to me about his romance. Escaping to the kitchen garden with a cup of coffee, even in winter, is my idea of a peaceful five minutes but today wasn't going to be my lucky day. Granny, it appeared had been meddling with a vengeance and Gordon was rather alarmed by the things she'd been saying to him. He's a good, reliable lad and a wonderful horseman, and I didn't like to think of him being upset, even if his girlfriend did give cause for concern.

He leaned against the brick wall and ran a finger over the pointing. 'She also said that I wouldn't be allowed to stay on in the yard, if I carried on seeing Christine,' he said, almost in tears.

I sighed with exasperation. Whilst I appreciated Granny's viewpoint, threatening the lad was not going to produce the desired effect. Her own daughter, Rupert's stepmother, had been so meek and mild that the old girl had probably forgotten that when you tell the younger generation they *can't* do something, it usually makes them all the more determined to thwart you at any cost.

'Granny is concerned,' I said slowly. 'And as far as the Coven is concerned, she has a right to be, but there is no need for you to worry about your job. We would never ask you to leave because of … your involvement with this girl.'

'But why doesn't anyone like her?' he naively asked.

'It's got very little to do with her as an individual, and every-thing to do with her family's beliefs. *They* will be the ones who won't let it rest. You shouldn't have told her you were a witch.' From what I could gather Christine was as dim as a Toc-H lamp, but I could hardly say so to Gordon's face. Neither did I want to admit that we'd heard the family had their sights set on bringing a stray lamb back to the fold and nailing him firmly to their cross.

Pentecostals, as far as I am concerned, are the most acrimonious, highly poisonous and malignant sect of all. And I should know, since they were a strong feature of Welsh religious life in the early part of the century, and my family came originally from that neck of the woods. The services are enthusiastic and rousing with a strong emphasis on music and participation on the part of the congregation, where 'speaking in tongues' is assumed to be a form of spirit baptism. And they'll damn anyone to hell and perdition for very little reason, even their own – never mind anyone who had admitted to being a witch. Gordon's naivety would be his undoing.

'But what do *you* think I should do?' he asked. After all, I was still Dame and he was still a member of the Coven. 'I'm getting flack from all sides.'

'I can't answer that, Gordon, but I do think you are much too young to be thinking about settling down with *anyone*, and so I can't see what all the fuss is about. Just don't let anyone put any pressure on you to do anything until you're 100% sure about how you feel. Not Granny, your parents, Christine … or her parents. It's got to be what *you* want but it will mean leaving the Coven were you to make the arrangement a permanent one. There's nothing we can do about that, I afraid.'

He pushed away from the wall and shuffled off back to the stables. 'I know. Just so long as I don't have to leave the horses,' he muttered as he walked away.

I sat back and closed my eyes against the sun. *Rooted and bound, rooted and bound …* I thought with a smug smile. Granny might be meddling to end the romance but it was far easier to tie the lad to something by love than through bullying or fear.

The following day Granny turned up at coffee time with a large tray of homemade cakes and buns for Pris to try out at the Witch's Kitchen. We were rather dubious about trying *anything* as they'd been on the back seat of her car, but they did look appetising. She'd been over to a nearby village to visit May

Butterworth, whose baking skills in the area were almost legendary. From what I'd heard, there had been some rivalry between the two women in the dim and distant past but I couldn't for the life of me remember what it had been about.

'I didn't think you liked May Butterworth,' I said, fishing for information.

'I don't, but she does make exceedingly good cakes,' replied the old witch with a cackle.

Later that day, as I was coming out of the newsagent's, I bumped into Gordon's father, who was known to all as 'Young' Joe, on account of him being 'Old' Joe's son. 'Do you know what that ol' bugger's up to?' he asked without preamble, and without having to think I'd guessed he was talking about Granny.

'What's she done now?' I replied, not really wanting to know the answer.

'I were coming home the other night, well past midnight it was, and I saw this great black shadow squatting in my garden. Can you guess what she were doing?' I shook my head. *She were pissing on the path!* All I could see were this great white arse gleaming in the moonlight! Gave me quite a turn, I can tell you.' He frowned for a moment and then went on. 'Mind you, if it's summat to do with getting rid of that daft lass of his, I'll not mind.' And with that he walked off. Loosely translated for the non-initiate, it appeared that Granny *had* started meddling with Gordon's romance with a vengeance.

With the start of spring, life on the farm works it own kind of magic. At Candlemas, we see the first of our lambs, which also heralds the old Imbolc – the start of the old Celtic lambing season. Although our lambs are safe and snug in the lambing sheds, it never ceases to amaze me that these fragile little creatures can withstand the freezing weather conditions that can bring snow and icy winds and driving rain. This is a true marker on the turning of the year.

Spring Equinox

According to most 'witchy' books, the Spring, or Vernal, Equinox always falls around 21st March but, owing to the idiosyncrasies of our calendar, the actual date is not constant and can vary anywhere around that time. The Equinox marks the moment when the Sun crosses the celestial equator, moving from south to north. For the next six months it will stay in the northern hemisphere of the sky, before crossing the equator at the Autumnal Equinox and returning to the south.

As we've explained before, this is why the Coven prefers to observe the equinoxes and solstices rather than the traditional Wiccan calendar dates; we work with the actual changing tides of the cosmos rather than some dubious Church calendar dates that now have Celtic names and a tenuous grasp on tradition. Sometimes traditions have to change and precession eventually alters the seasons, but the equinoxes and solstices remain constant and mark the times and tides of the year for us, exactly the same as it did for our early ancestors.

Spring Equinox was the date set for the grand opening of the Witch's Kitchen, and there'd been a great flurry of activity as we all pitched to help with the preparations. I didn't consider it to be an auspicious time to start a new business as, from personal experience, I've always found the tides around the Spring Equinox to be extremely dangerous and unpredictable, as Julius Caesar found to *his* cost. It's often a time for great changes and upheaval, with a knock-on effect that can last right up to the Summer Solstice.

The interior of the café was now crisp and bright, although the rest of us weren't convinced by the collection of stuffed animals peering out at the diners from their glass prisons but … well, Pris has always had a 'thing' about stuffed animals and it's her business. The collection had started when she decided to visit a similar venture she'd heard about some 70 miles away, and prudently (or so he'd thought) Adam had elected to wait in the car to read his newspaper while she snooped around.

Nearly half an hour had passed and as he turned the pages of the broadsheet, his eye caught sight of a female figure attempting to wrestle a 12-point stag's head through the narrow shop doorway. From where he sat, it looked as if the stag had the advantage. Adam slowly lowered the newspaper and open-mouthed watched as his wife advanced towards the car, presenting a surreal, anthropomorphic image of a stag's head on a woman's body – complete with mini-skirt and four-inch stilettos!

'How the hell are we going to get it in the car, love?' he said wearily.

'Don't be silly, of course it will go in.'

'You couldn't get it through the bloody shop door, so how do you expect to get it in a Metro?'

Pris stopped and stared, forgetting they'd borrowed their son's car for the day, but as we've often said before, once Pris gets an idea in her head, there's no stopping her. The long-suffering Adam travelled home lying flat in the back of the car, holding the stag's head in a meaningful embrace and trying to prevent the points of the antlers from impaling his wife whenever she applied the brakes.

We later discovered why the thing had been such a 'bargain'. The skin on the muzzle had shrunk, exposing a rim of white plaster underneath, and giving the impression of an advert for a well-known brand of toothpaste. Added to that, one of the glass eyes had a tendency to roll, which meant the 'ladies who lunch' would fall under the manic gaze of a leering stag – very Horned God indeed, but not over lunch! Another acquisition was a fox with a similar expression: only this was due to it having been rammed into a much smaller cardboard box, which had not only distorted the mask but had also given it a curly tail like a husky! The company (to date) was completed by an owl minus some tail feathers and a stuffed stoat, for whom time had metamorphosed its ferocious snarl into another manic leer. Adam's response to his wife's interest in a full-sized bull moose was: 'Don't even think about it!'

What the new waitress made of her employer's penchant for surrounding herself with dead animals, it was hard to say. She said very little but I had the feeling that she was listening to everything, and missing nothing. We didn't have long to wait.

It was the sort of filthy wet Monday that always took me back to my schooldays, when everywhere smelt of damp gabardine. The Witch's Kitchen was too far from town for any except the real die-hards to brave the weather, and so Rupert and I were summoned over there for a late lunch in order to minimise the waste. We were just sitting down to what looked like being a mammoth trenching session, when Rupert surprisingly asked Abi, the waitress, to join us. Not being the most sociable of folk, especially where strangers were concerned, it was most out of character.

We'd finished off Brenda Macinroy's French onion soup and were about to start on Buffy Lambert's *lamb marinade*, when a party of late lunchers arrived and the lamb was off … and onto their plates! The local farmers' wives were doing Pris proud and half the success of the place was the fact that she was offering freshly home-cooked food every day. Even the parsimonious antique stall-holders were coming down from their dusty eyries for lunch, even if it was only for a sandwich or a bowl of soup … and recommendations were bringing in visitors from further afield. Locals knew the cauldron and besom by the old range were for real; the visitors merely thought it quaint. By the time everyone had left, we were finishing off with coffee and Anna Robson's *rhubarb compote* … and nothing had gone to waste.

'So did you work with a group before moving here?' Rupert suddenly asked Abi without any further preamble.

'I'm not sure what you mean,' she answered hesitantly, looking uncertainly from me to Pris, and seeing that both of us were just as surprised by his question.

'I'm sorry,' replied my cunning old Man, 'I had the impression that you were a witch, albeit a young one.'

'I don't know if I am or not,' the girl replied nervously. 'I did belong to a group in the Midlands, but there was something ... not quite right about it. I couldn't say what exactly, but things just didn't *feel* right and so I left. That's why I'm here, they sent their fetch after me and I couldn't get away from him. They kept trying to draw me back in.'

'What form did it take?' asked Rupert, then seeing the girl's hesitation added, 'The fetch?'

Abi looked blank. 'It was just a member of the group. He was called 'the coven fetch'. Am I missing something?'

Pris snorted. 'These people are a bloody menace! What did *he* tell you he was there for?'

'His job was to act as a go-between, take messages and summon people to the coven, to 'fetch' them, I suppose. He was sent to coax me back and kept coming to the flat, banging on the door. In the end I had to move to get away from them.'

Before Pris could open her mouth, Rupert began to explain. 'A fetch isn't *human*, Abi, it's an astral entity created by a coven or individual to over-look, or carry messages between the different psychic levels. It's like having an astral working sheepdog, because they can run amok if not kept under control. It's something else belonging to traditional Craft that has appeared in books without the authors having the slightest understanding about the magical aspects. The meaning has been taken literally by people with no genuine magical training and applied to what they see as being their version of witchcraft, or Wicca. This is why the Old Ways are being plagiarised and turned into something completely bogus in order for the role-playing to continue. Unfortunately, there is a whole new generation of potential witches who have no access to genuine Craft because they don't know it exists, thanks to that lot.'

Abi looked around the table at each of us in turn, and the light slowly dawned. 'You lot *are* for real, though, aren't you?'

We said nothing and Rupert looked at his watch as a sign that it was time to go. 'How did he know?' whispered Pris in my ear, as we were leaving.

'How did you know?' I asked as we drove home.

Rupert just gave an infuriating chuckle and patted my knee. 'Oh, when you've been a witch for as long as I have, you learn to recognise these things,' he added, exasperatingly.

Once Abi began to relax in our company, she kept Pris amused for hours relating her experiences with the Midlands coven. It transpired that the couple who ran it were media junkies, who had recently appeared on television and not given a very good account of themselves, not to mention the rubbish they were spouting about paganism *per se*.

Now referred to as the 'Odd Couple', we learned that, although not the most prepossessing of sights, they insisted on working sky-clad on every occasion, with cold water being flicked on the women's breasts to make the nipples stand out. Pris was reduced to tears of laughter at the thought of the male OC prancing around stark naked, banging his drum to the midsummer chant of ...'*The sun has got his hat on, hip-hip-hip hooray ... the sun has got his hat on and he's coming out to play ...*'

On the occasion of an initiation, a newcomer was hauled in to take the part of 'initiatorix', when she'd only been a member for a couple of weeks and had just popped in to deliver a bag of cooking apples! The initiation consisted of the naked couple facing each other with the chap standing on the girl's feet, while the HP and his drum and limp lingam, banged out a chorus of '*Robin Hood, Robin Hood, riding through the glen ...*' from the old television series. By this time Pris was convulsing and had to be given a large slug of *Famous Grouse* before listening to any more.

What was even more insidious than all this clowning around was the fact that Abi is a natural witch (albeit an untrained one), and the Odd Couple hadn't been slow in spotting this. On the pretext of letting her experience *their* power raising, they encouraged her to open up and empower the Circle (under the OC's guidance, of course), while all the time they were drawing off *her* in the worst form of magical exploitation. No wonder they wanted her 'fetched' back! It was this raw, natural energy that Rupert had sensed when he first met her in the Witch's Kitchen.

Having convinced the girl that the Coven wasn't into exploitation, magical or otherwise, Pris and Adam took Abi up to one of our working sites in the woods, having assured her that robes and thermals would more than likely be the order of the day. In all the years she'd been a 'practising Wiccan', she had never once worked outside after dark, under the stars, and it all became very tearful. It looked as though we might have discovered a new Coven member.

We've often remarked that potential members are a bit like number 29 buses: you wait for ages for one and then two come along together. The second manifestation came in the form of the unfortunate woman Rupert had savaged in Castor & Pollux some months earlier, but this time it was Pris who had brought home the trophy, along with some tantalising gossip. She'd called into the shop for a coffee and Gerry was showing her some of the new merchandise that had been delivered that morning.

'Here, it says in this book that a curse can be lifted by a liberal application of white candles, clear quartz crystal and white lily essence,' said Gerry, deliberately winding her up.

'Not one of *mine*, it wouldn't,' she retorted.

'And what about this?' asked Gerry, handing her a box bearing the banner 'Witches Tool Kit'. On opening it, to reveal a pentagram-shaped display, the first thing Pris saw was the wand – a pencil-thin stick that came in two pieces that screwed together. The *Book of Shadows*, was an equally unimpressive paper leaflet which she couldn't even bear to open and read.

'Why on earth are you stocking this?' she asked.

'We're not,' he replied, 'but folk keep asking for them and so I thought I'd get one, just so I can put it in the middle of the display with a card saying: *Do you really think this will make you a witch*? A snip at 20 quid, don't you think? What do you think to the Magical Talisman?'

This was a bright blue printed card with a combination of different symbols on it, including ££££ signs and the new euro-dollar symbol. 'Ah,' said Pris, 'it's a Euro-witch Kit!'

The next item, which was probably the most impressive in the box, was a wooden altar pentacle – a three-inch diameter piece of wood with a pentagram scratched in it, and filled with gold paint. There were two white candles, a little larger than those used for birthday cakes, complete with a gold plastic holder and three incense cones complete with a 'consecrated incense vessel', which turned out to be a foil holder usually containing a tea-light.

By this time Pris was helpless with laughter but there was worse to come. There was a 'consecrated water vessel' and a 'consecrated salt vessel' (two more tea-light holders) and a bag of 'Salt from the Dead Sea'. Nothing else in the kit, however, compared with the final item ... the 'chalice'. This was a small wooden eggcup that looked as though any liquid poured into it would immediately soak into the wood. It was so badly finished that any potential witchlet would be chewing woodchips for a week, if they actually stopped laughing for long enough to be able to use it.

Almost crying with laughter, the banter continued for some minutes before they realised someone was listening to their conversation. 'Excuse me,' said a small, middle-aged woman, 'I didn't mean to eavesdrop, but do you think you could answer some questions for me? I'm becoming very confused.'

Her name was Carole, and she had some very interesting information to impart. When they both were firmly ensconced in the alcove (the sofas now replaced by cane chairs) with a fresh coffee each, Pris learned that this was indeed the poor soul who'd attracted Rupert's wrath over the triple goddess some months before.

'I didn't take too much notice of him, because you meet some really strange people in these sort of shops,' she said in a low voice, so as not to cause offence. 'But afterwards I got to thinking and so much of what he'd said actually made sense. Anyway, last week I went to a pub moot at the Duck & Ferret, which was being run by the manager, who was saying the most outrageous things ...'

Pris's senses were immediately on auto-alert. 'Such as?'

'He was telling the group that he could trace his tradition back to the Stone Age. Oh, it gets worse ... or better, according to your perspective,' she said, as Pris failed to suppress a laugh. 'Apparently, the founders of his tradition came from Atlantis, via a wormhole in the universe ... no, stop it! He *was* serious, but what I found even more frightening, was that most of the people there were taking it all in. Several of us made the excuse of going to the bar for a drink, but we legged it.'

'And this chap said he was the *manager* of the pub?'

'Well, relief manager, which is why I thought he should be okay. What I'm really trying to say is that it made me think even harder about what that man said to me in here. To be honest, I'd rather be thought a fool by him, than treated like a gullible idiot by that other one. Is there any way of getting in touch with him?'

'Grandad wants to see you,' said Gordon one morning. 'He said it was important.'

The old man had been ailing for some months and as it was me he'd asked for, I thought I'd better get round to the cottage as quickly as possible, but without showing any unseemly haste. The district nurse was already hovering around but there was a lot of shouting going on and finally she emerged with an expression like a smacked bottom. Obviously Old Joe wasn't one of her favourite patients, and his reputation for shooting crows and magpies from his 'hide' in the outside lavatory would have been common gossip. There was no sign of the shotgun, but he probably kept it under the bed.

'And just see that you take that medicine,' she called in an authoritarian tone from the front door.

The old man was propped up against the pillows with a mulish expression on his face. As soon as the door closed with a bang, he leaned over and emptied the glass into a chamber pot he obviously kept there for the purpose. At least, I *hoped* it was discarded medicine, since the colour of the liquid would have given medical science cause for concern!

'You know why I want to see you,' he said, and then carried on without any further preamble. '*You* won't beat around the bush and try to convince me I'm not dying. Well, I am and I haven't got long left, so I need you to do a couple of things for me and not let that daughter-in-law get her own way, like she did when the Missus went. The Old 'Un and May Butterworth were here yesterday, not that I'd ever expected to see those two together in the same room, and my bedroom at that, but they agreed that I should talk to you.'

'Yes,' I said thoughtfully. 'They're as thick as thieves at the moment and yet I always thought they loathed each other.'

Old Joe chuckled, obviously enjoying some memory. 'They fell out over *me*. Had 'em fighting like cats, clawing and kicking and biting. Took four blokes to haul 'em off each other.'

It wasn't easy to imagine Granny, or May Butterworth for that matter, rolling around in the dirt and fighting over a man. I looked at Old Joe with new respect.

'What exactly …'

He reached out and grabbed my hand, showing amazing strength for one so near death's door. But there was also fear. 'Gabrielle, I don't want to be buried in no graveyard by some vicar. The Missus … well, she didn't mind where she went but I do. The vicar can say what he likes over my coffin if it keeps the rest of the family quiet, but I don't want to be buried in no Christian soil. I want you to ask your Man if he'll find me a bit of a plot …' The brusque voice wavered, afraid of refusal.

'I promise we *will* take care of you,' I said gently, holding his hand. 'Give Joe a letter stating that you want us to arrange the burial and then there can be no disputing it when you've gone.' I didn't like to tell him that the dead have no rights over their own disposal, but I trusted Young Joe to do the right thing by his father.

'And I want one of them willow caskets … according to the Old Ways. I'll not be any trouble to him when I'm in the ground.'

Earth to earth.

It's always more heart-rending when a large, strong man or animal is reduced to a dependency on others. Old Joe had been a part of our landscape and many are the times he'd snuck-up on Rupert coming home from a teenage night out at the local pub, his cat-like tread making no sound despite those great heavy boots. The first Rupert had ever known that the old man was about, was when a large hand descended on his shoulder out of the darkness, which had never failed to scare him out of his inebriated wits. I knew there would be no hesitation on his part in granting the old man his first and final request.

Dust to dust.

None of us could ever remember there ever being any talk of Old Joe actually being a member of the Coven, as he had always occupied one of those shadowy realms that lie between witch and countryman. In the old days these functions would have over-lapped on numerous occasions, and much of what today is referred to as 'witchcraft' was once basic country lore. It might have been Granny who taught us to tell the maze and call the spirits, but it was the old man lying upstairs waiting for death, who had taught us the healing power of herbs and to divine using the behaviour of birds.

Ash to ash.

Roodmas

It's always a bit daunting when witches who have become familiar acquaintances unexpectedly ask you to take part in one of their celebrations. This is especially true when the invitation has come at a time when you have just announced that you are not doing anything on that particular date. Rather than trying to mumble some lame excuses, it's sometimes easier all round just to bite the bullet, and accept with as much good grace as you can muster. Of course, since the publication of *Coarse Witchcraft: Craft Working*, it's highly unlikely that any members of the Coven would be invited anywhere ever again, in case their hosts find themselves exposed in the next volume!

And so it came to pass that Guy and Gerry were neatly cornered into spending Roodmas in the company of five very queer witches (and *they* used the word advisedly) following the invitation from one of their very good customers. They were told it would be a traditional seasonal gathering, with just a simple ritual.

At the appointed time, our 'boys' arrived, resplendent in their elegant black robes, warm cloaks and bearing gifts of wine and one of Gerry's wonderful cakes, decorated with a spiral pattern picked out in silver balls. 'As we hadn't been asked to take part in any formal part of the rite, we were simply looking forward to being able to relax and let someone else take the floor,' explained Gerry.

'That was mistake number one. Mistake number two was in taking it for granted that everyone present knew what they were doing. I mean Gaby dear, *we* might be gay, but this lot were hysterical!

'We were greeted by our customer, clad in see-through silver muslin, a silver leather thong and an inordinate amount of body glitter. On a professional drag-queen this might have been passable but on a middle-aged, balding gentleman of more than ample proportions, it bordered on being frightening. Before Guy and I could exchange a glance, his partner, whom we'd only met on a couple of occasions, flew down the stairs and embraced us warmly. He clung onto Guy for a little longer than was necessary, leaving a generous application of Revlon foundation smeared down the front of Guy's immaculate little black number.

'Host Number Two was clad in a short Byronic nightshirt split to the waist to reveal a shapely pair of legs, shown off to perfection in gold mesh leggings. The fetching black French knickers, worn tantalisingly over the top, co-ordinated beautifully with highly polished leather jackboots. I looked away just in time to catch the look of abject horror on Guy's face. Swiftly, to the point of rudeness, and before he went into shock, I pushed him towards the sitting room where a welcome log fire crackled. I began to prattle on about the cold … anything in fact, to keep my mind off those French knickers, in spite of just having caught a fleeting glimpse of them vanishing back upstairs again.'

Apparently Gerry spent the next ten minutes plying Guy with *Grouse* until he'd smoothed his partner's offended sensibilities. Their *sotto voce* conversation was finally interrupted by the arrival of Dick Whittington, sporting an enormous codpiece and accompanied by his Cat dressed in fishnet tights and four-inch stiletto-heeled boots. In their plain black robes, it appeared that Guy and Gerry were distinctly under-dressed for the occasion.

'There was a sound of footsteps on the floorboards above, and Host Number Two re-appeared with a companion. It seemed that this young lady had gone to bed the minute she arrived (as you do in someone else's house) and Lord Byron had been tucking her in when the 'boys' arrived. They weren't introduced to her as she was painfully shy; a fact that wasn't immediately obvious as she was dressed from head to toe in scarlet and sporting a cleavage that would have rivalled Dolly Parton. Gerry was busy trying to decide whether she was supposed to be a little devil, or a circus clown, as the strategically placed pom-poms made it a difficult decision. Guy wondered through his haze of *Grouse* whether they'd got the dates muddled up and they were all going Trick or Treating instead.

Pris and I decided to call round to the shop for the next instalment. Pris, being highly delighted that someone else was on the receiving end of 'What Witches Do', settled down in a chair with a coffee, ready to gloat. Guy, as handsome as ever, reclined in another chair while Gerry re-opened the batting …

'Our muslin draped host handed out what looked like large green pencils, which confused us even more … were we going to be asked to knock up a quick sketch of the proceedings as they happened? A quick explanation followed, with instructions on how to bend these things in half when we were all in place. Bendy fluorescent wands were a new magical invention to us, but when in Rome and all that, and we meekly followed the small procession out into the garden, where a large need-fire was burning.

'It came as a bit of a surprise to be informed at the last minute that we were appointed to work two of the quarters, but girding our loins we prepared to do our bit. I've never witnessed the quarters being manned by a Dick and his Cat before but we'd been assured that all these people were Initiates, so who were we to question? At the centre of our little company sparkled our High Priest, while lurking in the shadows behind him stood Host Number Two, with his arms wrapped protectively around our shy little devil, Dolly. Her shyness must have been crippling.

'With a flourish of muslin that hovered dangerously near to the flames, our High Priest opened the proceedings. The familiar banishing pentagrams were flung in all directions as he left nothing to chance. Nothing untoward was going to get near this ritual; in fact nothing of any description was likely to either. *Surely* the invoking bit was going to come in a minute? As the last bastions of defence were left hovering in the air, the silence was broken by a bellowed instruction to bend!

'We all know that a certain amount of risqué fun happens at a lot of witchcraft gatherings, but it seemed a bit early in the night for any bending, especially in mixed company. Then we realised it was the green wands he was referring to. Dutifully we all waggled the hard plastic about and lo and behold the things burst into light. I was suddenly reminded of a group of giant glow-worms, all hovering at waist height. The Beltaine rite was truly underway.'

Guy took over the narrative in his smooth, dark chocolate voice. 'The Dick's glow-worm wavered in mid air for a second before the guardians of the eastern gateway were summoned. As spontaneous calls go, I had to admit that this was impressive. All and everything that could possibly be attributed to the eastern quarter was mentioned in almost poetic terms. The glow-worm took a nose-dive at one point, but it was soon aloft again and hovering steadily. After a respectful pause it was the turn of the Cat. Another glow-worm teetered above head height, and another beautiful call issued forth. Surprisingly, this glow-worm also took a nose dive at one point, but overall the performance was admirable ...'

'Then it was my turn,' interrupted Gerry, 'and turning outwards I raised my glow-worm and waited. The seconds ticked by and still I waited, sure that any minute now I would feel the old familiar inner stirring, which confirms to me that I have made my contact. I waited a few moments longer, with my throat tightening and absolutely nothing magical stirring whatsoever, the night air remained a blank canvass to me. I heard Guy discreetly clearing his throat (coded language for, 'Get a move on, I'm cold/bored/thirsty or need a piddle'). The awful realisation dawned that this gathering was totally and utterly devoid of any magic, the High Priest had seen to that with his flourish of banishing pentagrams.

'It seemed that the Wise Ones were making damned sure that I didn't go along with this charade. Improvising swiftly while making mental apologies to any affronted guardians, I drew what I hoped would pass as a deeply mystical symbol in mid air, and turned to face the centre with a benign smile on my face. A murmur of approval rippled around the Circle and I was relieved to see that everyone seemed duly impressed (including myself!).

'It was just a bit disconcerting to catch a glimpse of a twinkle in Guy's eye as he addressed the quarter. Credit where credit is due, he managed to give a good account of himself, the only trouble was that I happened to recognise just exactly *what* he was addressing. It's not for nothing that he shares that magical catchphrase with Adam,' said Gerry, glancing meaningfully in Pris's direction. '*If in doubt – get the old dark forces out.* Banishing pentagrams or no banishing pentagrams, *something* took great glee in turning up at the party.

'Suddenly the peace of the sacred space was shattered. There was a loud four-lettered expletive from the Cat as she wobbled on a broken flagstone and pitched into a rose bush, laddering her tights as she fell. Undeterred our High Priest launched into a long spiel taken straight from the *Gospel of Aradia*. This was a tad unexpected but by now we were learning to roll with the punches. The Dick had leapt to the Cat's rescue and felt compelled to drag her into the darkened undergrowth to administer some emergency first aid. From the ensuing noises, which were reminiscent of a sink plunger unblocking a drain, I can only imagine that he had insisted on kissing it better.'

Guy crossed one slim leg over the other and took up the tale. 'Aradia was well into his stride by this time, and a long garbed speech ensued about the meaning of the night's gathering. It didn't seem entirely accurate to me given the gender ratio of the company but by that time I was so cold and angry with Gerry for getting us into this farce that I seized on it as a welcome sign that things were drawing to a close. Sure enough, the moment came to bless the feast, and at this point Dolly, the little red devil got a shock. As you know, when the Horned God is summoned by an imperious Aradia, he does not argue.

'Dolly was unceremoniously thrust away to fend for herself as our hosting Horned God dived to his knees and slid gracefully across the grass, arriving at the billowing muslin folds of Aradia, encased in that silver thong. Mutely, Dolly turned her eyes on me but I gave her a glowering look from under my hood and that was warning enough. In fright she turned towards the Dick and, kindly though he might have been feeling, a piercing scowl from the Cat soon put paid to any altruistic tendencies *he* might have been going to have. Retreating further into the shadows, Dolly had to be content with hugging the dead stump of a tree.

'At last, the rite, such as it was, ground to a halt but not before we'd all been instructed to jump through the flames to ensured continued fertility for the coming year! This seemed quite incongruous considering that there were two gay couples, the Dick and his Cat and Dolly the Clone in the company! Host Number Two began with a flourish and at the fire's edge he took off in quite a spectacular leap, with arms and legs flailing, and those French frillies sailing uncomfortably close to the flames. But it is the sight of middle-aged flab exposed under ruched-up muslin, genitals held snug in a silver posing pouch and skimming through the firelight, is one I will carry to my grave.

As we filed indoors, I chanced to pick up some crumpled sheets of paper from the shrubbery. Written out neatly, in print just large enough to read by the light of a glow-worm, were two lovely calls to the guardians of the east and south. So much for our experienced Initiates, then? As coven gatherings go, this one was certainly different, but I can only hope that this lot are never involved in the re-making of *The Wicker Man*. I don't think I could stand to see Edward Woodward playing the part in black French knickers and jackboots.'

Despite the popular concept of farmers being callous and exploitative when it comes down to livestock and wildlife, no self-respecting countryman will pass a fatally injured animal without stopping to put it out of its misery. I pulled back the curtains early one morning to find a sickly rabbit sitting in the middle of the lawn. It was suffering from that scientifically-created disease known as myxomatosis and there was only one solution.

'Rupert,' I said, 'there's a poorly bunny out on the lawn with 'myxy', can you go out and sort it?' A grunt came from under the duvet. I went downstairs to the kitchen to make the tea and each time I looked out, the poor shivering creature was still there. 'Rupert,' I said, a little more forcefully, banging the tea-tray down on the bedside table. 'Will you *please*, go and deal with that rabbit?'

In exasperation, he flung back the duvet and I followed the noises of him stomping downstairs and out into the boot room. There was the rattle of the gun cabinet keys, the sound of the back door opening and the crunching of footsteps on the gravel. There was a loud bang and the poor rabbit keeled over, its suffering at an end. Then I heard a cheerful voice call out in greeting, 'Mornin' Mr P. A grand day for a bit o' shooting.' It was the postman, totally unfazed by the sight of a stark naked man, walking around wearing just a pair of wellies and brandishing a shotgun.

But that's the country for you.

Things were a bit more confrontational at the Witch's Kitchen later that day, when 'arfa Kinsman showed up and threatened to test Pris's resolve not to belt him even if she got half the chance. Fortunately, it was before the café opened and only Abi and Carole were there to bear witness. Kinsman strolled in and, completely ignoring the two women, who were setting the tables for lunch, made straight for Pris.

She glanced up but his opening gambit caught her by surprise. 'Pris, you and I need to get one or two things sorted out. You can't refuse to recognise me as a member of your Tradition because the Old Man himself gave me access to your teachings.'

'I can, because you are *not* an Initiate. And you well know the Old Man's not been himself for quite a few years. Whatever he gave you doesn't make you a member of our Tradition.'

'Oh, we'll see about that!' he responded, leaning forward across the counter, all pleasantry now evaporated. 'If you don't accept me, I can make life very awkward for you, believe me!'

'Is that a threat?' spat Pris, now equally as angry. 'Because if it is, you'd better give it your best shot. If you know anything at all about *my* Tradition then you'll know we don't take kindly to ill-wishing, or threats of cursing. And it will be returned to you in ways you've never dreamed possible.'

While this exchange was taking place, Carole had positioned herself near the old fireplace and was ready to wield the besom; Abi had fled to the office to get hold of me on the phone. By the time I got there it was all over and Kinsman was nowhere to be seen. Pris, shaken and angry, was nursing a large mug of coffee with its traditional 'rescue remedy' – a large *Grouse.*

'Can you manage on your own for a while?' I asked Abi. 'I think Pris could do with some fresh air.'

We drove up to the woods and sat on a fallen tree, Pris still clutching the dregs of her coffee and drawing heavily on a cigarette. 'By the gods, I wanted to hit him,' she said. 'I wanted to wipe that smug, smarmy smile off his face right there and then. What do I do, Gaby?'

Some advice is hard to give … especially when it applies to someone else's Tradition, but as I saw it, there was only one course of action. 'You've got to let it go and walk away, Pris,' I said. 'It's a problem that's only going to get worse, and you know that Kinsman isn't the only one who claims your lineage. The Old Man's been more than a little indiscrete over the past ten years and who knows what else is waiting in the shadows. You're not turning your back on your roots or your Ancestors, but you can distance yourself from those who are currently bringing your Tradition into disrepute.'

Pris sighed and threw the last of her coffee into the bracken. 'Yeah, you're right. I've tried to remain true to my oath but it just isn't possible anymore. You can't remain loyal to something that's no longer loyal to you. Thank the gods we found the Coven, or we'd really be out on a limb.'

'You and Adam took Initiation with us, but it was only really an affirmation of your existing oath. There's very little difference between your ways and ours. We know you have always remained true to your roots, and that's all that matters. It's nothing to do with outsiders ... let them speculate. Besides,' I added, 'do all these pretenders *really* know what they're getting by taking your Tradition as their own?'

There were some dark, shadowy things that have come out of the Forest of Dean and Pris's Tradition was certainly 'overcast'. There were repercussions in making the Old Ways public property, and I doubted whether any of the folk so desperate for those particular Old Craft roots would be aware of the very *real* dangers lurking in the darkness. The anger and sadness faded from Pris's face, to be replaced by a knowing grin and I knew she was already one step ahead of me. The malediction had been made many, many years before and it had never been, nor could ever be lifted: the Tradition was doomed and the malice and malcontent it bred was manifesting in the political in-fighting between those who would claim it for their own.

'So mote it be!' said Pris getting to her feet and heading back to the car with a much lighter step. She even danced a little jig along the woodland track.

On their heads be it.

And it is not until the air is perfumed with the evocative scent of the hawthorn that we actually celebrate 'May' – it's a peculiar musky, female smell that hovers on the breeze and assails the senses. The days had been quite chilly around the beginning of the month and the buds on the may refused to break; then there was the sudden warmth of spring sunshine and the trees were heavy with the sensuous white blossom.

'And after April, when May follows, And the whitethroat builds and all the swallows! Hark, where my blossom'd pear-tree in the hedge Leans to the field and scatters on the clover Blossoms and dewdrops – at the bent spray's edge ...' as Browning would have it.

Summer Solstice

The local Game Fair had grown out of the pagan camp held on our land a couple of years before. As with most things, the original organisers had moved on, and so the local countryside agencies adopted the idea and developed it into an annual event to showcase rural sports and offer everyone a good day out. It was still held on the weekend nearest to the Solstice and included many of the same people who had played such an active part in that first camp.

Now, three years' later, it was a fully-fledged Game Fair, with a centre show-ring, surrounded by craft and country goods stalls, clay-pigeon shooting, lurcher and terrier racing, show jumping and the traditional bonfire with hog-roast. This was more our sort of event, with Richard, Adam and Rupert being the current champions in the team shooting stakes. Not to mention our lurcher being the fastest thing on the block for the second year running. Gerry and Guy had entered their dog but, being a real couch potato, it merely lay down as the others hurtled out of the trap, leaving ours the undisputed champion.

It was a beautifully sunny day as Pris and I strolled round the Fair, the dog sporting his ribbons, proudly attached to his collar. I happened to glance down and saw white foam dribbling from his mouth! Panic set in, until I realised that he was lurcher-height to small children's ice cream cones and that he'd been taking a surreptitious swipe each time he passed. The last lick had removed a whole scoop and he was desperately trying to swallow the evidence before the crime was detected.

The centre show-ring was taken up with the judging of the best-kept children's pony and to our surprise we saw that Rupert had been roped in for the judging. He's not exactly a children sort of person, and actively loathes Shetland ponies, which he considers to be nasty, evil-tempered little brutes. This event was pure Thelwell, as diminutive tots bustled around the ring, on ponies that were almost as wide as they were high. Rupert's face was giving nothing away, but he wouldn't meet my eye.

A black, leg-at-each-corner Shetland ambled past and Pris gave a bit of a sniff. 'It's not *that* cute!' I said, referring to the child.

'It looks just like Lightning,' she replied, with a lump in her throat.

Now Lightning has a tale all to himself, and it's to Pris's credit that she's kept him for nearly 30 years, despite times of great financial hardship, when he's been an awful drain on her resources. We've known about Lightning for years, but he'd continued to live in the valley where Pris grew up and so we'd never actually seen him. In her much younger days, a teenage Pris had been sent to do the weekly shopping, but had hung around the horse sales instead. One lot had been a mare, with her foal being sold separately. The mare had been knocked down to the local knackerman and as she was led away, the foal began screaming and flinging himself about in terror. The knackerman started the bidding, but being a good witch even then, Pris ensured that he had a choking fit, which prevented him from continuing.

The foal was knocked down to Pris, but as she explained: 'There I was standing in the emptying sale ring, with a hysterical foal, and nothing but a bit of baling band to put round his neck. On top of that, I'd only got my Mother's Morris Minor and I'd spent the housekeeping. [It's nice to know that *some* things don't change!] but I promised him there and then, that I'd never, ever put him back in the sale ring, or part with him.'

I knew by now that the old lad must be getting on a bit, but the sight of the little Shetland in the show ring had planted another idea in Pris's head. Further discussion on the subject was prevented when a young man, who was manning one of the stalls, nabbed us. He beamed in a familiar way, and we were just about to head off in the opposite direction when he called us by name. I frowned for a moment and then realised who he was.

'It Rupert's disciple,' I said to Pris. She looked blank. 'You remember … the drummer? He and Rupert were joined at the hip during that first pagan camp, and I thought we'd land up having to adopt him. He burned his drum.'

'Gotcha.'

It transpired that Scot (for that was his name) had taken Rupert's teaching to heart and had gone off to learn more about the countryside before trying to become a witch. Gone were the long, scraggily locks and beard and we were confronted by a fresh-faced young man in clean chinos and a Tattersall shirt. He'd got himself a job with a country sports firm – hence his presence at the show – and was hoping to be promoted to manager of a new shop opening up in the area. He'd already bumped into Rupert, who'd promptly invited him to join us for supper later that day.

'Rupert's getting rather gregarious these days,' said Pris, as we moved off. 'Another number 29 bus, do you think?'

Needless to say I made sure that Adam and Pris were also on parade for supper, as Rupert obviously had some hidden agenda in asking a stranger into our home and inviting them to 'take our salt'. It was another illuminating episode in the political intrigues that were constantly dogging our steps these days, despite the fact that we rarely venture far from home, or get involved with the pagan scene at large. Scot had arrived promptly and left at a reasonable hour, leaving the four of us to chew over the information he'd unwittingly revealed during the meal.

'This is getting too ridiculous for words,' said Rupert, 'and I deeply resent the inference that the 'pustular postulant' was forced to leave because I couldn't keep my hands to myself!'

'Yes,' said Adam gloomily. 'Few men would want to admit to sliding his finger around *her* knicker elastic. The thought is positively frightening.'

'The real issue,' said Pris pointedly, 'is to decide whether this chap is a plant, or not. After all, on his own admission he confessed to having slid more than just a finger under the elastic!'

'Unless he just happened to be in the wrong place at the right time. There was no way that Jackie Pratt could have known he'd met us previously, when he first turned up on her doorstep.'

'No, but she didn't waste any time with the name dropping once she'd known he'd been to that first pagan camp. Or with the inference that she was more intimately acquainted with us than she was,' said Rupert. 'Scot was convinced that she had worked with the Coven, and he seemed to know 'arfa Kinsman as well, so I propose we keep him at arm's length until this is all sorted out. It's a pity because it looked as though the boy had put in a lot of effort with the sole purpose of coming back to us in a more knowledgeable frame of mind.'

'And it's a shame if she's queered his pitch with us,' said Adam, 'but I don't want to be looking over my shoulder, wondering who else is waiting in the wings.'

'I agree,' I added. 'Since the book came out we've attracted far more attention to ourselves than we could ever have expected. I'm not exactly sure why, considering it was supposed to be a spoof, but I propose we don't take anyone else into the Coven until the interest dies down.'

'What about Carole and Abi?' asked Pris. 'Adam and I could carry on teaching them without any close Coven involvement, at least until we're absolutely sure of them.'

'And Scot's job isn't supposed to happen until next year, so that gives us some breathing space as far as he's concerned. It's a damned nuisance having all this attention,' said Rupert, 'but I suppose we've brought it on ourselves by going into print, even with such an innocuous title as *Coarse Witchcraft*.'

Rupert had guessed Pris wanted to ask something of him, by the way she kept hanging about and virtually rubbing her shoe up the back of her sock. And because it's the nature of their relationship, he deliberately kept out of her way, just for the sheer delight of winding her up. By tea-time she was nearly in tears of frustration.

'For goodness sake,' I said to him. 'Can't you see Pris wants to talk to you privately?'

'Of course, I can,' he answered with a grin, helping himself to a large slab of fruitcake. 'She wants to ask if she can bring that moth-eaten old pony of hers onto the yard, and knows what I think about Shetlands.'

'How did you know?' I asked, experiencing another feeling of *déjà vu*.

Lightning arrived a week later and it was a sorry home-coming. The poor little chap could hardly put one foot in front of the other because of laminitis, and it took half an hour to get him down the ramp. He was dull-eyed, with sore patches on his skin, and all-in-all had the appearance of a badly-stuffed sofa.

'It might be kinder to have him shot,' said Rupert, looking at the pensioner with a horseman's eye.

Pris shook her head firmly, but I knew he was in a worse condition than even she'd remembered. 'I've got to give him a chance,' she said, leading him into the stable that had been set aside for him. The door closed behind them and I knew a few tears were being shed.

'Isn't there anything you can do?' asked Adam.

'Of course, but there are no guarantees, especially at his age.'

In fact, most of the problems had been caused by the wrong sort of care for an aging pony, rather than any deliberate neglect and, compounded by loneliness, he was suffering from a form of depression. The people who had kept him on loan had done their best but a lack of real experience had allowed a lot of problems to develop in the old boy.

Although Pris knew Rupert disapproved of keeping Lightning alive, there were several occasions when she's caught him in the stable administering pig oil and sulphur to help clear up the pony's skin complain, and she often found fresh chopped herbs that she couldn't identify had been added to the feed. By the time, we'd got around to writing this part of the book, the little chap has been given a new lease of life, a different diet and was running around with the other horses, despite his advancing years. Pris had kept her vow and the old pony was home to stay; she had kept to her promise.

Granny's actions, however, were also giving us cause for concern because, to put no finer point on it, she was on the warpath. In all fairness, I think between the Pentecostals trying to poach Gordon and 'arfa Kinsman threatening Pris, she could see the Coven fragmenting and falling apart. Perhaps she thought none of us were doing enough to combat these disruptive elements but we all have our own way of doing things. For some unfathomable reason, Granny and May Butterworth were now inseparable and Granny's marketing efforts on her new friend's behalf might have got her nominated for the Chamber of Commerce 'Businesswoman of the Year' if her motives weren't so downright suspect!

Not only was May Butterworth now making cakes and pies for the Witch's Kitchen, she was also regularly supplying the pub where 'arfa Kinsman was acting as relief manager. It also meant that the scurrilous old bat was busy behind the scenes at the pub, as well as in close attendance when May made her deliveries to the private households in the village. One look at Granny's greasy mitts would have been enough to put any self-respecting trencherman off food for life but luckily for May, the Health & Safety people weren't around to slap a Government Health Warning on her bosom pal!

None of us had a clue what the old girl was up to and, even when asked directly if it concerned Gordon, she stared back with those bright blue eyes and refused to answer. If she'd bothered to find out how things were going at the yard, she would have learned that Gordon had jumped at the chance to go up to a small National Hunt yard for a few weeks, when their head lad went on holiday. A few months earlier he would have been reluctant to leave his 'true love' even for a day. *Rooted and bound, rooted and bound* ...

Six of us made the long trek across the fields to the remotest of our working sites. It was Midsummer Eve and as we negotiated the final part of the journey, we stopped to watch the sun disappear behind a distant hill. Summer is actually the worst time to look at the stars, because it is never truly dark; the sun is never more than 15 degrees below the horizon and its glow brightens the sky, even at midnight. In fact, full summer is only said to have begun when the star, Spica, appears in the South-West.

Tonight, however, the sky was stained a glorious red-gold, with only a few flecks of cloud floating aimlessly past. We waited with anticipation as we realised that something spectacular was about to happen. Refraction had created a vertical spectrum of colour that seemed to be sinking below the horizon with the sun in the direction of the sea. Because the blue tints were scattered by the air and fragmented, we caught just a fleeting glimpse of that rare green brilliance, known to occultists as the 'green ray', before it disappeared completely. In the deepening twilight, the evening star twinkled towards the West.

This added to the sanctity of the evening's working and each one of us continued walking in silence ... until we came to the clearing. The silence continued, but it was due to dumb-struck horror not reverence. Our magical working site had been defiled in the worst possible way. There were used condoms, empty beer cans and traces of burned foil littered about. The centre of the clearing was scorched from where a large fire had been lit, and the ancient split beech tree had offered a convenient chimney for an impromptu barbeque, the inside of the trunk was now charred and blackened.

Pris bent to pick up a crushed beer can.

'Leave it!' said Rupert angrily. 'I'll come back tomorrow and clear it up.'

Everyone stood around miserably for a few moments, and then we trudged back the way we had come, but this time in anger and not in any mood for celebration. Not only had our own personal sacred space been defiled, but our land had also been desecrated by morons not fit to be in close proximity to Nature. And the powers that be at Westminster want to open the countryside up for all and sundry to rampage across.

It would take Rupert more than just an hour's work in clearing up the rubbish, he would have to spend a considerable amount of time in the magical cleansing – and that would not happen overnight. In fact my worst fears were confirmed a couple of nights later when I took a phone call from Pris only moments after putting the receiver down on a call from Gerry. They were both asking the same question ... what did Rupert want with their partners?

'Boy's stuff,' I answered.

It would be a long time before we could use the site again for magical working but I hated to think what would be conjured up and left there as a Guardian. Woe betide anyone who ventured there again with vandalism in their hearts! As Pris had commented, even she would think twice about venturing up there if the combined energies of Guy, Adam and Rupert had put the protective boundaries in place!

Lammas

It was Lammastide when we received word that Old Joe had died. The old man had done as I'd asked and left written instructions about his funeral, so it was only a question of deciding who would do what, between us and the family. In the end it was agreed that Young Joe would take care of the arrangements up to the coffin leaving the church, and we would take over from there. There were a few protests from Gordon's mother, who thought the willow casket no substitute for the undertaker's best, but for once she was over-ruled by both husband and son. That she objected to our involvement went without saying.

Nevertheless, he was one of our own, even though he'd not been an active member of the Coven in our memory: and promises had been made. As kids we'd learned our woodcraft from him and as gruff and unbending as he was, there was a kindness concealed beneath the rough exterior. His family had put the funeral arrangements into the hands of Diggit & Bend, a local funeral parlour, so Pris and I slipped in to discuss the plans and to make sure there was no hitch when we took over after the church service.

We also discovered that Old Joe's daughter-in-law was lavishing more attention on the old man in death than she'd ever done in life. The black hearse, three black limos and masses of flowers. The only fly in the embalming fluid was the willow casket.

Gordon had insisted that his grandfather's wishes had been carried out and compromised by allowing his mother to buy him a smart new suit for the occasion. The undertaker had received explicit instructions that the casket was to be covered by a heavily embroidered throw so that the perceived parsimony of the family would not excite comment from the neighbours.

All the mourners were seated by the time we made our entrance and I must confess we created quite a stir: four black riders, in polished boots, pristine breeches, and hunting-black jackets, with riding caps carried on the arm. Rupert, Adam, Pris and myself stood in a row at the back of the church, waiting to escort Old Joe on his last journey. Adam was looking particularly nervous. He doesn't mind the odd slow hack across country but he wasn't that confident in the saddle. He was fidgeting about, then suddenly he was missing and we assumed he was fighting a losing battle with his bladder, or gone outside for a cigarette to calm his nerves.

A couple of minutes' later his place was taken by Gordon, who had decided to defy his mother and take his place as the fourth rider. And judging by the speed with which Adam had disappeared, there wasn't going to be any argument or discussion. Gordon looked particularly handsome in his riding kit, but a middle-aged couple and their daughter, who were sitting just in front of us, didn't appreciate his fine appearance. I would have thought Christine would have been proud of her good-looking young man, but somehow Gordon's gesture seemed to have thwarted their sense of propriety. I don't know if it was at that precise moment the girl's parents sensed they were losing the battle for Gordon's soul, but they certainly raised the stakes after that day.

As the pall-bearers lifted the casket, which up until then had been covered by an embroidered purple throw, Old Joe's family led the stampede for the waiting limos. Obviously they were not going to accompany the old man during the final stage of his funeral. The four of us left the church and mounted the horses that had been held at the ready by a groom. We'd managed to borrow an old-fashioned hay-cart, complete with a grey Shire mare, to carry the casket to its final resting place on the ridge overlooking the river. The cart was draped in black and Adam was already on board, holding Old Joe's broken shotgun that was to be placed on top of the casket and buried with him. I don't suppose they'll worry too much about a gun license renewal in the Afterlife.

Young Joe and Granny were helped up onto the cart and, once they were seated, we were ready to move off. The slow rumble of the wheels on the road, the creaking of the old wooden frame, and the steady tread of five sets of horses' iron-shod hooves set a sombre tone for the hot summer morning. At a slow, walking pace the horses and riders marked the four points: Rupert and I in front, with Pris and Gordon riding behind.

There were more people lining the route of the cortege as it made its way towards the fields and instead of breaking up as the cart rumbled passed, they fell in behind and slowly followed on foot. By the time we turned into the hay field to make our way to the ridge where Old Joe was to be buried, there were over a hundred people walking in silence. When Young Joe turned and saw how many had turned out to pay their respects to his father, he was unable to hold back the tears.

Rupert's men had dug the grave during the previous day and there were six burly farm workers ready to lift the coffin from the cart. They'd all in their time been sworn at, cuffed and bullied by the old man but like the rest of us, most of them had learned their skills under his tutelage. The lid of the willow coffin, with its symbolically broken shotgun, was woven with sprigs of rosemary and as it was lowered into the ground, the mourners clustered around to throw hand-picked cottage flowers on top.

Rupert and I consigned Old Joe's body to the grave and our eulogy was a highly personal one since he was not only an important part of our lives, he was also one of the last true links with old country Craft. Rupert had sat up most of the night, working to get the words right and when he delivered them over the open grave, there was hardly a dry eye on that hillside. The local kennel huntsman blew 'Gone Away', and as the long, haunting sound echoed across the land, the mounted hunt staff and hounds came passed to pay their last respects.

As the mourners slowly filed away, the farm lads began filling in the grave and only when the last spade-full of earth had been thrown did Young Joe and Granny take their leave. Gordon handed the reins of his mount back to Adam and walked with them down the hill: three of them united in grief and their differences forgotten. We learned later that when they reached the last gate, they'd stopped and looked back. There on the ridge, the sight of the four riders, silhouetted against the clear blue sky of the summer skyline made Granny burst into tears.

If Beltaine is generally the time for rampant sexual urges, those of Lammastide were obviously taking their toll on Gordon. In the weeks following his grandfather's funeral he began looking tired and drawn, and by the end of the month he was looking downright ill. Finally, Rupert found the boy sitting on a bale of straw with his head in his hands, and felt obliged to ask what the problem was, which was just as well really, since we were entering into the realm of the Horned God.

'Nothing. I'm alright, really I am.'

'It looks like it,' replied Rupert bluntly. 'There's obviously something wrong with you.'

The boy answered wearily. 'Just after granddad's funeral, Christine … well, she suggested I stayed over because her parents were away. And … well, you can guess what happened.'

'You've not got her pregnant?'

Gordon shook his head. 'I'm not that daft.'

'Well, what the devil *is* the matter with you?' said Rupert in his best demanding manner that few can ignore. 'Are they trying to force you to join their infernal religion?'

Gordon sighed and surrendered. 'They want me to, of course, but the problem is Christine. She wants me to do it every night, and not just once. I'm not getting any sleep and it doesn't matter where we are … it's out in the fields mostly, now that her parents are back. She won't leave me alone and I don't know what to do.'

'Pray for the weather to change,' answered Rupert dryly.

Gordon responded with the first smile he'd shown for weeks. 'Are all women like that?'

'No, thank god,' said my unsympathetic spouse.

Lammas had always been a strange time of the year. It was the old festival of the wheat harvest and its name came from the Old English *hlafmaesse,* from *hlaf,* loaf and *maesse,* mass = 'loaf-mass'. It was also one of the old quarter-days and the name derives from the custom of each worshipper presenting in the church a loaf made of the new wheat, as an offering of the 'first-fruits'. Although this observance had been incorporated into the church calendar as early as the 8th century, there is evidence for it being much older.

In truth, Lammas celebrations have always been subdued affairs in comparison with the other festivals but for the early farmers, the harvesting of the 'first-fruits' would have been an early indication of feast or famine for the community. These offerings would no doubt have been accompanied by a collective sigh of relief that there *was* a good harvest to come. Despite the fact that Lammastide represents the busiest period in the agricultural year, there is still the element of sacrifice lying just beneath the surface.

In some circles there is the belief that King William Rufus was killed on 2nd August while out hunting in the New Forest in 1100, as part of a pagan sacrifice. There are a number of accounts of his death, including that of the historian William of Malmesbury, who recorded that the king's blood dripped to the earth during the whole journey, in keeping with the old tradition that the blood of the 'divine victim' must be spilt on the ground to ensure the continuing fertility of the land.

True or not, the story symbolises the deep spiritual bond the people have with the land and the deep-seated belief that if the first-fruits are poor, then some form of propitiation must be made now, rather than being left until it's too late. In some parts of the country, Lammas marked the end of hay-harvest, and if this was poor, then there would be insufficient fodder for over-wintering the animals. These harvest customs have survived unchanged for centuries and mirror the sense of belonging and responsibility that is needed in this gruelling partnership.

Several years ago, we lost our entire wheat crop due to bad weather. The incessant rain turned the golden ears to a horrible black mildew and all we could do was to cut it and fire the stubble. I don't know why, but Lammas always represents feminine energies for me and I decided that under the next full moon, I would walk the boundaries of the farm as a propitiatory gesture.

I'd just stepped out of the back door when a shape detached itself from the shadows at my side, making me almost jump out of my skin.

'Nervous tonight, aren't we?' said a familiar voice.

'Pris! What the hell are you doing here?' I whispered.

'If you think for one moment that I'm going to let you go galli-vanting off into the night dressed only in a thin, woollen cloak, you've got another think coming.' Pris is nothing if not loyal.

'Look, this is my penance, not yours. You don't have to come,' I argued in a loud whisper.

'If you don't shut up, I'll bang on the door and let Rupert know what you're doing. And you don't want *that*, do you?'

I didn't, as he would only pour scorn on the whole operation. So in the end I agreed to allow her to accompany me, but the thought of Pris, stark naked under her cloak, save for her hip flask of *Famous Grouse* in her garter, is a memory I shall never forget. We slithered and slipped, tripped and tottered around the boundary as the contents of the hip flask diminished in order to keep the cold at bay. I don't know if the Old Ones were influ-enced by our gesture but I bet it took them until All Hallows to stop laughing!

'Her parents are hoping the lad gets Christine pregnant, and then he'll have to marry her,' beamed May Butterworth as Pris encouraged her to enjoy a good gossip. 'At the old man's funeral they could see where his loyalties lay and they weren't with 'er.'

'But why all this determination to net Gordon?' asked Pris. 'He's a smashing chap and a first-rate head lad but that's all he's ever going to be. Financially he's not a good catch.'

May Butterworth's cackle was too reminiscent of Granny's to be comfortable. 'He's a lost soul and the preacher-man wants to save 'im, even at the expense of his daughter's virtue. Not that the girl could have done anything about it.'

'What do you mean?'

'Well, Granny Jay saw to that. I told her that the girl has a regularly order, twice a week, for my vanilla slices and so she used to come over a slip a bit o' summat into the filling.' Pris eyed the vanilla slices on the stand with some misgiving. 'Oh, those are alright, it was only the ones I saved for Christine that she tampered with. Don't know what she put in 'em but I could do with some of it m'self.' The old girl cackled again and leaned forward in a conspiratorial manner. 'Young Gordon's been working away for Mr Percy, ain't he? Well, the girl ain't been staying home knitting, I can tell you. She's got a taste for it, and most of the youths in the village have had a generous helping of it by now, I should guess.' What was it Granny had said about May Butterworth making 'exceedingly good cakes'!

Without further ado, Rupert despatched Gordon to another yard in the north of England on the pretext that the owner needed someone to yard-sit while he was in hospital, in the hopes that Christine's behaviour would become public knowledge. This is what we mean about looking after our own, even though none of us approved of Granny's methods. At least we now knew what she was up to as far as the Pentecostals were concerned but it still didn't answer the question of what the old girl was doing at the pub!

Autumn Equinox

It was late afternoon when Adam phoned to ask if we'd seen or heard from Pris. She'd gone out for a ride earlier that day and hadn't returned. By the time we'd all met up in the stable yard to set off to look for her, a very bedraggled horse and rider came in by the field gate. Pris is a highly competent horsewoman but we could all see she'd been badly frightened. The words tumbled out but her relief to be back in one piece was all too obvious.

'I didn't realise how late it was, so I decided to come back along that double hedge at the top of the hay field but within about twenty yards from the end, the horse suddenly shied violently and began rearing. There was nothing at all that I could see to have startled him but it took me all my time to keep my seat and settle him down. Then he began to shake violently and to back up in an attempt to spin round and make off in the direction we'd come from. After a considerable battle, I had him standing still and tried to urge him forward but he just refused point blank to walk on.

'As a last resort, I dismounted, dragged my jacket off and threw it over his head, leading him back, away from whatever it was that frightened him. I took the jacket off and remounted but at this point he plunged up the bank and through the hedge into the field. It took me all my time to hold on. What on earth made him behave like that, I just don't know ... but it was pretty scary ...'

'You can't take a horse down the Hag Track,' said Rupert unsympathetically. '*Everyone* round here knows that. Even the hunt gives it a wide berth because the horses refuse to go along there no matter how fast the chase. Hounds don't like it either, that's why old Charlie makes for that part of the county if they've picked up his scent. The foxes have lived up there undisturbed for as long as I can remember. I thought you knew.'

'I *didn't* know,' said Pris crisply.

'Well, you do now,' answered Rupert with a grin but before he could move out of the way, a piece of well-aimed horse dung took the cap clean off his head.

Bending to pick up another piece, Pris caught one in the bustle. Adam looked at me, and I looked at Adam, and we silently agreed to go back to the house and leave them to it. Pris was obviously over her fright and the muck-fight would end over coffee laced with *Grouse*. Adam and I are used to this kind of behaviour from our respective spouses. At one dinner party, Rupert produced a margarine tub full of Bart Simpson water pistols and before the astonished guests, he and Pris engaged in a water fight ... reverting to childhood is an excellent way of relieving tension!

The 'track' that Pris tried to ride down is, in fact, an early earthen boundary marker thrown up to separate land owned by different families and believed to date from pre-Christian times. This method created a track wide enough to allow a cart to pass, with high earthen banks on either side, which could run for miles or just a few hundred yards before suddenly coming to an abrupt end. Over the years, these parallel mounds create a 'double hedge', which can be very magical places if they have been left undisturbed. Our 'hag track' is almost a continuous tunnel of hawthorn dotted with oak and ash trees, with gaps here and there where livestock have pushed their way through. It no longer marks any boundaries, simply because Rupert's family owns the land on either side and has done so for many generations.

Primitive man believed that there was a 'life spirit' that resides within all animate and inanimate things, and happenings such as Pris's encounter are a constant reminder that we do *not* control these natural forces. And it was this 'force' that Rupert and the others had empowered at our sacred site. The weather was still fine and the evenings warm enough to tempt people into staying out of doors, which meant it wasn't long before we heard of the strange goings-on that had affected a group of local teenagers. Fortunately for us, St Thomas on the Poke remains an unspoiled market town, and the inhabitants usually know what's happening in their midst.

It was Gerry who first alerted us to the possibility of identifying the culprits whose profanity was responsible for our ruined Midsummer rite. If this were the case, then we also knew that they had returned to the woodland clearing again, *after* Rupert had been back to cleanse and magically charge the place. Over a beer in the Fox & Hounds, one of the local mothers had asked for Gerry's help and advice when her teenage daughter had suddenly started to have terrifying nightmares.

Gerry asked all the right questions before offering any constructive advice and it was only a day later that the mother came back into the shop with the pertinent information. Apparently her daughter and a group of friends had gone out for another all-night party in the woods, but when they arrived at the place where they'd met previously, they all had the feeling they were being watched. With typical teenage bravado, the group handed out the beer but half-way through the evening something had spooked them so badly that they panicked and fled.

At first they put it all down to a drug-induced reaction but when the nightmares continued some felt the need to talk about their experience. It was soon apparent that none of those affected could give an exact description of what it was that had terrified them, and the impressions were slightly different for each of them. For weeks afterwards they were still being plagued by the fear of being followed, and some were even requiring counselling to help them overcome the fear of being stalked.

Gerry, of course, knew exactly *what* it was that the teenagers had encountered, but he'd been one of the Coven who had seen the defilement of the sacred site, and was less than sympathetic although he wasn't about to express this sentiment to the worried mother.

A witch of our acquaintance also had a similar experience in recent months, when his own personal site was desecrated by vandals. He pushed on through the undergrowth and eventually came to a previously unknown clearing and in the centre sat a large brown hare. Despite this auspicious sign, there was an overwhelming sense of foreboding and he retreated. Some days later, however, he decided to return with offerings and as soon as he'd made his obsecration, the 'guardian' removed the barriers and he was bade welcome. This type of manifestation is characteristic of 'guardians' and many other kinds of nature elementals and the Adept must learn to recognise, identify and treat with them accordingly.

As far as we were all concerned, the crass behaviour of these teenage litter-louts warranted these extreme measures. The land is privately owned and they were, in law, trespassers; the litter they'd left behind could have been harmful to all manner of wildlife. Incongruously, the girl whose mother had enlisted Gerry's help, claims to be a 'pagan', as do several of her friends who were there in the woods that night.

This incident perhaps goes a long way to illustrate why we distance ourselves from the so-called 'pagan' scene … simply because we are not speaking the same language. Or holding the same beliefs. Once Gerry knew who the girls were, he recognised them as regular customers in the shop, who were always twittering on about Nature, the goddess and being vegetarian. They bought the books and cultivated the talk but they could still go to a pristine woodland site and leave rubbish behind that could inflict a slow, painful death on any poor creature who, for example, happened to get caught up in one of those plastic beer-can holders!

Here we return to the Old Craft concept of protecting our own, because we cannot – and will not – take responsibility for those who come onto our patch uninvited and desecrate a traditional magical working site. On the other hand, we do know of another magical group who work in the area because we often come across a site that has been recently (although discreetly) disturbed and the obvious signs are there for those with the eye to see. We do not know who they are but we have no objection to them using our woods for their observances because they obviously respect the land. They do not use our personal site for the very same reason. Perhaps they come from a nearby town and do not have any other access to woodland; perhaps they belong to a different Tradition to ours. It doesn't matter, simply because they show themselves to be true witches who do not come to wreak havoc but to pay homage to their gods in time-honoured fashion.

Feigning innocence as to the real cause of the girls' night-mares, Gerry suggested to a couple of them that perhaps they should perform some act of atonement and help clean out a culvert that had become blocked with rubbish during recent heavy rains. After a lot of suppressed sniggering and face-pulling, he was eventually told 'not to talk so bloody silly, that's got nothing to do with *real* magic' and they flounced out of the shop. All we will say in response, is that the 'guardian' remains in place in our neck of the woods and if any venture there with vandalism in their hearts ... well, as Pris said earlier 'So mote it be!'

The year had nearly come full circle and it wasn't long before we discovered what Granny had been up to in her dealings with 'arfa Kinsman. We often find that long-term magical situations or problems resolve themselves between the Autumnal Equinox and All Hallows in a general tidying-up before the end of the year. And prior to the forthcoming Equinox there seemed to be an awful lot of tidying-up that needed to be done.

The two main issues – Gordon and 'arfa Kinsman – were still unresolved and while there had been some significant develop-ments on both fronts, they still remained a problem for the

Coven and its members. Christine's behaviour was now public knowledge and 'Young' Joe had wasted no time in informing his son that he was being made a fool of in the eyes of his mates — most of whom had already enjoyed Christine's favours.

Gordon, to his naïve credit, still wanted to believe the best about the girl who'd set his heart aflame and appeared deaf to his father's revelations. That said, he made no move to ask for Rupert's help in ending his three-month stint working away from home. In fact, he made it quite plain that he was more than happy to be a long way from the machinations of Pentecostal pressuring and was more than happy to stay on for a while.

'Arfa Kinsman, however, had been around long enough now for everyone in the Coven to be heartily sick and tired of him. His presence in the area was like a winter malady, inasmuch as his malevolence was quiet and non-specific, but the effects were proving to be – if not deadly – certainly unwelcome and unpleasant, and possibly long lasting.

When Rupert discovered that Granny had been tampering with May Butterworth's cakes he was, in the well-publicised style of the Prince of Wales, 'incandescent with rage' and the rest of us made sure we were conspicuous by our absence when he delivered his edict. Not only was Granny's method illegal, she had gone against a specific directive of the Man in Black and that was tantamount to heresy in our eyes. That meant she was formally banished from the Coven and the rest of us were forbidden to intercede on her behalf.

Granny, of course, is *old* Old Craft and a law unto herself. She had set in motion a sequence of cause and effect that was almost impossible to reel back in, even if she'd felt so inclined … which we were pretty certain she wasn't! The rest of the story filtered through to us via various different channels, the first being Pris, who volunteered to call at the cottage one evening just to make sure the old girl wasn't suicidal or, worse still, homicidal.

She found Granny sitting with her feet nicely tucked up

against the old Rayburn, and holding her customary mug of strong tea. Pris pulled up a chair and a mug and they sat in companionable silence for while ... then began to chuckle over a series of gruesome endings for 'arfa Kinsman. Much as it was tempting to go for something permanent, Granny reflected aloud, he wasn't actually worth *that* much effort. The fact that he had to go was without doubt, although the fact that he should be allowed to live she considered to be an inconvenient by-product of Rupert's *edictum*.

The old clock laboured heavily on towards midnight, and the shadows deepened, but still they pondered on the problem. 'What about a plague of boils of biblical proportion?' suggested Pris, her thoughts running over Kinsman's attachment to the pustular postulant, and reflecting her own loathing of the pair. The clock's discordant chimes rang out in the gloom, but it was closer to two o' clock before a satisfied grin suddenly lit up Granny's lined face. With a satisfied grunt, and some grumbling about old bones, Granny unceremoniously showed Pris the door and shuffled off to bed, no doubt to sleep soundly.

According to her custom, the following morning saw Granny up and about as early as ever. A lifetime of late nights and midnight cogitations has conditioned her body to grab whatever sleep it can, yet she is still awake early enough to be abroad before anyone else. A cup of tea, strong enough to double as paint stripper, always does the trick, and after two steaming half-pint mugs of the stuff, Granny was, as usual, ready to face the day.

Gossip told us that her first port of call was at a small holding some quarter of a mile away, which still went by the quaint local name of Farmer's Bottom. When the new owners moved in two years previously, Granny had made a point of calling and introducing herself. Regular (though uninvited) visits had succeeded in Granny fooling the new folk into accepting her as a well meaning but slightly dotty local character. If the truth be told,

Granny, as usual, had her own agenda.

This five, unfarmable acres adjoined Rupert's land, and as an infrequently used right of way ran across a corner of the bottom field, Granny wanted to keep both eyes and ears open for any talk of future building plans. The new people were 'townies' as she disparagingly described them – and pleasant though they may be, they would never be accepted and fully trusted by the present generation of locals. A modest Lottery win and a flashy 4x4 did not compensate for having the 'land in the blood', was the general consensus of opinion.

The one thing that had Granny really rattled was the fact that the couple were raising their two children as vegetarians. It wasn't so much the fact that they chose not to eat meat, as the fact that this enforced diet did not appear to be doing either of the children a lot of good. Pale faced and whining, the two boys were rarely seen playing outside, and when they did, they appeared reluctant to engage in any of the 'normal' games that country children play. The joys of slinging cow pats, chasing hens, climbing trees and falling out of a rope swing were unknown to them – and Granny often muttered to Pris that 'it wasn't normal for kids to be so clean'. Privately most folk felt that it wasn't normal to be quite so *unclean* as Granny – but these opinions were firmly left unsaid. Dropping a small pot of un-labelled salve into her copious pocket (according to the postman), the old witch had set off with a firm tread in the hope of catching her neighbours having breakfast. There would be no chance of a decent bacon sandwich, but Mrs Norman did make rather good homemade jam and a few rounds of hot toast would save Granny the chore of having washing-up to do later.

It transpired that the previous day, Mrs Norton had seen fit to mention that the children were suffering from a very unpleasant form of eczema, which seemed impervious to anything the local doctor had prescribed. Granny's skill with herbs was known far and wide, and today's visit was geared round taking something to cure the affliction. No doubt Granny chuckled to herself as she walked – the Old Gods had never failed her yet when it came to solutions – and her 'mission of mercy' was a convenient beginning to solving the problem of 'arfa Kinsman once and for all. We should have known better than to believe her reluctant promises!

At the Farmer's Bottom, Granny peered closely at the children's heads and faces: it was a nasty case of scald-head and no doubt about it. The cracked skin on the ears, lips and even their eyelids, was weeping and red, and the accompanied itching had the two boys whining even more than usual. Granny having whispered something to them, they both nodded, round eyed and silent, making no protest as she swirled a crooked finger round the pot, before anointing every trace of redness. In less than a minute the boys were running around looking much more cheerful – yelling that they 'didn't tickle' any more.

As she later told a neighbour, Mrs Norman was, of course, genuinely grateful and, insisting Granny stay for toast and a cup of tea, offered to buy the salve. This had, however, vanished back into the darker regions of the waxed coat pocket. 'Oh, now I can't go letting you 'av that one, m' dear,' smiled Granny, camping up the local accent, 'but I'll surely drop you another pot in tomorrow.'

Mrs Norton was bemused. 'But it's such a trail up the long field – surely I could buy the ointment and save you the trouble of another walk?' she queried.

But Granny wasn't to be persuaded, she simply smiled and said, 'Oh no, you see this one is promised,' and with that she took her leave.

By the time Granny had walked down into the village, the front door of the Duck & Ferret stood wide open, and May Butterworth was just arriving in her old van stacked to the gunnels with trays of homemade pastries. The one-time rivals nodded and exchanged the traditional village greeting which sounded something akin to *'Nah'all'*. No one could remember just what it had originally meant, but roughly translated it was something close to, 'How are you?' – but as Granny always said – intention is everything.

'What brings you down here?' May had asked, eyeing her with some suspicion.

'Oh, just thought I'd give you a bit of a hand,' smiled Granny, as she sallied forth into the dark interior of the pub, carrying a tray of pasties.

The autumn sun not having reached the front windows, the interior was still cold and dark, and Granny had to squint to see that the figure behind the bar was indeed 'arfa Kinsman. He appeared to be checking an invoice, and only looked up when she suddenly manifested in front of him out of the gloom. Before he had time to escape, this terrifying old woman was peering closely at his face, and exclaiming: *'What's that!'*

In the narrow confines of the bar 'arfa Kinsman had little chance of retreating further than a foot, and in some alarm he put his hands to his face. 'What's what?' he squeaked, before clearing his throat and attempting to assume a degree of dignity.

Granny shook her head slowly, sucking on her startlingly white teeth in true Crone-mode, and with a worried frown, replied: 'Oooh, you want to be careful about *that,* lad. There's a lot of it going about at this time of year. Why only today I seen two children fairly afflicted with it.' According to the ever-observant May, you could have cut the 'local dialect' with a knife!

By now Kinsman *was* worried, and would have whirled round to look in the large mirrored wall behind him, except that when he attempted to – he found his tie caught in Granny's unwholesome grasp. Before he could react, she'd fumbled in her pocket and produced the pot of ointment. With one finger she flipped open the jar and without further ado, daubed a hefty dollop of goo onto his ear, followed by a liberal application all over his face and neck.

'There,' she said, relinquishing her hold on his tie and breaking into a menacingly pleasant smile. 'That will sort you once and for all, my lad ... oh aye, sort you good that will ... never fails to sort doesn't this stuff.' And with that, she snapped the lid closed, jammed the jar in her pocket, and left without looking back.

May Butterworth wasn't privy to Granny's 'cunning little plan' but she knew that something had passed between the manager and the old witch, so she hung about to watch developments. 'arfa Kinsman felt at his face, it didn't feel sore, and whatever weird substance the old woman had daubed on him had already soaked into his skin. Examining his reflection, he couldn't see anything wrong, and shaking his head he smirked to himself, obviously thinking that she was as nutty as a fruitcake and probably hadn't a magical bone in her body. The arrival of May's pastries was far more important, and Granny was soon forgotten as he busied himself in the kitchen.

Gossiping with one of the barmaids, May Butterworth discovered that the next morning Kinsman had woken up, full of the joys of self importance, and eager to make a good impression. A large party had booked in for lunch, and he was keen to start chivvying the kitchen staff into an important sounding bustle of activity. The party was made up of Licensed Victuallers, and if he could give a good demonstration of his managerial skills, there may even be a chance of a permanent place at the Duck & Ferret.

A lot hinged on the success of the luncheon and, fastening the cuffs on his best blue shirt, he whistled as he took the stairs two at a time. He could shave and finish his toilet later – but first he wanted to make certain that the kitchen *was* a hive of activity. He burst through the swing-doors and was nearly blown back out again by the heat from the ovens, but he was gratified to see the preparations were well under way. Bottles of wine stood ready, gleaming cutlery was waiting on steel trays, and the smell of roasting beef was already permeating the air.

He mopped his brow, and backed away to the safety of the bar. The heat in the kitchen had made him itch, but the cool air soothed the burning, prickly sensation that was beginning to irritate him. He mopped the sweat away once more, but the itching increased. With some annoyance he ran his handkerchief under the cold tap and mopped again – this time the itching seemed to die down, and he promptly got busy restocking the bar. He didn't want to risk the slightest thing being at fault when the Licensed Victuallers arrived for lunch.

At twelve o' clock sharp, a mini-bus rolled to a halt, and a dozen or so smartly dressed gentlemen made their way into the Duck & Ferret for lunch. Kinsman straightened his tie and went forth to meet his public. A shriek from the barmaid focussed all eyes on Kinsman's face. It was not a pretty sight: from hairline to collar it was a livid with weeping pustules that seemed to break out almost as they watched. His ears stood out like beacons, while his pale eyes looked most peculiar against the angry blotches. Suddenly aware of a strange sensation, he rubbed frantically, which only triggered off the awful itching, and 'arfa Kinsman was forced to retire to his room with the worst case of scald-head ever seen in the village.

The Licensed Victuallers, having taken one look at this awful spectre, had turned on their heels and left, vowing to find another venue – even if they had to settle for fish and chips. Words like 'disgraceful', 'revolting', and 'unhealthy' were overheard, and two days later a rather terse letter arrived announcing an impending visit to the Duck & Ferret by Environmental Health officials. The best laid plans of mice and men can always come unstuck, and a week later 'arfa Kinsman was last seen leaving in a taxi – a small removal van following behind – and leaving no forwarding address. His short reign at the Duck & Ferret had come to an untimely end – while his eczema lived on unchallenged – and impervious to anything the dermatologists prescribed.

As Pris later commented, he and the pustular postulant now didn't spoil a matching pair. Rupert heard the tale in silence but it was obvious that he was desperately trying not to laugh as he tacked up the horse for a morning ride out.

It wasn't until I was clearing out the usual debris that accumulates in farmhouse kitchens that I re-discovered the fetish that Rupert had found concealed in his saddle earlier in the year. It had been stuck on top of the dresser in a sealed glass jar so, in effect, the ill-wishing that had probably come with it was contained in a traditional 'witch bottle'. As it was impossible to determine the precise nature of the hex it was pointless attempting to return 'it' ... whatever 'it' was, and so it was best left alone and buried somewhere well away from the house and yard.

It was important that the witch bottle remained sealed ... a fact that had completely escaped one witch of our acquaintance. On removing a similar object from a victim's home, he had promptly taken it down to the canal and emptied the contents into the dark sluggish waters, and then chucked the bottle in after them! This meant that the hex was completely uncontained and uncontrollable and if he thought that stretch of the Trent & Mersey possessed the cleansing properties of 'clear, running water' then he needed to re-assess his magical training!

On a more personal level, I'd my own personal axe to grind over the pustular postulant. True, she'd tried to inveigle her way into both our Coven and our lives, but also had several attempts at trying her hand at seducing Rupert. I'd actually overheard a couple of the exchanges and my old Man had been positively rude to her but it didn't dampen her ardour – or her determination to be accepted into the Coven by fair means or foul. Thoughtfully, I weighed the witch bottle in my hand and visualised the spotty mess that was the pustular postulant's face.

Without further ado I dropped the jar into the old slurry pit.

It briefly floated on top of the foul-smelling liquid, then the thin crust parted and the witch bottle disappeared from view with a highly appropriate burp. It was consigned to the murky depths of the slurry pit with a few well-chosen words of my own. Vengeance is mine, sayeth the Dame!

No matter how many so-called festivals are now included in the pagan calendar, for our ancestors there were only two important divisions in the year: summer and winter ... the seed-time and harvest ... the turning out of livestock and the bringing it back in again. These were the ancient divisions of the year in all parts of Britain although, because of the differences in regional climate and temperature, the festivals could be observed several weeks apart.

Summer would have been heralded by the flowering of the hawthorn and the sprouting of the spring grass; winter would have come when the last of the harvest was gathered in and the stock brought home for culling. All the hard work through the long summer months would be celebrated and nature's bounty acknowledged. There were times, of course, when the harvest was poor and there would have been little to celebrate ... even in our time there have been years when the harvest has failed.

But this year there were no such fears for the future and for the Coven there is no celebration more important than the Harvest Home. It is an occasion we share with our fellow coveners and those who work for us on the farm. It's often been observed that there have always been two religions in the British Isles: the doctrine of the church and the old, pre-Christian religion followed by those whose lives depended on the land. This is why the early church was forced to adopt many of the old indigenous traditions and bring them within the framework of the religious calendar.

Many of these old practices remained outside the parameters of the church, however, and still survive today in what has been called the 'rural underground'. A farmer can take all care and precaution humanly possible but still harbour the sure knowledge that he is powerless against the vagaries of Nature, should she decide to thwart him. Although these beliefs may appear out-dated and irrational to some who call themselves pagan, we nevertheless continue to observe them. For this reason the Man in Black will pour the last drop of the 'harvest cup' onto the ground as a libation.

Pris had volunteered to do the catering for our Harvest Home and so we decided to clear out the big barn for the occasion and hold a good old fashioned barn-dance to round off the evening. It was the very morning of the Harvest Home when we heard that Christine had eloped with a pharmaceutical salesman, who called regularly at the chemist shop where she worked. To me it sounded like something that only happened in a John Steinbeck novel but I hoped she'd be happier wherever she was than continuing to be used as a pawn in the religious chess-game played by her parents. At least the girl now had her freedom, but I still felt that Granny had been playing a dangerous game.

Gordon was making coffee in the tack room when I finally managed to catch him alone. 'I hope you're not too upset by Christine running off and leaving you like that,' I said.

'Well, she didn't exactly run off,' he answered. 'Her folks kept nagging me to leave the stables and get a better job and a couple of days ago, her father said he'd got me a job in a factory. I told him I wasn't working in any factory, and he said he wasn't having any stable lad marrying *his* daughter. I just said that was fine by me and if he was forcing me to choose between Christine and the horses, then there was no contest. This is where I belong and if they can't see that … anyway, next thing I know she's gone.'

'I'm glad if that's what you feel is right,' I said, thinking that here was a chip off his old granddad's block and perhaps Rupert should let him have the old boy's cottage once the short-term lease was up.

'It's in my blood, Mrs P,' he was saying. 'This ... the stables ... the horses ... and the Coven. It's just that I'd never ... well, let's just say she glamoured me and I'm over it now. I think I'm going to be like granddad,' he said, almost as if he were reading my thoughts. 'You'll have to carry me out in my box.' *Rooted and bound, rooted and bound ...*

Later that evening the trestle tables were groaning with harvest fare and the fifty or so revellers were showing their appreciation by clearing their plates and not refusing a second-helping. A thick game soup with fresh crusty bread and butter was followed by a choice of baked ham and homemade pickles, or huge slices of May Butterworth's game pie, with baked potatoes and salad. May's apple and blackberry pie was served with lashings of fresh cream, followed by a selection of local cheeses. Pris had done us proud.

This was a 'working' meal and offered the type of food that would have been waiting in the farmhouse kitchen following a long day in the fields. Tonight, however, everyone was spruced up and taking full advantage of the copious supplies of beer, cider and robust red wine. At the end of the meal, before the tables were moved for dancing, Rupert proposed a toast to the bountiful harvest and was joined in a rousing rendering of *John Barleycorn, The Lincolnshire Poacher, John Peel* and *The Farmer's Boy,* all with varying degrees of inebriation.

Madeleine and Robert had flown back from Dubai, expressly to join the party; as had Richard and Philly, who had taken time off from their studies. Gordon's fling with Christine and his subsequent temporary job with an important racehorse trainer had given him a new-found confidence. He'd gone off a likeable lad and returned a handsome young man, who'd been surrounded by a bevy of local girls throughout the meal. We have to let them go ... so that eventually they come back.

A local folk-group provided the music and the evening was in full swing when Granny sidled up to me, having been allowed back from her brief exile now that Christine and 'arfa Kinsman had left the area.

'How did you do it?' she asked between sips of cider.

'Do what?'

'Prise the lad off that girl. I took care of her all right but he was a bit of a sticker. Thought for a time we'd lose him.'

'Just a matter of knowing the right application,' I replied in a non-committal way.

The old girl glanced at me sharply and I knew I'd hit a raw nerve. She obviously thought I'd not heard about her deliberately infecting 'arfa Kinsman with scald-head, but May Butterworth hadn't been slow in seeing an opportunity to pay Granny back for all the grievances that had piled up over the years. They might now be good pals on the surface but these old country women can harbour a grudge worse than any Borgia.

Granny had merely overlooked the obvious in her approach to the problem but it wouldn't hurt her to wonder about what kind of magic I'd used to bring things back under our control. She'd judged us all incapable of sorting out the problems and taken it upon herself to show us how things were done in the Old Ways. In doing so, she had broken a hundred-year-old tradition of not going against the express order of the Man in Black, and if we *were* still operating under the laws of the Old Ways, she would have been strangled with her own cord!

Rooted and bound, rooted and bound ...

There was one last task to perform and this was to be a symbolic gesture of sowing wild-flower seeds in the grass margins. In the old days, the sowing of the corn was attended by all manner of rites and observations before the land was considered fit for drilling. In these times of modern agricultural methods many of these methods have fallen by the wayside but there are those that still endure. To test if the land is ready, the farmer simply walks across his fields and 'to feel it through his boots' as he takes up a handful of soil, in just the same way as they did back in the 16th century.

Sound like superstitious nonsense? A 16th century writer on agriculture named Fitzherbert wrote: *'Go upon the land that is ploughed and if it synge or crye or make any noise under thy fete, then it is to wet to sowe. And if it make no noyse and will bear thy horses, thanne sowe in the name of Godd.'*

We decided to sow the wild-flower seeds as an offering after the Harvest Home simply because in the wild, the seeds were already in the ground, and many of them benefit from being frozen during the winter months as an aid to germination. Another old country belief is that all seed should be sown while the moon is waxing and harvested when the moon is waning.

The new moon was only two days away and it was on this late September night that Rupert and Adam made their way through the darkness of the yard to where an old hay turner partially concealed the fiddle drill. Rupert glanced at Adam and grinned – his teeth showing unnervingly white in the gloom. 'Okay, which of us is going to make the biggest prat of ourselves then?' he asked. Without hesitation Adam volunteered Rupert for the job of shouldering the strange instrument. Rupert chuckled good naturedly. 'Suits me fine. It just means that you get to haul that bloody great bag of seed along while capering in an unmanly fashion behind me.'

The two men guffawed like schoolboys, having fortified themselves for the ordeal with a hefty portion of *Grouse*. Then they both became serious. The same thought crossed both their minds as they shrugged out of their clothes and decided to cheat by putting boxers, socks and boots back on. 'It's all very well keeping the faith,' muttered Adam, 'but I for one don't want to find some bloody abandoned needle through my foot.'

Rupert nodded. 'Yup – common sense in all things these days, I'm afraid – besides we've got to have somewhere to keep the first aid flask.'

Without another word he shouldered the cumbersome drill, and looked to see if Adam was ready. Adam hoisted the half sack and giving the 'thumbs up', they stepped out of the barn into the chill night air, glancing up at the moon. Light clouds scudded across her face, but it was otherwise clear, and with a sense of purpose the two men set off along the hedgerow. In the distance a dog barked, but apart from the slight swish of their own feet in the long headland grass, the night was calm and quiet.

Rupert began to work the drill, and soon fell into a rhythm that Adam had no trouble in following. As the last sounds of civilisation fell away into the night, Adam began the old chant of the fields. The whirl of the drill strings was a two-time beat, and the two men fell easily into step with it, Adam maintaining the chant, while Rupert took up the chorus. In the damp night air, a steady spray of seed fell silently to earth, and the chant became more insistent.

To a casual onlooker the sight of two grown men in boxers and boots, pacing steadfastly through the darkness, while muttering some gibberish may have appeared more than mildly ridiculous. Especially as the arm-action required to work a fiddle drill bears an uncanny likeness to what Adam insisted on referring to as 'unnatural practices' and which never failed to inspire a great deal of mirth and ribald comments among those who witnessed it. Granny had once muttered darkly at this childish humour and bit back saying, 'Why the devil do you think it *is* used, you clowns!' which was quite a sobering thought.

Against the backdrop of owls hooting, and the odd scream of the fox, Adam and Rupert worked steadily round the boundary fields. The chanting became hypnotic and they walked on in a strange state of mind. The whirl of the drill, and the fall of the seed, created an eerie musical background to the old words of the charm. As they approached the almost total blackness of the top spinney, the spell was suddenly broken.

Rupert let out a howl as he lost his footing on the slope and skidded on the wet, churned up mud that formed the cows' favourite watering hole. Adam came to with a start just in time to see Rupert slithering down the embankment towards the stream – legs splayed out and the fiddle drill halfway over his head. His own whoop of laughter was cut short when his own feet shot out from under him, and in spite of a valiant effort, he too went sprawling in the mud. Face down and travelling at what felt like warp speed, he cannoned into Rupert, knocking the drill out of his hands. The two men just gave in and rolled about, helpless with laughter.

'Well, that's one way of honouring the age old custom of testing the earth to see if it's ready for sowing,' said Adam dryly, referring to the practice of testing the warmth of the earth through the most sensitive part of the anatomy. Suddenly, it dawned on them that the water was actually *very* cold – and what they were sitting in wasn't simply mud.

'My God you stink!' roared Rupert, to which Adam replied, 'Yeah, well, they always reckon that foxes smell their own first.'

The banter went on as they hauled themselves up and scrambled up the banking. Filthy, smelly and decidedly dishevelled, they examined the drill. 'Thank the gods there's no harm done,' Rupert commented.

Adam looked ruefully at the depleted seed bag. 'I think the old spinney's got a bit more than its fair share, but c'mon, there's still enough here to see us round.'

Rupert shielded his eyes in a mock gesture. 'Onwards and upwards then … c'mon soldier let's get finished, I'm frozen stiff.'

As they were about to set off Adam let out a yell. 'Damn! Where's the flask?' The thought of his beloved hip-flask basking in the stream was too much to contemplate. Without thinking he plunged back down the embankment and began grovelling about in the dark. Suddenly there was a loud whoop of success. 'Got it! Give us a hand up or I'll drink it all myself.'

That threat alone was an inspiration in itself; Rupert held out a muddy hand and hauled Adam back up the banking. Once on terra firma again they wasted no time in knocking back the contents of the flask. The hypnotic mood had been broken, but as both the drill and they were still in one piece they decided to press on and finish the job.

'In for a penny – in for a pound,' Rupert grunted, as he shouldered the drill and struck out again along the hedge.

Adam topped the drill-bag up again and nodded. 'What is it that these modern pagans say about rituals of love and laughter? Well, the Old Bugger is certainly having a laugh at us tonight.'

Rupert grinned as he replied. 'We must look a bonny pair, let's press on before dawn breaks and someone catches us looking like this.' Resolutely they set off again: after a few minutes they fell back into step, and the chanting continued – albeit a bit more subdued than before. It was a tired, cold, hungry and footsore pair that crept into the yard just as the light was breaking towards the east. Moving stealthily, Rupert pressed the latch on the old kitchen door, and opened it very slowly without a creak.

'Thank goodness the Aga's still going full pelt, I'm frozen,' I heard him whisper as he crept across the kitchen. He let Adam close the door and just as he set off towards the welcoming warmth, the overhead lights snapped on.

'Hold it right there!' said Pris. The sight that met our eyes was one that we would never forget and, thanks to a disposable camera, it was one that neither Rupert nor Adam would ever be allowed to. 'Out to the trough, *right now*,' she bellowed. 'If you two think for one moment that you're skulking in here smelling like that, you've got another think coming.'

Without a word of retaliation the two men turned and sheepishly made for the door. The sight of the two behinds, clad in muddy, wet boxer shorts that drooped and slapped against two small cold bottoms sent us both over the edge. Weak with laughing, but still sharp enough to spot the moment, I made sure the camera flashed again, and the men bolted for the safety of the yard to undergo further humiliation.

'Do we call this 'one for posterity'?' howled Pris, but the best was yet to come.

Our lurcher, woken by the noise, had come out to see what all the fuss was about and with a quizzical look, plonked his haunches down on the cobbles to watch. Now in his time he had enjoyed rolling in just about every revolting concoction available to a dog. From dead sheep to fox droppings, he had wriggled with delight in them all – only to have to suffer the discomfort of being hosed down before being allowed back in the house. Hosed down, in fact, at the side of the very same trough that the two men now dithered beside. He licked his lips and settled down to watch. Without further ado, Pris turned on the hose and the two men reluctantly struggled with caked-on mud and streaks of 'nervous cow'. Dripping from head to foot, boxer shorts clinging pitifully to their legs, we eventually took pity on them.

'Oh enough, I can't stand to see a grown man suffer,' I giggled.

'Oh, I can,' Pris replied, 'I haven't laughed so much since Walter Middleton tried to take that old gelding of his wife's hunting. It must have galloped four miles with him – trouble was it was *away* from the field and then came home without him, having deposited the old boy in a slurry pit.'

Her reminiscing was broken by Rupert. 'I'm frozen stiff and I have every intention of entering my own home right now.' He strode haughtily away towards the kitchen. Adam only hesitated for a second before bolting after him.

Pris and I exchanged sidelong grins and winked. 'Okay boys, a joke's a joke, but you two are cold. The water's piping hot, so dash off and have a shower before you catch your deaths.'

'We'll get on with breakfast,' I added, 'and we'll ask them how they got in that state later.'

It might not have been the most sophisticated ritual in the

history of Craft, but it was one in time-honoured tradition. Pris and I had performed a similar women's rite during the previous year, and it says a lot for our menfolk that they were willing to subject themselves to the cold and humiliation that only the Old Ones can inflict on us when they wish to amuse themselves at our expense. Few people today give them the opportunity since most contemporary rituals are conducted behind closed doors.

All Hallows

The night was clear and sharp. Immediately overhead the Milky Way stretched from the eastern to the western horizon and the huge full moon hung low and orange in the south. This was a very special occasion since it marked not only our All Hallows gathering but was also a 'blue moon' – when there are two full moons in a calendar month. And, with the coming of winter, we could see at last the return of the Hunter, followed by the Dog Star, climbing in the South-East.

It was to be a full Coven meeting – all those who had undergone Initiation and, for the first time in many years, included Granny. She'd muttered something about 'seeing if Old Joe were alright' and wasn't going to be put off by the fact that it would mean walking across several fields, climbing stiles and negotiating stepping stones across a small stream. It was on the way home from this site that Pris had encountered the bull at last Winter Solstice but this time Joseph was safely penned back at the farm.

Another year was over and we'd managed to come through it reasonably unscathed, although Rupert admitted that he was becoming more and more jaded by Craft with each passing year. He still enjoyed working with Pris and Adam, simply because we know each other so well, but a full Coven gathering was something he could well live without – especially as Granny was coming too!

'It will sound like a bloody Salvation Army band, traipsing across those fields,' he grumbled. 'And some idiot is sure to fall in the stream … And what does that silly old fool want to come for, anyway? She's just out to cause trouble, I know it. Probably because you outsmarted her over Gordon … She'll be up to her old tricks, you mark my words.'

'We can hardly refuse her under the circumstances,' I replied, mentally ticking off who would be coming to the gathering.

Apart from myself and Rupert, there would be Pris and Adam, Gerry and Guy, Madelaine and Robert, Gordon and Granny, which made ten in all. With a place laid for the 'dumb supper', we were only two short of a traditional Coven – but it was enough. It would have been nice to include Philly and Richard (who weren't old enough to take Initiation) and Abi and Carole (who were only beginners) but Coven rules are there to be observed, not broken.

By way of a compromise, Rupert had been up to the site earlier that afternoon and collected enough firewood to see us through the long night. He had also lugged Pris's huge cauldron containing a rich beef stew since one vessel large enough to feed ten hungry witches would have taken some carrying, and none of us were getting any younger. The rest would have to manage carrying the bread and wine between them, he said.

By the time we'd all arrived at the working site, the fire was glowing and the cauldron bubbling away, wafting the smell of stew out under the trees. Drawing on his woodman's skills, Rupert had set the fire-pit earlier and the food would be ready for when the ritual ended. Although it wasn't a cold night, the welcoming glow from the fire meant that we could all robe in comfort, instead of shivering behind the bushes. Usually *someone* falls over when hopping from one leg to another, trying to remove boots under the cover of darkness … that is, if they haven't gone in the stream first.

'What do you reckon Granny's up to?' whispered Pris as she pulled on her robe.

'Rupert reckons she's only here to cause trouble,' I answered softly, so as not to be overheard.

'She wouldn't dare,' said Pris. 'Not here, not tonight. She's too much respect for the Old Ways, even if she hasn't any for its officers.'

'Well, brace yourself Myrtle,' I replied, 'we'll find out soon enough.'

One by one, ten cowled figures formed the Circle around the fire, each standing with their heads bowed, hands folded inside the sleeves of their robes. This was the quiet-time needed to separate the mundane from the spiritual, and at this point all tom-foolery ceased; each person drawing on the teaching of the Old Ways according to their own individual lights.

Everyone has their own way of preparing themselves for Circle and I glanced around at my fellow coveners, wondering what was going through their minds at this precise moment in time. Immediately opposite me stood Gordon, his handsome features accentuated by the flickering firelight under the shadow of the cowl. Was he thinking about Christine, or had he put all that aside now that he knew where he belonged. And Granny. Was she thinking about her youth when she and Old Joe had their little fling?

It was a glorious night and if we'd have tried to create a blueprint for the perfect conditions for an outdoor ritual, this could not have been bettered. The moon was veiled by a slight haze, which meant the woods were bathed in a muted light as we waited for the signs that we were welcome. One by one they came. One by one those standing at the Quarters acknowledged the acceptance and the rite was allowed to begin. The Horned Keeper of the woods and dales was being summoned ...

It seems like a contradiction in terms to say that the ritual was carefully choreographed and yet each individual acted according to the spontaneous impulses of his or her nature. The power was built and the Circle enhanced: outside a dog fox called to the vixen, while overhead owls hunted and called. Pacing the Circle, the Old Words rose and fell in a rhythmic chant, we all began to feel the razor-edge of the psychic cold enveloping the sacred space.

The power was building and flowing in outward-circling spirals, as the gaps between the trees glowed with a faint blue, luminous light. On the periphery of my vision I could make out a vaporous, cowled figure pacing on the outside of the Circle in unison with our own rhythmic steps. One by one the Coven members noticed it and slowly all movement ceased as we silently welcomed our visitor – whoever it may be.

As the others admitted later, it was probably the most exhilarating experience any of us had ever had during an All Hallows ritual. We pay homage to our Ancestors but rarely do we get the opportunity to meet them cowl to cowl, as it were. The previous year Granny had told us of the war-time ritual that had gone so horribly wrong, and that she had never since managed to make contact with anything ever again during group work. Now, on the very night she was with us for the first in years, it had happened again.

Pris must have been thinking about the same thing, because at that moment we both glanced at Granny. Under the shadow of her hood, tears were streaming down her cheeks but the look of rapt wonder was a sight we'd never seen before on the old witch's face. Unconsciously she wiped her nose on her sleeve but never took her eyes from the Old One as she sunk to the knees on the hard ground.

PART THREE: COLD COMFORT COVEN

GABRIELLE SIDONIE

Curtain Call

Coarse Witchcraft 3: Cold Comfort Coven is the third and long-awaited, last in the series. In the country, it has always been considered good manners to know when to leave and, after three rollicking titles about what it's like to belong to a good, old-fashioned rural coven, we've decided to call it a day.

This decision has been influenced by certain unforeseen events that have had far-reaching repercussions on both the Coven and its members. The choice was not taken lightly but it was the Will of all, since we valued our privacy and felt that this was being infringed by the continual seeking out of our where-abouts by those who should know better. In short, the unwelcome attention that the Coven generated became untenable and so the move was made to go back into the Shadows.

We ticked along behind closed stable doors and tried to keep as far 'from the madding crowd' as possible, in order to keep our families free from the prying eyes of those who would expose our true identities to the pagan world. This goes against the old magical adage of 'Keeping Silence' but few appear to respect the fact that we did not wish to become public property. Even those close to us had been guilty of indiscretion.

It has also came to our notice that certain well-known pagans were claiming to know us personally and regaling others with claims of having actually been in Circle with us. At risk of causing offence and embarrassing them, we would say lies, lies and more lies! We have no knowledge of those outside our own Old Craft tradition, and we have no desire to impart our working methods to 'cowans', i.e. non-witches. There are no casual or 'honorary' members of our Coven because everyone has 'done their time' and proved their worth to the satisfaction of the Elders according to *our* ways.

Those of us left will, of course, continue to work our Craft in tune with the seasons. The continual cycle of birth, death and rebirth is ingrained in our souls and we could no more abandon that way of life any more than we could alter *what* we are. The Land, and the Old Lad, will always be the prime focus of our ways, for we can never leave it ... it has been said many times before, you can take the man out of the country but you cannot take the country out of the man. And without the Land there can be no Old Craft for us.

When we wrote *Coarse Witchcraft: Craft Working*, there was the honest intention of trying to reveal some of the Old Ways without becoming too dogmatic about the manner in which things should be done, or breaking any oaths. To a certain extent this idea worked and the majority of readers have laughed with us (and at themselves) but several years down the line the mood has changed. To make no bones about it ... it's no fun anymore.

Gabrielle Sidonie

Forever Autumn

Through autumn's golden gown we used to kick our way,
You always loved this time of year.
Those fallen leaves lie undisturbed now
'cause you're not here …

The radio announcer's voice cut abruptly through the lyric to give an update on the current world banking crisis, and I stared bleakly out of the window. That had always been Rupert's favourite song but it had now taken on a new significance. Philly had finished her inspection of the cottage and now leaned against the sink in my pristine Smallbones kitchen, waiting for coffee and Danish pastries.

'Never had you figured for a minimalist, Ma,' she said, 'but I approve. The unspoken words, however, hung in the air between us. Rupert would have hated it!

There was hardly anything to remind us of the Farm, except for a handful of carefully chosen pieces of furniture, a couple of pictures and the large bronze greyhound from the hall table that Rupert had given me as a wedding anniversary gift. The cottage itself was almost unrecognisable from the hideous pink blancmange and sea shells of the previous owners. Even the name had been changed from 'Pixie Cottage' to plain and simple '3 High Street' – despite the neighbours' plea that the nauseous reconstituted stone fairies should remain on the verge! We might have a splash of faere-blood in our veins but we're certainly not of the gossamer winged variety.

Philly's off to Newmarket in November to complete her equine veterinary studies, while her brother oversees the transformation of the Farm from general purpose farming to high-tech Stud for racehorses, eventually with its own veterinary clinic. At least this way there's no question of breaking it all up for inheritance, and both have always been good mates – I just didn't want to stay there now that their father was gone. It's actually good fun having a grown-up witchlet for a daughter and we've been having some amazing 'magical conversations', which demonstrates just how much she's really learned about Craft over the years. It's also reassuring to know that the next generation of Old Craft has been well-grounded in the Old Ways, despite their progressive ambitions. And I was missing Pris's company less and less as the weeks slipped by.

Life had shattered into fragments like the crystal bowl I once dropped on the flagstone floor – totally irreparable but each fragment shimmering like a tiny diamond amid the devastation. Those of us with witch-blood, however, know that the dead are always with us and there's very little they don't know about 'on the other side'. I'd been agonising over what to do and had turned to a bit of comfort reading in an old Agatha Christie mystery when the words leapt off the page … 'To know when to go – that was one of the great necessities of life. To go before one's powers began to fail, one's sure grip to loosen, before one felt the faint staleness, the unwillingness to envisage continuing effort.'

Magic works in mysterious ways – and I'd previously sent out an astral call for direction – the secret is the knowing *how* to recognise and interpret the answer. Most pagans expect the 'message' to come through with blinding flashing lights and a clap of thunder, but things are usually much subtler than that. More often than not, the solution appears to have little or no bearing on things magical in the slightest and, as a result, the sign is ignored and not acted upon. I knew this was *my* 'sign' because the novel was called *Cat Among The Pigeons*, which was one of Rupert's favourite sayings. It was time to leave the Farm.

And so here I was in a tiny cottage in St Agnes On The Pull, a few miles from the Farm and starting anew in Crone-mode, as Philly called it, away from all the heartbreaking memories. Hopefully, in this cottage in a country village I could reconstruct my life, piece myself together again and draw on the toughness of body and mind, like the heroine of Francoise Sagan's *Wonderful Clouds* … it was *my* unquenchable optimism that at the moment was the only constant element of my nature. And I spent a lot of time reading old favourites that I hadn't looked at for years.

'Do you miss Pris,' asked Philly as we drank our coffee.

'I miss what we had, not what it became,' I replied evasively. 'There was a cuckoo in the nest and with all the tittle-tattling, the lies and half-truths, it got so tangled that it was impossible to straighten things out again. The Coven became too confused and angry, and with your father gone, I really couldn't be bothered to get involved with the in-fighting. Why do you think the Old Craft motto is: Trust None! We trusted and that trust was turned against us. But if I'm honest, yes, I will *always* miss Pris being around. Pris and Adam will always be fondly remembered as part of the good times.'

'So what now?'

'You should know by now that you don't stop being a witch because there's no working Coven. We are what we are, every single day of our lives … the ethos of the Coven will always be with us as long as we remain tied to the Land.'

The drone of farm machinery hummed in the distance, gathering the last meagre pickings. In contrast with last year, farmers were facing one of the worst harvests in memory, with rain-sodden crops rotting in the fields and standing wheat beginning to germinate on the stalk. Despite the family's grief, by the Autumn Equinox last year, ours was all in the barn. This year, the surrounding fields that should have been harvested were turning black and half the wheat crop was still in the fields because the machinery kept getting stuck in the mud. Even on sunny days the ground has been too soft and so our neighbours will soon have to decide whether it's worth collecting, or writing it off.

Apparently, our immediate neighbour had to plough in

hundreds of acres of oil seed rape that didn't germinate last autumn because of the dry conditions; this year more has had to be abandoned because of water-logging. This is the reality of Nature and in times gone by, our Ancestors would have faced a bleak future when the harvest failed ... famine was one of the great exterminators in ancient times and whole communities would have lived or died on the strength of the harvest.

That's why when Old Craft talks about Nature and fertility, it is referring to the perilous relationship that mankind has with the elements, not an individual human's (or animal's) ability to breed. Look at any of the old pagan beliefs of the common folk and at the core you will find the religious observances and propitiatory rites had their roots in *agriculture*. The common people didn't concern themselves much with the mighty State gods, they remained true to the 'numen', the power or spirit dwelling in each natural object and this is the root-core of *all* pagan belief – not the great gods so familiar within modern Wicca. Unfortunately, this deviation has caused a great deal of ill-feeling among town-bound pagans, who resent the implication that they cannot be true Old Crafters if they are not country born and bred.

Nature is about harmonising with the spirit of the landscape, learning the language of the fields and hedgerows, and being in tune with the tides and seasons. It's all about being a participant rather than a mere observer. As a solitary these sensations were becoming even stronger, more pronounced and I have to confess I was enjoying this 'walking along old paths' and reconnecting with Craft at a much more basic level that I hadn't experienced since I was a youngster.

Philly and I had walked down to the local pub, The Black Pullet, for a late lunch and marvelled at the contents of our remarkable village shop that supplied everything a villager might need, from a pound of nails to Greek vine leaves. On the way back we had run into Old William, the local poacher, with his two greyhounds. I'd already been warned to steer clear of him by several well-meaning neighbours who were all obviously frightened to death of the old countryman who, the villagers confided, was a *witch*!

'Afternoon ma'am,' he said as I stopped to pat the heads of his dogs. I can never pass a long dog without having a word. 'A grand day for being out and about.' His pale blue eyes twinkled beneath straggling bushy brows and a dirty ratting hat, and we agreed that it was indeed a grand day, with Philly desperately smothering a fit of the giggles. Here was probably one of those 'secret people' who have lived in English villages for hundreds of years, acting as healer for both livestock and locals.

But as Mickey Spillane once observed: 'One dog can always tell another dog. They can see them, smell them or hear them, but they never mistake them for anything but another dog. They can be of any size, shape or colour, but a dog is a dog to a dog. Dog was meeting dog. Nobody knew it but the dogs and they weren't telling.'

'Oh God!' gasped Philly struggling for breath as we reached home. 'We've been sussed by the local poacher! Talk about always recognising your own. Granny would have loved him! They would have made a matching pair.'

Harvest Home

The Lammas rite of baking a loaf from the first cut corn was particularly poignant, particularly because this was the first serious observance I'd made since leaving the Farm. Although it wasn't *our* corn, we'd jointly decided that it was appropriate to start to make the customary observances that had been dormant since Rupert died. There would be no community Harvest Supper in the old barn this year ... but Life has a habit of getting in the way of even the most modest of plans.

The original intension had been for me to finally accept and celebrate my new role in Craft as a Crone or Elder – there was no longer any responsibility for the Coven, and as a widow, I would now have to be self-sufficient both socially and magically. This step isn't as difficult as it sounds, since it merely means doing what the hell you like, when, where and how you like – both socially and magically. For some strange reason few Craft-women relish this relinquishing of power but traditionally, it isn't possible to remain 'in charge' once passed child-bearing age. One should step aside and make way for a younger woman – hence Maiden (new moon), Mother (third quarter) and Crone (dark of the moon). Not that Granny had ever obeyed the rules.

None of these thoughts, however, were quite as blasphemous as they appear. I could easily recall Rupert striking a manly pose by the fireplace when he echoed a similar idea not long before his death. 'Do you realise that we've running the Coven since we were only a few years older than Richard and Philly are now?' he'd said. 'I'd hoped we'd be able to keep going until they could take over but I don't think I can do it for much longer. I want us to be able to do our own 'thing' before it's too late and maintaining responsibility for the Coven has always got in the way of us progressing magically on a personal level.'

'And it's too much of a responsibility to dump on the kids,' I'd replied firmly, sitting on the arm of an overstuffed chair. '*You* resented it and besides, they're not anywhere old enough for initiation, so it's out of the question.'

'Neither were we,' he'd answered mulishly.

'Only because no one dare argue with Granny.'

I knew he was about to deliver one of his diatribes, so I'd settled down and waited to find out what the real problem was. Rupert's 'questions' were usually purely rhetorical and one wasn't supposed to *participate*, just keep quiet and listen. At some later stage he'd become convinced that we'd actually discussed the matter although, in fact, he'd delivered a monologue – but I was used to his ways and it was easier to let him have his rant.

He'd stooped to throw another log on the fire and kicked at it angrily as it threatened to roll back into the hearth. 'It's time to get out, love. Enough is enough. We have always done our best but the rot goes too deep. The whole thing is ruined – let's salvage what we can from all this and call it a day.'

It took me several minutes to understand the full implications of his words. 'But the Coven, the family ... our oaths. We can't just turn away from what we are!'

The sitting room was silent and neither of us spoke for a long time. The clock ticked slowly and the log settled in the grate. The enormity of the meaning behind all this was impossible to grasp and neither of us wanted to accept that Craft (as we knew it) would have to go back into the Shadows if it was to survive for future generations. Now, with both Granny and Rupert dead, it didn't seem such a big deal after all!

I also remembered a letter sent to me by old chum Evan John Jones some time before his death, in which he'd expressed similar sentiments. We'd been discussing what the next step would have been for Robert Cochrane, had he lived to develop his own inimitable style of magic.

'I'd been wondering how long it would take before someone asked that question,' John had replied. 'I've a shrewd suspicion, having more or less followed in his footsteps, and eventually finding myself in more or less the same position as he was.'

The letter continued:

The surprising thing is, it can in many ways lead to a break with traditional Craft and eventually lead on to a highly individual form of devotional workings that in one sense, reverses everything Tubal Cain has to teach. In a sense you belong, yet not belong. You break away from being a member of the group as such and embark on a highly individual way of working, yet at the same time you remain rooted to your Clan tradition. The other oddity is, you never actually pass on anything in the sense of the working techniques. Instead, people have to find their own way there and develop their own particular mystical bent and experiences.

Robert once said that Tubal Cain should not be the be-all and end-all of a person's Craft experience, as each one of us should be capable of reaching far beyond that. The more I think about it, the more I feel he was right, none of us should be led by the hand all our occult lives, but should be free to reach out and find our own spiritual reality without destroying our Craft roots. It's something so many people fail to grasp and take the attitude that 'If you're not with us ... then you're against us'. I suppose they hate to lose what they think of as control over the followers.

Magically, these are interesting times for a post-menopausal witch because this is when our powers are at their greatest, and where we have the advantage over the males of the (witch) species. From an historical perspective, powerful witches have always been depicted as old hags or crones and in the good old days, a 40-year-old woman would have been a museum piece! Whether it's something to do with a chemical reaction in the brain, or a channelling of different energies within the endocrinal system but all the senses seem to be more alert ... more 'attuned', somehow. Our solitary state brings more than its fair share of rewards on a psychic level, but the 'signs' aren't always what we would expect.

Philly and I were taking a leisurely stroll along the lane when half a ton of horse pitched over the hedge, minus its rider. Having got rid of this unwanted encumbrance, the animal did a lot of snorting and prancing before allowing Philly to catch hold of the reins and quickly calm it down. It was a magnificent animal; the kind of Thoroughbred normally seen over the 'jumps' rather than the Flat, and no doubt its owner would shortly come looking for it. On the other side of the hedge and out of our view, however, the situation was far from calm. A strident female voice was lambasting a male who was being less than complimentary about her equestrian skills.

'You arrogant prick, Kieran! Don't tell *me* how to handle a horse!'

'You couldn't handle a bloody yard broom! Have you stopped to think where the horse is now, or whether it could be injured?'

'That's *your* problem …'

Suddenly the lane became very congested and noisy. Just as the battling riders – one mounted, one on foot – emerged through a gateway, a muddy Land Rover screeched to a halt. From the driver's side there appeared an embodiment of a thunderous Jove, looking as though he were about to hurl a thunderbolt, but not quite knowing where to aim it. He glanced at Philly holding the horse and then back at the riders as the female flounced towards the Land Rover; although it's very difficult to produce an effective flounce when your rear end has made obvious contact with a wet cow pat!

'Take me home, Raulf, I won't ride out with this arsehole again …' she said, slamming the passenger door.

'It might be a good idea if one of you helped that poor child with the horse, instead of squabbling,' roared Jove. The 'poor child' remained silent and amused.

'How the hell am I supposed to get Badger home on my own?' demanded the younger man. Badger presumably being the recalcitrant racehorse.

The woman mouthed something like 'Up yours' through the glass, as the 'poor child' interrupted with a noticeable degree of authority in her voice.. 'You lead and I'll follow ... as long as you drive me home afterwards.'

The young man looked at her for the first time and obviously didn't have any faith in this chit of a girl. 'I don't think ...'

But I'd already given her a leg up and for all her diminutive size, she sat well in the saddle. What neither of the men knew was that when most little girls were happily playing with 'My Little Pony', my daughter was avidly devouring *Summerhayes' Encyclopaedia for Horsemen!* The 17-hand monster responded willingly to her heels and without another word the two riders disappeared back into the field.

'Well I'm damned!' thundered Jove.

The woman's face was murderous, and even more so when the Olympian turned to me and asked whether he could offer me a lift home. I declined on the grounds that I only lived five minutes' walk away ... and would rely on Philly to provide the outcome of the adventure upon her return. It's another Crone's prerogative to enjoy village gossip, if not to actually promote it!

It was late before Philly got home and I was already tucked up in bed with a book. She flung herself down on the duvet still smelling of the stables and began her narrative. Apparently the disgruntled female had flounced off again by the time the riders returned to the fold, leaving the field clear for Philly to be invited for supper and get to know our neighbours without let or hindrance. As a result of all this activity, we found ourselves the guests of Raulf (traditional pronunciation 'Rafe', largely restricted to the English upper classes and generally taken to mean 'wolf'!) Layne at the local Harvest Supper two nights later.

In a curious twist of Fate, from unknown newcomers we'd been elevated to rubbing shoulders with the County elite who held the local Manor and surrounding estate. Flanked by Philly and the flouncing Vanessa, Raulf Layne held court, with myself and his son Keiran on the opposite side of the table. She was a silly woman, not unlike that other Vanessa that Rupert's brother was knocking off some years ago, and who had come to grief having mortally offended my late husband's sensibilities.

It quickly became obvious that she had her sights set, not on the son, but on becoming to the Manor re-born, and once discovering that we were better connected than she'd first supposed, launched an all-out assault on the Squire's attentions. Apparently, our host had known Rupert from various point-to-points and the hunting field and he was quite happy to recount some of those stories. Vanessa hung on every word, laughing gaily and patting his arm in encouragement – it would have been funny if it wasn't so pathetic, and even Raulf himself was obviously a little discomforted by these unfamiliar attentions.

Similar to our own family custom, the Harvest Supper was being served in the old tithe barn at the Manor and the ladies of the parish had provided acres of white linen tablecloths for the occasion; not to mention the excellent food and gallons of Layne's traditional cider and apple juice. With Raulf paying more attention to his guests than she deemed necessary, Vanessa was drinking more than was good for her – and her behaviour pissed me off. I was no more interested in Raulf Layne than he was in me but the embarrassing antics of this stupid young woman brought out the witch-bitch in me. Her obvious insecurity gave me the only weapon I needed and in the words of that Chinese military genius, Sun Tzu: 'I never seek to defeat the person I am fighting. I seek to defeat his confidence. A mind troubled by doubt cannot focus on the course to victory.'

I was wearing another anniversary gift from Rupert – my highly prized star sapphire. This was of the blue-grey variety that usually displays a much more distinct star than the darker stone, and is highly prized magically. I began tapping my ring finger on the table in a series of morse-like movements: without realising it Vanessa fixated on the flashing star and quickly reacted to its power. She became more animated and vocal; to add to the attraction, a large piece of vivid green parsley had become wedged between her front teeth and re-appeared with each flashing smile. With Vanessa well and truly under and quaffing cider with gay abandon, I proceeded to 'glamour' Raulf and ratchet things up a bit there as well. Any witch worth her salt can produce this effect whether she's eighteen or eighty and the Squire was captivated, even though we were only talking farming and horses. In a last ditch attempt to hold the field, Vanessa aimed to put her hand on his thigh but it ... sort of slipped and she caught him full in the crotch! Philly and I exchanged looks and remembered the other Vanessa committing a similar misjudged assault on Rupert and having the fire bucket emptied over her head. When we eventually left and politely thanked our host for his kind invitation, *this* Vanessa was last spotted throwing up in a fire bucket.

'What the hell was that all about?' snapped Philly as we drove out of the gates.

'She pissed me off,' I said lamely. 'We were having a completely normal and civilised conversation and she kept sending me 'Keep Off' signals. The man hadn't shown even the remotest interest ...'

'Well, he will NOW!' interrupted Philly darkly.

'Don't be daft,' I said but I had a horrible feeling that she could be right. It was a stupid thing to do and a dreadful breach of Craft etiquette, but it was done and I would have to suffer the consequences. 'He'll forget all about it in a day or so,' I added hopefully.

In the darkness Philly gave a giggle. 'No chance because I know that my Mum is a *real* witch. I just wonder what will happen next without Dad here to hold you in check!'

The Rose Bay Quadrilles

After the Harvest Supper we kept rather a low profile, so we had no idea of what the outcome of my little excursion into psychic manipulation had been, although Keiran Layne had phoned to ask Philly to ride out on her day off. The week passed by peacefully enough with no repercussions, although the villagers' attitude to us had warmed considerably since our appearance at the Squire's table. The difference between living in St Thomas and St Agnes was that previously we were involved in the day-to-day activities of the village and were part of the community. Perhaps that would also begin to change …

I can recall one neighbourly instance where Rupert and I were just having our morning coffee when the local bobby turned up. We usually only heard from Roy if was a matter of livestock escaping, and then it was just a phone call to alert us as to where the offender could be located. For him to turn up on the yard in full dress uniform and an official car meant serious business, but Roy wasn't bristling with officialdom … he was shaking with fear.

A strong coffee, laced with four heaped spoonfuls of sugar and a slug of *Famous Grouse* and we were ready to get down to business. 'I need your advice, Mr P,' he'd said, sipping the scalding brew. 'There's a warlock in the next village.'

Rupert looked puzzled. Getting increasingly hard of hearing, he thought Roy had said *warthog*, which explained the constable's horrified stare when he replied, 'Well, what do you want *me* to do, shoot it?'

'I wouldn't want things to go *that* far, Mr P,' said Roy hurriedly. 'After all, you're the best person to deal with a warlock, being as you are as you are, if you get my drift?'

'Ah … a *warlock*, you say!' repeated Rupert, with a twinkle in his eye. 'Perhaps you'd better tell us the whole story and we'll see what we can do to help. Purely in an advisory capacity, you understand … and no artillery?' he added, much to Roy's relief.

It transpired that this 'warlock' had rented a little terraced house in the next village and was putting the fear of God up the villagers, by a series of publicly-pronounced curses and the threat of sticking pins in dolls to bring about all manner of unsavoury results. When Roy had called in response to a complaint from a panic-stricken pensioner, the warlock had promptly cursed him, too. It seemed rather incongruous that the local populace were quite happy to have a full Coven of *witches* as neighbours but had been sent into a superstitious frenzy by the appearance of a self-styled warlock in their midst. It was obvious that he was a member of the pagan lunatic-fringe but we promised to look into the matter and Roy went off as happy as Larry, having deposited the problem on someone else's altar, so to speak.

The next we heard of the warlock was when he turned up in the shop, Castor & Pollux, run by two of our Coven members, Gerry and Guy. He and his side-kick turned up one wet Wednesday afternoon, in a flurry of swirling capes and shaven heads. At least *he* was shaven, she was cloaked and hooded and the 'boys' couldn't tell since she never raised her eyes from ground level. Gerry took one look at the pair and fled into the Gallery in hysterics, handkerchief stuffed into his mouth, and so Guy was left to sort them out.

Guy is a beautiful creature but as Gerry frequently says: 'Bent as a nine bob note, sweetie, and he's all mine!' He's also an imposing six-footer and quite able to hold his own, as it were, in the face of magical adversity. Not a lot fazes Guy and certainly not a five-foot nine Bela Lugosi impersonator in a cheap polyester cloak! As he said later, it was only an imp and not a fully-fledged demon.

What was highly significant was the fact that the warlock was eager to barter over an imposing antique dagger on display in the shop. As we all know, one should never 'haggle over a black egg' … i.e. never try to knock down the asking price for any form of magical equipment or books … and the warlock offered Guy a fraction of what it was priced at. This was the first 'positive' proof we had that he wasn't genuine, since no magical practitioner worth their salt would go against this form of personal 'sacrifice'. From then on the warlock and his companion were referred to as Bela and Lugosi.

It wasn't going to be difficult to sort them out and the only real problem was which one of us would 'corpse' from laughter, as they say in theatrical circles. One dark and stormy night six of us piled into the Land Rover in full regalia and drove over to their hide-away. The wind was lashing itself into a frenzy when Rupert delivered three loud raps on the front door with his staff and we all huddled there in the shadows, Adam having thoughtfully removed the porch light with a well-aimed brick! The door opened and revealed six robed and hooded figures, much to the obvious consternation that showed on Lugosi's face – Bela was nowhere to be seen.

Before he had a chance to speak, Rupert opened the performance in a grave baritone. 'Who dares to enter the realm of the Clan of the Hooded Crow!!?' (Where the hell had he got that from? I could feel Pris beginning to shake with laughter next to me.) 'Answer!' To back him up a bit the rest of us started a chant that was actually the lyric to *The Lincolnshire Poacher* with lots of 's's in it, which all sounded rather sinister and hissy when distorted by the folds of our hoods.

Lugosi was opening and shutting his mouth like a goldfish with several attempts at 'I … I … I …' He'd never seen anything like it in his life, and to be truthful, neither had we.

In his best sepulchral voice Rupert was banging on about being cast into the Abyss and the curse of the Nine, while we droned on – I think Adam was improvising with something from White Stripes, but I can't be sure. These idiots weren't worth a legitimate Craft ritual and we were just giving them a taste of the gobbledy-gook they'd been handing out to their neighbours. With a final: 'And if ye are not gone from this place by cockcrow tomorrow, it will mean DEATH!' His pointing finger stopped just inches from Lugosi's chest and in response the friendly neighbourhood warlock slammed the door in our faces.

We managed to reach the Land Rover before collapsing in hysterics and as we drove away, Pris choked out: 'I think I've wet myself.' Surprisingly enough this attempt at amateur theatricals worked, and the warlock was seen no more on Roy's patch.

I'd had an itchy left palm all morning and as it was a 'sign' that never let me down, I was wondering where the unexpected money was coming from. Guy and Gerry had paid a surprise visit and, as always, came bearing gifts – the gift in this instance was a large modern oil painting of a huntsman and his pack, with the image reverse in the dark swirling clouds above. It was rather a dramatic piece but, as Guy pointed out, there wasn't much call for the subject since the wretched hunting ban. After a great deal of argument it was decided to replace the picture in the sitting room, which was long overdue for a clean – the result was certainly breath-taking and the light from the French doors brought out the colours on the canvass.

'Perfect,' said Guy but he was examining the painting we'd taken down. 'Where did you get this?'

'It came from the Farm and had been hanging in the old breakfast room. I brought it with me because I needed a big picture in the sitting room and it wouldn't have been missed. Why?'

'It looks like a Caspar David Friedrich. One similar is in the Louvre … his *Tree With Crows* …'

'The Clan of the Hooded Crow!' spluttered Gerry, and of course we fell to reminiscing about the Bela and Lugosi saga that I'd been thinking about earlier that morning. The 'boys' were scaling down prior to their move to the coast; Guy was expanding the Gallery and Gerry had finally had enough of selling incense sticks, crystals and tarot cards to 'amateurs', as he referred to his customer. Together with the painting, they'd also brought our invitations to the new Gallery opening in a month's time.

'Had a phone call from the poison dwarf the other day,' said Gerry, referring to the person generally held responsible for breaking up the Coven. 'Wanted us to go to the newly reconstituted coven and meet the members. Why she thinks she can run her own show, I really don't know. She asked if I had a number for Pris and Adam, but of course, I didn't. If they'd wanted to keep in touch with her, they would have done, so it's not up to me to act as go-between. Anyway we're moving in a fortnight's time and closing the door on St Thomas for good.'

'Yes, we've all had to do that,' I answered, and we changed the subject.

Guy took the old painting with him for cleaning and valuation, and said to keep my fingers crossed that it was by the artist he'd mentioned. As they drove away, the old left palm started itching again and I rubbed it vigorously on the wooden door frame. Wedged in the letter box was an envelope and on opening it found a cheque for £75 in payment for my article in *The Countryman* magazine.

I sat staring at the new painting on the opposite wall and as the sun began to sink, it cast an eerie glow on the canvass, altering the whole perspective of the picture, and imbuing it with a life force of its own. Suddenly, I was aware of the floating, astral- cold sensation that heralds the start of a pathworking, and allowed myself to be carried away on the current. I was being draw towards the painting, and recognised the figure of the distant huntsman as being that of Rupert, waiting for me on the ridge overlooking the Farm …

Suddenly, a loud rapping on the front door broke the spell and I was brought back to earth with the feeling that I'd been pitched down in a fast moving life. With a queasy stomach and trembling limbs, I got to my feet to answer the summons. Standing in the porch was a rather scruffy youth holding two greyhounds on a bit of bailing twine. 'Uncle William said I wus to bring 'em here,' he said by way of explanation and before I could reply, he was gone!

Embarrassed, the dogs shifted about under my scrutiny and were obviously aware that while they might be welcome, their attendant livestock *wasn't*. I hurried them through to the garden before any opportunistic flea could take advantage and viewed them through the windows of the conservatory. Why William had left me with his dogs, I could only guess ... he'd either gone into hospital or prison, since anyone else would probably have had the old poacher's dogs destroyed while he was out of the way. They were sleek and lean hunters and had been reasonably well cared for.

It was getting dusk before Philly came home and the greyhounds were beginning to panic. 'Well, they can't come in here like *that*,' said the vet in her best professional manner and promptly produced all sorts of fungicide shampoo, wormers, flea treatment, nail clippers ... and the ubiquitous rubber gloves. An hour later *we* were soaked to the skin and the greyhounds were drying off in front of the fire as though they'd live here all their lives. They were also producing some disgustingly smelly farts but then there was no telling what Old William had been feeding them on.

'Black Shuck and a Gabriel hound,' remarked Philly as we fortified ourselves with a hot whiskey. This observation being due to one dog being all black, and the other white with red-brindle patches over his ears and mask – and well documented in British folk-lore.

'I think he's dead.'

'Who?'

'Old William. He wouldn't give up his dogs like that to a

stranger, if things weren't desperate.'

Philly looked at me strangely but she wasn't about to argue. She knew me too well. 'So what are *you* going to do about them?'

'They've been given to me in trust by one of our own kind. I don't really have a choice, do I?'

'Oh, Christ!' said Philly pouring another drink, but I knew she wasn't displeased.

We'd always had dogs about the place and it was the one thing that was missing to make the cottage really feel like a home. Like everything else of late, the decision had been taken out of my hands. Life was beginning to feel like an emotional Cresta Run and was gathering momentum with every twist and turn. I was just about to say that I was dreading what was going to happen next when I felt something snag against my sweater and looking down found that the gold band of my wedding ring had snapped and caught in the fibres of the wool. It was all happening too quickly and to my daughter's concern, I burst into tears. The Circle was finally broken.

Hunter's Moon

Shortly after Rupert's death I found an anonymous news-clipping in his wallet and could see why he'd kept it. 'As the wounded WWII veteran said of the critic who denounced the atomic bombing of Japan, 'I don't demand that he experience having his ass shot off. I merely note that he didn't.' There is a similarly galling naiveté in those, far removed from Nature, who see in hunting the exploitation of animals and who imagine that anyone who disagrees with them is either the unenlightened slave of unquestioned convention, or of base self-interest. This is not a demand that those who would dictate to hunters on how to treat wild animals, should witness the death agonies of a starving or injured creature from so-called natural causes; neither should they be forced to see the aftermath of a fox attack on a poultry run or lambing shed, I merely note that they haven't.'

There were parallels to be drawn between the sentiments in the clipping, and the views often expressed by outsiders on all aspects of traditional witchcraft and country living. We, the participants in Old Craft teaching and country people, have had the benefit of that ancient wisdom – the observers haven't. Since the publication of the first edition of *Coarse Witchcraft* the Coven had become the object of prurient interest and speculation on the internet with the 'observer's' judgements aired without any of the participants' knowledge.

Nevertheless, if the content of these blogs and forums were anything to go by, contemporary Craft is doomed and already dying. Not because of any flaws within itself, but purely and simply because the majority of its followers had evolved into shallow, small-minded eco-darlings without the strength of character to ever uphold the Old Laws. The heart could never go out of true Craft, of course, but true loyalty and the trustworthiness of spirit was a dying element in those who would seek it out.

Cocooned in the security of the farm and the family, I'd never considered how anyone could possibly be so interested in us that it would warrant spending so much time amassing bogus information about the Coven and spewing it far and wide. The thought gave me the creeps, and it wasn't too difficult to think of the situation as being akin to having a personal stalker. For the first time in my life I had felt vulnerable. My privacy and that of those I cared about had been violated.

'It's not worth getting upset over,' Rupert had said. 'These damned fools can't even attempt to live a *real* life. They are so inept, their only existence relies on becoming like a fungicide growth on the front of a monitor screen. The longer they sit there, the bigger they grow. They've nothing real in their lives. It's a fantasy fungi based on lies, spite and a pathetic insecurity that leaves them clinging like cleavers to a rotting tree. They are full of sentimental bullshit on a good day – and spiteful crap on a bad one. We've just become victims of our own success ...'

'Victims of pure unadulterated jealousy, more like,' had been Pris's view. 'Let's face it, we thought we were giving a bit of subtle, good-natured instruction under the guise of humour but all we've succeeded in doing is drawing unwelcome attention to ourselves. Look at wot's his name, the one with his four and twenty Wiccans down from Inverness ... he's publicly claiming that he knows us all well and that he's worked with us on numerous occasions. Lying bugger! Strikes me that he'll initiate anything with a pulse, judging from his track record. And if he's such an important 'high priest' with all these nubile wenches running around, why does he even want or need to align himself with two old Crones like us!?'

This rather long-winded explanation is to demonstrate why I'd begun to respond to the advances of certain pagan magazines and publishers – I now *wanted* to put the record straight. So many people wrote about what they *thought* Old Craft was about, but slowly a few Old Crafters were beginning to record for posterity the true approach to these Old Ways. And I was seriously considering writing about the fundamentals of what we believed and practiced, without giving away any secrets. After all, having finally evolved naturally (and magically) into the Crone-state it was my responsibility to preserve and pass on our Wisdom – and our differences.

To quote one example where we differ quite considerably from Wicca and the pagan community at large, is on the subject of cursing. Most pagans are adamant that they don't and won't curse. In Old Craft we *do* curse – not very often but when it is necessary to resort to a Higher Law and we have exhausted all other methods of obtaining justice, a fellow Crafter will comment: 'You (or We) need to sort that bugger out!'

This does not mean that we go around cursing with impunity. There is *always* a price to pay and any experienced magical practitioner accepts the consequences of their actions. A curse thrown in a fit of rage or jealous pique might be extremely effective, but a knee jerk reaction might also rebound on the sender if the proper procedures aren't in place. The old saying about revenge being a dish best served cold suits the witch's approach to cursing but, more often than not, they will not expend the energy necessary for a successful curse when a bottling or binding can be just as effective. Cursing, like most areas of magic, is a question of personal responsibility and/or morality but once thrown cannot be retracted, and is not always the answer to an insult or injury.

We learned that Old William *had* died and so the responsibility of ownership for his two greyhounds did fall to me. I can't honestly say I was displeased either. They are lovely dogs and had given me the excuse to roam far and wide, reconnecting with that obscure language of the fields and hedgerows we learned as children. As we progress magically, we move away from this fundamental knowledge to explore more intellectual pastures: until something happens to send us back to the security of our roots. It's like viewing the Qabbalistic Tree of Life as a gigantic game of 'snakes and ladders'. One moment we're quite happily working towards the pinnacle of our magical or mystical abilities at Chesod – when suddenly we're catapulted back to Malkuth where we now view things from a completely different (and hopefully, wiser) perspective from the first time we passed through that particular *sephirah*.

Autumn is a great time for this kind of thinking: spring and summer are much too busy for such introspection. As I've mentioned before, being a great reader, I often find that 'signs' leap off the page and provide me with a form of answer in the nature of classic bibliomancy or rhapsodomancy. I don't choose a book or page at random, the passage suddenly stands out in the normal course of reading a perfectly ordinary novel – after all, we can always find 'signs' in sacred or magical books! Yesterday, for example, I came across this paragraph in *Memoirs of a Geisha*:

We human beings are only a part of something very much larger. When we walk along, we may crush a beetle or simply cause a change in the air so that a fly ends up where it might never have gone otherwise. And if we think of the same example but with ourselves in the role of the insect, and the larger universe in the role we've just played, it's perfectly clear that we're affected every day by forces over which we have no more control than the poor beetle has over our gigantic foot as it descends upon it. We must use whatever methods we can to understand the movement of the universe around us and time our actions so that we are not fighting the currents, but moving with them.

I marked the page and carried on reading ... only to come back to it later and reflect on the wisdom encapsulated in the words. In response to the thought patterns that had recently been passing through my mind, the direction was clear – I was to go with the flow and *not* fight against the current. In my altered state of consciousness I accept that in my *personal* universe everything can and does have an effect on my future actions wherever they may lead.

It's been quite a gloomy, wet autumn but I've still been out and about in the woods with the greyhounds, who seem to have got used to their non-hunting lifestyle – although I'm wary of letting them off the lead. The beauty of grey wet days is that we have the woods to ourselves, since the fair-weather riders and dog owners don't seem to venture out in the rain. Having been used to walking where I liked, it seemed strange to be walking on someone else's land – even though I'd asked permission from our neighbour who owned it. But it doesn't seem so peculiar for a woman to be out walking dogs at any time of day, whereas a solitary female abroad at dawn or dusk might draw unwanted attention. The dogs provide the perfect cover.

In the silence of the empty woods I found myself remembering a story of Pris's about when she and Adam took a party of newbies out for their first outdoor ritual. Although the site was fairly near the road, it was only approachable by clambering over ditches, dykes and stiles and therefore in the dark appeared much more arduous than it actually was. While Pris had decked herself in her special HPS finery behind a tree, Adam set the fire, cunningly concealing a whole box of firelighters in the centre – just in case! The Circle nervously gathered round and as the fire caught with a whoosh!, a series of shots rang out through the trees.

'Bloody poachers!' Pris had related, 'but as they'd no more business there than we had, the situation was hardly going to be confrontational. The newbies were white with terror but my only concern was that someone might be hit by a stray shot. I cast the Circle, flung evocations about like confetti and got the chant going – somewhat discordant and half-hearted but the shooting stopped. I knew that the poachers were watching from the bushes but I figured they would be too frightened by a group of chanting, cowled figures to risk hanging around to see if we were going to throw another virgin on the fire. I felt their energies slink away and eventually the 'ritual' – if you can call it that – reached its conclusion. We raised bugger all, in terms of magical energy that night, but I bet it's an experience none of 'em will ever forget!'

I was chuckling to myself and glad that I could still savour the memories of an old friendship, even if the friendship itself had passed into nothingness. Friendships that endure in Old Craft are as rare as hen's teeth and we appear to shed them like a snake sheds its skin – probably so that we can move on to the next stage of our magical development without encumbrance. And as painful as that shedding seems at the time, we take with us valuable lessons and, if we are truly honest, fond memories of those times that were. Perhaps it is merely another stage on our journey – the learning to let go and find the courage to travel the Path of the Mysteries alone.

Memories are certainly like the dappled sunlight through the branches of the woodland – light and shade – I was thinking, when I noticed a vehicle up ahead blocking the fire access. Darker thoughts intruded. There was no one else around on this gloomy autumn afternoon and before I could make a decision as to whether to plunge into the trees or soldier on, the driver got out of the Land Rover and with relief I recognised the figure of Raulf Layne. Perhaps I greeted him a little too enthusiastically but the long and the short of it was that he gave us a lift home, although he eyed the greyhounds with some misgiving. Even more so when we got back to the cottage and I removed their new water-proof coats.

'I wondered what had happened to them,' he said as I made the coffee. 'I've lost count of the number of times I've threatened to shoot the damn things.' The greyhounds made themselves scarce and slunk off into the sitting room, rather than wait for the biscuits to be produced.

'My legacy from Old William,' I answered in defence of *my* dogs and challenging him to raise an objection.

Perched at the breakfast bar of my compact designer kitchen, this man looked immense. I've mentioned before that Rupert was 'small and beautifully made' but Raulf Layne was reminiscent of the proverbial bull in Fortnum & Mason's china department. He would be impressive enough striding around his Gothick Manor but he was distinctly out of place at the former Pixie Cottage!

'I suppose they're company for you. It's too easy to get used to living alone, don't you find?'

'I don't know, Rupert's only been gone just over a year, and I've just moved here from the Farm,' I answered brusquely.

'Of course, I'm sorry ...'

What he was sorry for I didn't find out because Philly arrived with Keiran Layne in tow, and the kitchen became even more congested. My daughter had thoughtfully bought a bag of fresh scones from the local shop, so we all settled down again for afternoon tea and any further direct conversation with Raulf was conveniently diverted. Why I was giving him such a hard time was inexcusable, after all *I'd* 'glamoured' *him* at the Harvest Supper and he was only unconsciously responding to the power of the witch. It would have to be sorted if I didn't want to spend the rest of my life avoiding him, so I'd have to carry out a 'de-glamouring' job – or move! It was a problem of my own making, and it was my responsibility to solve it with the least upset to my unfortunate 'victim'.

Overture for a Happy Occasion

For the next week Philly and I were back at the Farm. There were all sorts of things to discuss, both business and personal, and it was easier for us all to be under the same roof while we made our decisions. Although the twins had inherited the Farm, their legacy had been drawn up in such a way that it gave me a percentage of the business, so whatever we did, we had to do as a family agreement – even prenuptial arrangements for any future marriages! Rupert's forward thinking was safeguarding the Farm, the Land, and our individual security.

The building work at the Farm was progressing nicely with a big American-style barn for the horses, and lots of paddock already fenced and reset with grass; although I'd insisted that we keep the old stable yard intact, where our old horses could live out their years in familiar surroundings. Some things needed to stay as they've always been out of respect.

It was good to be together again and of course, there were lots of occasions for: Do you remember? That was when Richard mooted the idea of buying a neighbouring small-holding that was on the market, since at a time of recession we might be able to get it at a reasonable price due to it being in a derelict state. Several years ago a 'drippy' commune had taken it over cultivating a few feet of vegetable plot, planting all sorts of agricultural debris with nasturtiums, and added insult to injury by painting the buildings bright lavender with purple doors and window frames. They had eventually been arrested for growing tons of cannabis in plastic tents in one of the barns and were currently being detained at HM's pleasure.

'It would be perfect for Philly's equine hospital. There's plenty of room and she'd have her own house to live in. Take years to put it right, of course, but then you don't want to miss out on your Newmarket experience, do you?' he asked his sister. 'What do you think? We'd both be completely independent but still next door.'

'We could look at it, I suppose. Can we get the keys ...'

'No problem,' interrupted her brother, waving a set of keys in the air. Like his father, young Richard never lets the grass grow under his feet either.

'Do you remember when they moved in?' giggled Philly. 'Really set Dad up for a week's moaning over the breakfast table ...'

Rupert had been busy spraying the grass verges along the lane between our property and this small, run-down small holding that had recently been sold, although the new owners hadn't yet put in an appearance. The previous occupant, an irascible octogenarian (who had finally been carted off to a home after assaulting a DEFRA representative with a 12 bore!), had assiduously cultivated some four acres of ragwort despite mounting pressure from his neighbours.

Eco-campaigners deny ragwort is dangerous to livestock, despite the extensive veterinary reports to the contrary. Its yellow flowers can be seen throughout July and August, but the plants can be in flower at almost any time of the year somewhere in the British Isles. Hay containing ragwort is potentially lethal and as the plants are capable of spreading more than 150,000 seeds with an expected germination of more than 80 per cent for the next 20 years, it is obvious why farmers are duty-bound to eradicate them. In fact, since 1959 every landowner has been required to control ragwort, either by direct spraying, or by lifting and burning, but up until the last decade, prosecutions for failing to control it were few.

It had been a bright summer morning and all was right with Rupert's world until his peace was shattered by a strident voice addressing him from the tarmac. 'What on earth do you think you're doing!!!?'

He turned to find himself confronted by two androgynous figures, whose curiously draped forms suggested some strange cult-invasion from the suburbs. 'Good morning,' he responded. 'Lovely day.'

'It would be if you weren't spraying the filthy stuff all over the countryside,' came the response. 'You farmers are all the same. No respect for Nature. All you're interested in is making money and destroying *our* natural heritage.'

He'd eyed them curiously for a few moments and then, beside himself over the boundless extremes of their urban ignorance and arrogance, he responded with a stream of invective that would have left them in no doubt as to the grave error of judgement they'd made. No doubt the content of this diatribe was heavily littered with agri-jargon but the fury of its delivery would have left nothing to the imagination. The two figures had wheeled like spooked starlings and hurried off down the lane, from time to time looking back over their shoulders to see if they were being pursued by this madman in a ratting-hat. Finally they disappeared into the gateway of the small-holding – the new neighbours had arrived.

'They never did speak to any of us after that,' I added. 'And they certainly didn't do anything to improve the property, never mind objecting to a bit of ragwort spraying and growing that crap in the barn.'

Surprisingly, it was Richard who raised the question of the Coven. It appeared he'd been 'giving a lot of thought to it of late' and felt that some sort of statement needed to be made about its existence. 'I don't mean going out on a recruitment drive,' he said, seeing the expression on my face, 'but just setting up a website with some pertinent information about Old Craft and stating quite categorically that despite the rumours we're still alive and kicking. And I think that eventually Philly and I should take over where you and Dad left off …'

I looked at Philly but she wouldn't meet my eye. 'If that's what you want to do, but remember we're not hereditaries …'

'I have been reminded of that in no uncertain terms on numerous occasions,' he replied sharply.

'Richard, it's a big responsibility and it ties you without any respite and you're just starting out with a new enterprise. Once you assume that responsibility, it's for life. That's what your father resented at the end, and that's why he wanted us to step down and get a life of our own before it was too late.'

'And that's what killed him,' said Philly. 'He broke his oath, even though it was due to outside pressure.' Her voice wobbled slightly.

'Don't talk nonsense,' I snapped. 'Your father had a massive heart attack, brought on by overwork, living too well and high blood pressure. We tried for years to keep Old Craft from floundering but the only place it truly exists *is* in the Shadows, where it's always belonged. Your father knew this and despite the antagonism between them, he only kept the Coven going for Granny. When she died there was no reason left for carrying on the charade. That's what the others didn't want to understand.'

A Coven is a state of mind. Like Old Craft itself. There really isn't such a thing left any more. It exists in the memories of the Old Ones and in the misconceptions of the new ones. It's on the map of history and in the pagan vocabulary, but the thing that made traditional British Old Craft and the Coven has long since gone, although thousands prowl the places where they once existed, looking for the reality but finding only the Shadow. One day my children will also realise this.

'So you don't want me to keep the Coven going?'

'Richard, if that's what you wish. Use the internet by all means – after all that's what destroyed us in the end – but decide on a sensible approach in agreement with your sister. All I ask is don't expose the family to any more public scrutiny ... but why this sudden interest?'

At least my son had the good grace to look shifty and I guessed there was something he *wasn't* telling me. *Cherchez la femme?* Was that why he wanted Philly living some distance away when she finally finished her training? Did we have an ambitious 'high priestess' on our hands, pulling strings behind the scenes?

How the Stars Were Made

The pressure was also on from the publisher for me to sign a three-book deal. I think publishers have come to realise that there's been nothing new coming out for years concerning genuine witchcraft, simply because after the first enthusiastic flurry, few pagan authors have the experience to write past a certain magical point. As a result, one more enterprising of the breed tracked me down to my lair and offered me the opportunity to set the records straight, as it were. And since copies of the original *Coarse Witchcraft* were now selling for ridiculous prices, it was worth considering as there was obviously still a demand for what we had to say.

I did what we always do in matters such as these and consulted the Ancestors – All Hallows was only a few weeks away and so I appealed to Rupert and Granny to offer up their advice. The Ancestors are an integral part of a witch's world and even the recently deceased have a part to play. Granny was buried up on the Ridge next to her old flame, and Rupert's ashes had been scattered in the bluebell wood but there was still only the thinnest of veils that separated us.

It was a lovely mild late autumn evening and out there, only visible in the hours before dawn, Orion was beginning to make his return journey to the northern hemisphere. A pipistrelle bat uttered a shrill little squeak and I recognised this as a 'sign'. It took me back to my teens when Granny was trying to teach me the art of telepathic image transference. At a pre-designated time I was to focus my mind on an item, and project the image into her mind from a distance.

I forget what the intended image had been but a pipistrelle bat kept on invading my line of vision and I must have subconsciously focussed on the bat instead. The result was that Granny had misguidedly chosen this exact time to go to the lavatory, and mid-action found a bat persistently flapping around her head as she squatted on the bowl. It took a moment for it to register that the bat was an astral image, and where it had come from. 'You daft young bugger!' she thundered at me down the telephone line later that evening, but I knew she was secretly pleased that one of her 'young uns' was showing such promise. Obviously the auspices were favourable …

Philly's decision to go against her brother's plan, however, would *not* have met with the old girl's approval. Something had been festering since our return from a week at the Farm, and after the initial excitement of the prospect of buying the small-holding had worn off, there was obviously still some unfinished business to attend to. It took almost another week before she decided to say what was on her mind.

'Ma, I don't want to belong to the Coven. I want to work on my own. How do you feel about that?'

'It's okay by me, but would you explain why you've come to this decision?'

She filled the kettle and I knew we were in for a session. 'Basically, we can't turn the clock back and recreate what we grew up with. And I really don't want to be responsible for other people's magical development. I was hoping Richard would tell you himself but I've given him long enough and he hasn't – but the main reason is because he's met this girl. Well, woman really, who's pushing him into 'assuming his rightful position' unquote.'

Cherchez la femme! 'What's she like? Kosher?'

'I think so, from what I've seen. A bit older than him, which is good but I couldn't work with her and have another you and Granny, and Gwen and Vanessa scenario. We'd land up with more Dames than a pantomime production!'

'I wasn't easy,' I agreed, with a grin. 'What else?'

'Well, although we were brought up in the Coven, I've not made any formal oath, which I feel I would be breaking. And we'd never really talked about Dad, until last week,' she said meaningfully. 'I've served my time, and I reckon I'd like to work on my own – if you'll help me. I *know* there's more than observing calendar rituals and group dynamics.'

'Wait a minute,' I replied, rummaging around for EJJ's letter in my briefcase. 'Read that and see if it gives you the right answers. Whatever I say will not carry as much weight as this will.'

'*In a sense you belong, yet not belong. You break away from being a member of the group as such and embark on a highly individual way of working, yet at the same time you remain rooted to your Clan tradition* ... yes, that's exactly how I feel. So I'm not being disloyal, or anything?'

'No. That's how we felt at the end. We'd done our time, to the detriment of our own magical development. Your father didn't have his chance.'

'And that's what you're doing now?'

'Yes. Belonging to the Coven doesn't make you a witch, and no longer belonging to the Coven doesn't mean that we cease to be witches. Traditionally, true Craft has always been solitary but the experience of belonging to a group can teach the technique of those group dynamics and the ability to work with other people should it become necessary. But 'disloyal'? Not at all.'

'Can I work with you?'

'*Yes, my darling daughter!*' I answered, singing the lyrics from an old song to hide my emotions.

'Shit! I've been putting this conversation off for months, first with Richard and then with you. And now it seems so simple and straightforward.'

'Things usually are,' I answered. I was so proud of her at that moment; probably even more so than when she would finally nail up her brass plaque with all her qualifications. Our daughter ... whose name had been given when Rupert had announced that he had 'a colt and a filly' when the twins were born ... and the name had stuck.

The situation with Raulf Layne, however, was far from simple.

He turned up again late one afternoon with an enormous basket of fresh vegetables (surplus to requirements in the kitchen!) and a crate of wine (just collected from the off licence and thought you might like to try it!!). Since my daughter was out that evening with his son, I didn't feel that it would be polite to turn him away, and so he stayed for supper. He talked about how difficult it had been rearing Keiran after the boy's mother had 'bolted'; and the problems in unexpectedly inheriting the Manor after his older brother had been killed on active service. All through the evening he kept staring at the huntsman picture as if there was something about it he didn't understand. Finally he got up and stood in front of it in silent contemplation for about five minutes.

'I noticed this when I was here last time, and I haven't been able to get it out of my mind. I don't like modern painting but this bridges the gap from primitive hunter to today – and the way that it changes with both natural and artificial light. It really is a remarkable piece of work; magical in fact.'

'Yes, it is,' I agreed but for different reasons. 'Friends gave it to me as a going-away present. Their going-away, that is.'

'Perhaps you should introduce me to more contemporary painting,' he said.

Without thinking, I found myself inviting him to the new Gallery opening in a couple of week's time and making a mental note to ensure Philly and Keiran were there too. Gerry would probably frighten the pair of them to death; I could just hear him cooing in my ear: 'Gaby, darling, so-o-o distinguished.' Or they would take complete umbrage at me turning up with a chap, since both Gerry and Guy had been devoted to Rupert.

Rites of Passage

'Ma! The car's on its way down ... can you get up here straight away? There's been an accident!'

'Are *you* okay?'

'I'm fine.'

'I'm on my way.'

We come from a household where you don't hold a steward's enquiry when you get a summons like that. I grabbed a jacket, shoved the dogs out in the garden for a quick pee and was waiting on the verge when the car pulled up. The young lad driving wasn't very communicative but I managed to learn that it was Keiran who'd had the accident, and by the time we got back to the Manor, the paramedics were loading the patient into the ambulance.

Philly bounded over and thrust a plastic carrier bag in my hands. 'Look after that! I'm going to the hospital with Keiran ... and look after Raulf, he's in shock.' And she was gone in a swirl of exhaust fumes.

I instructed the housekeeper to make a strong brew and armed with a bottle of *Famous Grouse* (Rupert's favourite cure-all after pig oil and sulphur), I went to find my patient. 'They think he's broken his neck ...' his voice wobbled, on the verge of tears. There's nothing more pathetic than a large, powerful creature reduced to fear and trembling, whether human or animal.

The neck was about the only thing Rupert *hadn't* broken but so many of our National Hunt and hunting chums had, that I knew it wasn't always as bad as is first feared. 'What happened?'

'He fell off!' he said incredulously and shaking his head, as though his son had never taken a tumble in his life.

The housekeeper arrived with a tray and there was a lot of rattling and pouring before we could resume the conversation. 'Where did this happen?'

'He and Philly were in the exercise yard. Luckily she had her

249

mobile with her and could direct the ambulance straight to where he was.'

We lapsed into silence and sat there in the drawing room by the log fire, him holding both of my hands. It was strangely comforting and I made no attempt to move, since I knew he needed this human contact. An hour passed. The housekeeper came in to remove the tray, make up the fire and light the lamps, but still nothing was said until my mobile shattered the silence. It was Philly.

'Well, he's wiggling fingers and toes, so that's a good sign. He's having scans at the moment to see what needs doing. So I'll hang on for a bit longer and call when I know something more definite. How are things your end? (Silence) … Have you looked at the bridle in the bag? (No) … It's *very* interesting (OK) … Talk later.'

I relayed Philly's conversation to Raulf, who allowed himself to relax a little. Then I went to hunt for the plastic bag she'd thrust into my hands. With all the excitement I'd not given it much of a thought – until I pulled the bridle clear of the bag. With hindsight, it must have been important for Philly to remove the bridle from the horse before the medics arrived and even while her friend was lying critically injured. Then I saw why. Both buckles fastening the reins to the bit had been undone so that the pin of the buckle had dug deep into the leather rather than going through the hole. It had held for a time but eventually worked loose and Keiran had fell.

An experienced rider checks his (or her) tack after every ride and one buckle might have been misaligned in a hurry – but not two. This was no accident and Philly had preserved the evidence before anyone could interfere with it. With all the excitement it would have been easy to replace the pins of the buckles in the correct holes and no one would have been any the wiser.

Suddenly, I got the impression that Rupert was beside me and telling me one of his stories. It was going back to his days in a racing yard as an amateur jockey and work rider when it was discovered that someone had been interfering with various riders' tack. He was always assigned a particularly dangerous horse as the first ride out of the morning, and it was discovered before leaving the yard (and crossing a busy main road) that *both* buckles had been undone on his reins, and carefully looped back, so that the pin did not go through the proper holes in the leather. Any pressure on the bridle and the reins would have come away in his hands.

This malicious little trick is tantamount to severing the brakes on a car, but there was no way of knowing for sure who the perpetrator was. Rather than make a fuss with the trainer or the police, Rupert called on his Craft skills and threw a curse in the tack room where the deed had been done. Suspicion had fallen on one particular person who had left another yard after a similar incident but the curse had to be placed in a way that safeguarded the sender from targeting the wrong person. It was so simple:

Let the hands that do the mischief, be the hands that take the fall.

From that day, Rupert kept a hagstone in his riding bag, and silently repeated the curse each time he entered the tack room, while holding the hagstone. Whether the malicious actions were meant as a joke was immaterial, sooner or later there would have been a serious, if not fatal, accident. Eventually, the person who had been suspected took a nasty fall on the gallops and was injured so badly they couldn't continue to work in racing. But there were no more incidents involving the tack.

'It was no accident,' I said to Raulf, holding up the reins and bridle separately. 'Philly gave them to me for safe-keeping before the culprit could put them back together.'

If I'd previously considered him to be a mild-mannered man, the burning anger that blazed in his eyes told me otherwise. Jove had manifested again. His beloved son (in whom he was well pleased) could have been killed and I hoped he wouldn't lay hands on the guilty party with this wildness upon him. Luckily my mobile rang and diffused the situation: it was Philly with an update.

'I'm on my way home. They're keeping him in for a couple of days until the swelling subsides but it looks like a cracked vertebrae that will keep him out of the saddle for a few weeks, that's all. How are things your end?' I passed the phone to Raulf and Philly repeated our conversation. Visibly his anger subsided a little.

'Who?' he asked. 'Who would do this? Everyone likes Keiran?'

'Who has access to the yard, and with an axe to grind?' I replied, but thinking more along the lines of who had a grudge against Raulf himself, and knew that the best way to get back at him was through his son. My witch's instinct had one candidate in mind.

Since Philly was riding out every day, she took on the task of placing her father's tack room curse on whoever had interfered with the bridle, and by the time Keiran returned home, things were sorted. Raulf had been tempted to call in the police but was realistic enough to know that it would be a difficult case to prove – although I think he suspected the same person. As an added precaution, I made light of Rupert's superstitions around the stable yard and asked if there were a pair of old shears lying around. The young lad who had fetched me the day of the accident recalled seeing some in the tack room, and curiously hung around to see what I wanted them for.

'A little charm to protect the horses …' I said by way of an answer.

A Charm for the Stables
Hang up hooks and shears to scare
Hence the hag that rides the mare,

Till they be all over wet
With the mire and the sweat;
This observed, the manes shall be
Of your horses all knot-free

'My Gran used to use them in the cattle sheds,' said the boy. 'Always maintained shears stopped ill-wishing and interference from the fairy-folk.'

Here was probably another descendant of the 'secret people' of rural England. That strange breed of people that were commonly referred to as cunning-folk – practitioners of folk magic but with a strong Christian bias, who used spells and charms in their magic to combat 'malevolent witchcraft', to locate criminals, missing persons or stolen property, fortune telling, healing, treasure hunting and to cause people to fall in love. Although many of these practices were gradually absorbed into the growing neo-pagan movements of the 20th century, it was this Christian element that caused its decline; only to be found nowadays among the elderly people of rural Britain while Old Craft remains as strong as it ever was.

Raulf was watching me as intently as the boy. 'Oh, Rupert had all sorts of superstitions,' I prattled gaily. 'It was amazing what he would do with horseshoe nails. There were shoes nailed up in weird positions, strange potions in the feed room, hagstones dangling from the rafters. You name it we had it!'

'You know who tried to harm Keiran, don't you?' asked Raulf, interrupting my flow as we walked back to the house.

'I've got a good idea, but let's wait to see if Rupert's little bit of magic works,' I answered non-committally and knowing he'd think I was referring to the charm. 'It won't take long before we get a result.'

He looked at me quizzically but with a gleam of under-standing in his eye and refrained from commenting further. To quote the sentiments of that retired geisha: 'I now felt as though

I'd turned around to look in a different direction, so that I no longer faced backward toward the past, but forward toward the future.' I could remember old friendships without bitterness or rancour. Our particular branch of Old Craft seemed to be in the safe hands of the next generation, even if those branches were spreading in different directions. There was also rather a welcoming feeling spreading its tendrils around this village and the people connected to it. Perhaps it was worth taking a few risks to find out if we really fitted in rather than going quietly into the night of retirement and obscurity.

But perhaps the final words should be those included in the funeral service of a fine horseman and polo player, Paul Clarkin, who died as a result of a freak accident. He had once told his wife, God forbid he should go to any heaven where there are no horses, and at the funeral, on the back of the service card she'd had printed: 'Life's journey is not to arrive at the grave safely, in a well-preserved body, but rather to slide in sideways, totally worn out, shouting ****, what a ride!!!'

It's a sentiment that Rupert would have agreed with wholeheartedly.

Moon Books invites you to begin or deepen your encounter with
Paganism, in all its rich, creative, flourishing forms.